An excerpt from
EVENING HOURS

Life was good, and Kaylee had learned early to treasure such moments. After nearly losing her life at such a young age, nothing had ever been the same, and she never wasted one precious moment.

That thinking gave her all the more reason not to waste one second contemplating a particular man. Her heart did a sudden somersault as she admitted to herself that she had thought about that cowboy off and on all night.

Unsettling?

Absolutely.

Crazy?

Absolutely.

A waste of time?

Absolutely.

Lethal.

Absolutely.

So why couldn't she get him off her mind?

Also by MARY LYNN BAXTER

IN HOT WATER
PULSE POINTS
HIS TOUCH
LIKE SILK
TEMPTING JANEY
SULTRY
ONE SUMMER EVENING
HARD CANDY
TEARS OF YESTERDAY
AUTUMN AWAKENING
LONE STAR HEAT
A DAY IN APRIL

MARY LYNN
BAXTER
Evening
Hours

MIRA

ISBN 0-7783-2231-9

EVENING HOURS

www.MIRABooks.com

Printed in U.S.A.

This book is dedicated to my
friend and gym buddy
Walter Bates
who should be writing instead of running.
Thanks for all your plotting expertise.

Prologue

She looked dead.

For a second Edgar Benton's heart beat uncontrollably against his chest cavity. When he leaned forward and placed a trembling hand on the exposed arm and felt her warm flesh, a breath of relief seeped out of him. Thank God she wasn't dead. Not yet anyway, he reminded himself as fresh tears dribbled down his face.

This was the first time he'd seen his daughter since she'd been whisked away to surgery several hours ago. His precious sixteen-year-old lay like a beautiful corpse on the sterile hospital bed. Panic seized him and his knees buckled.

He pulled a chair close to the bed, his eyes never leaving her face. Edgar took several deep gulping breaths, then whispered in a garbled voice, "Please, Kaylee, hang on. I can't bear to lose you, too."

No response.

His baby, *his only child,* remained unmoving and unresponsive. His tears kept coming. What had he, *they,* done to deserve such an awful tragedy? His twisted, angry face looked toward the ceiling, silently cursing God. He couldn't fathom how he was going to survive without his wife. As he thought of her lying on a cold slab in a morgue, another onslaught of pain ripped through his gut.

How would he tell his daughter that she might not ever walk again and that her body would always be scarred?

"Oh, God, why?" Deep sobs racked his body.

After realizing he'd cried aloud, Edgar peered at Kaylee to see if the sound had aroused her. It hadn't. Taking several shuddering breaths, he felt a semblance of rationality return. His daughter was not going to die, not right now anyway. She faced an uncertain future, but at least she was alive.

If only he had been driving instead of Kaylee, who had just gotten her beginner's license and was testing her moxie behind the wheel for the first time.

If only she'd had more experience, then maybe she could have dodged the car that had barreled through the stop sign as if it owned the road. As it was, Kaylee had plowed into the side of it. His wife, Vera, had died on impact while his daughter had flown through the windshield, her lower extremities ripped to shreds by the broken glass.

If only he had taken the vehicle into the shop and had the seat belt repaired. If he'd taken care of that, the latch might not have popped open. His good intentions would certainly not have prevented the accident, but it might have prevented Kaylee's serious injuries.

He recalled the investigating officer's words at the scene of the accident as the paramedics loaded his daughter into the ambulance.

"I'm so sorry for your loss, sir."

Edgar couldn't respond, torn between staying with his dead wife and going with his injured daughter.

"It's one of those freak accidents when neither of your loved ones should have been seriously injured, much less killed," the officer added.

God, it's my fault.

"Sir, the ambulance is about to leave."

Without thinking, Edgar had run toward the vehicle.

Focusing on the moment at hand rather than replay the darkest moment of his life, he sank his head into his hands. Despair threatened to overwhelm him, but he knew he had to regain control. He hadn't been with them, and he couldn't change that. Even if he had, things would've happened in exactly the same way. He would have given in to Kaylee's plea to drive just as his wife had. Rarely had either of them denied their daughter anything.

Kaylee was a great kid, a popular teenager whose many friends were now gathered in the main waiting area, solemn-faced and afraid. Not only was she well liked, but she was a straight A student and was involved in various school activities. Her favorite was the drill team.

Another sharp pain sliced through Edgar, and his groan deepened. If what the doctor said turned out to be the truth, then she would never perform again, never strut her stuff, as she was fond of saying in order to get a reaction out of him.

He could hear her teasing words and see her rolling her eyes as he pretended to be perturbed with her choice of words. It was a silly but fun game they played.

Another stab of pain took his breath even as he felt a hand on his shoulder.

"Mr. Benton."

Edgar jerked his head around and squinted up at Dr. Chester Wainright, the surgeon who had only hours before operated on his baby, putting the pieces of her broken body back together. He was a tall, dark-haired, dark-complexioned young man who was as competent as he was good-looking.

"Are you all right?"

Before Edgar could force a reply, the doctor went on, "Sorry. Forget I asked that. Of course you're not all right."

Edgar rose to his full six-foot-plus height and ran a hand through his thinning dark hair while he blinked the tears from his eyes. He was only forty-two; before this morning that had seemed so young. Now, in light of how his life had been turned upside down, he felt like an old, old man.

"Is Kaylee going to be all right?" His voice croaked like a bullfrog before he cleared it.

"How 'bout we step outside," the doctor said, shifting aside for Edgar to precede him.

Once they were in a small adjacent waiting area, Dr. Wainright didn't waste any words. "Your daughter is going to live."

"But?" Edgar knew there was more to come, and it wouldn't be good. He felt himself visibly flinch.

Wainright sighed. "You're right. There is a but. She won't ever be one hundred percent."

"Don't beat around the bush, Doc. Spit it out. Will she walk again?"

This time Wainright didn't so much as blink. "If she does, it won't be without a significant limp. And perhaps a leg brace. Her right pelvic bone was crushed and she suffered a multitude of internal injuries. I anticipate some scarring in that area, disfiguring her."

The room reeled, and for a moment Edgar thought he might retch.

"Please, Mr. Benton, do me a favor. Sit, then put your head down."

Minutes later Edgar felt the room right itself; then he whispered, "What…what about a family? Children?"

Dr. Wainright hesitated. "It's a good possibility that she will never have children."

A cry erupted from Edgar's lips, a cry that was reminiscent of a howl.

He felt the doctor's hand once again squeeze his shoulder. Finally he lifted his head, unashamed of the tears running down his face. "My baby's alive and that's all that counts."

"That it is." The doctor cleared his throat, then went on in an exhausted voice, "I'm not trying to tell you what to do, but as Kaylee's doctor, I recommend she get counseling while she undergoes intense physical therapy." He paused as if unsure how to continue. "Her life as she knew it will be no longer."

"Oh, God." Edgar ground out the words, rubbing the back of his tight neck with an unsteady hand. "I can't bear the thought of her not walking again."

"Yes, you can," the doctor said in a stern tone. "If that's the way it is, you have no choice. You have to be there for her and you have to be strong."

Edgar took a heaving gulp. "I know."

The doctor stood. Edgar followed suit, their eyes locking once again.

"I'll be back later to check on you both," Wainright said. "Kaylee will sleep for most of the remainder of the day, so don't get worried."

Edgar blew out a harsh breath. "And when she wakes up, I—" He couldn't go on. His vocal cords constricted, shutting off further words.

"When she wakes up, you will have to tell her the truth, but only if she asks."

Edgar nodded. "Knowing her, she'll ask."

"Then you level with her."

Edgar nodded again, feeling his throat constrict even more. Once he was alone, he straightened his shoulders and walked back into Kaylee's room. For the longest time he stood beside her bed while wave after wave of anger, pain and remorse swept through him.

He finally got control of his emotions and sat beside her. Yet the words were so hard to come by. Reaching for her hand, he whispered, "No matter what happens, I'll never let you down again."

Suddenly his heart leaped. She had squeezed his hand. God had not deserted him. He had been given a second chance and he would make the most of it.

One

Sixteen years later

Man, did he ever have a great tush.

The way he swaggered when he walked merely accentuated it, and the white shirt, boots and tight jeans added style.

She figured he was an uninvited guest, as no one else at the party was dressed so casually. No one she knew would dare. This man was either a country bumpkin who didn't know any better or he had so much self-confidence he didn't give a rip.

If she were placing a bet, she'd opt for the latter. He seemed to be totally at ease with himself and his surroundings.

For a moment Kaylee Benton was held utterly captive by this stranger's rear—a first for her. Oh, she'd admired men's looks and physique, but never had she been blatantly fascinated by a specific body part.

Suddenly realizing where her mind was and what she

was doing, Kaylee was about to look away, when his gaze locked with hers.

She had seen movies and read books where two people met and eyes held across a room—but never had such a thing happened to her. Swallowing, she jerked her head around. Her cheeks and body suddenly stung.

Thankfully she realized that she was alone. At least she could regain her composure without an explanation. Taking several slow, deliberate breaths, she still found it hard not to sneak another peek at the man with the great tush.

"Stop it," she muttered to herself just as her insides settled back to normal. This was so out of character for her. It was bizarre behavior.

Dismissing the entire episode from her mind, Kaylee concentrated on the party around her. It was given in her honor at The Garden Room of the luxury hotel in the heart of downtown Houston. The room was abuzz with the sound of voices, laughter and music, and redolent with the smell of flowers flowing from the glassed-in section out onto the patio.

Kaylee certainly wasn't immune. She took great pleasure in the fragrances that encircled her, inhaling the scent from time to time. The shindig had been in full swing two hours and this was the first moment she hadn't been surrounded by people.

She loved being the center of attention. Being named Woman of the Year was an honor as intoxicating as the strong floral scent. Yet she was grateful for the respite. It wouldn't last long, she knew, since one of her models had just gone to refill her glass of wine.

She was used to having people constantly being in her face, especially beautiful people like those who now milled about. After all, she made her living off beauty. She had successfully launched a modeling agency several years ago, an accomplishment that hadn't been easy, especially since her idea had come under attack from the beginning. Her critics had told her she was crazy to think that an agency such as she envisioned would ever get off the ground in Houston, Texas. New York City, yes. Houston, no.

Thank goodness she hadn't listened to the naysayers. If she had, she'd probably be an embittered young woman chasing a dream that could never be.

Kaylee's gaze strayed to the cane that lay on the floor beside her. Even after all these years, her heart still constricted with pain when she saw it. She quickly reminded herself that even though she would never walk the walk, she had proved she could talk the talk. Her business was booming, a fact that the chamber of commerce had recognized. The ache in her heart eased.

"Hey, where's your devoted audience?"

Kaylee looked on as her friend and assistant, Sandy Nelson, plopped down in the chair next to her, a smile creasing her face right along with a devilish twinkle in her blue eyes. She was a tall, busty woman with, as Sandy described it, a widening ass and a mop of curly black hair that capped her head like a crown.

Kaylee adored her and knew the feeling was mutual. They made an awesome team. Without Sandy, Kaylee's career wouldn't be nearly as successful as it was today, because Sandy had an eye for who could enter the highly competitive world of modeling and survive, a gift that she, Kaylee, lacked.

"Barbie is getting me a refill," she said, breaking the momentary silence.

"You're probably enjoying the peace and quiet. You've been covered up all evening. I know how squirrelly that makes you sometimes."

Kaylee quirked an eyebrow and smiled. "It's scary how well you know me."

"Not to worry." Sandy grinned as she reached over and touched Kaylee on the arm. "Your secrets are safe with me."

"I know." Suddenly a lump appeared in Kaylee's throat and she didn't know why.

As if she sensed the poignancy of the moment, Sandy switched the subject. "This is some blowout, my friend."

Kaylee acknowledged her statement with a grin. "That it is. I still can't believe it's happening to me…to us."

"Whoa, there's no us to it. Tonight is all about you and your successful career. Just wallow in it up to your tonsils."

Kaylee smiled with a sigh. "You know that's hard for me to do."

"Get over it. Being in the spotlight for one evening is hardly lethal."

Kaylee laughed. "What would I do without you to keep me on the straight and narrow?"

Sandy laughed with her, then cocked her head sideways, a light appearing in her eyes.

"What?" Kaylee asked.

"You look great tonight. Actually, I don't think I've ever seen you look better."

Kaylee was taken aback. "You think so?"

"I know so. Your skin has a flush to it. In fact, your cheeks look like a ripe peach."

Giggling, Kaylee rolled her eyes. "That's gagging."

"It's the truth. Is there something going on I don't know about?"

Kaylee froze as thoughts of that stranger's ass came to mind. Grappling to regain her composure, she looked down and pretended to smooth a wrinkle out of her gown.

"And the gold in your brown hair, I've never seen it shine so much."

"Now I know I'm going to throw up."

"How dare you make a joke out of my compliments."

"Get out of here," Kaylee ordered with another laugh.

"I can take a hint." Sandy squeezed Kaylee on the shoulder. "See ya later, my dear."

Her assistant had barely disappeared into a throng of people when Kaylee looked up and saw Barbie Bishop headed toward her. The model wasn't alone. Walking beside her was none other than the cowboy Kaylee had eyed earlier.

Despite her efforts to remain calm, Kaylee's heartbeat quickened. Surely Barbie would detour any second now and bypass her she told herself. But the two never veered off track. Before Kaylee could find her next breath, they were in front of her.

"Kaylee, my friend here wanted to meet you." Barbie looked at her companion before turning her gaze back to Kaylee. "Kaylee Benton, Cutler McFarland."

Though she was loath to do so, she held out her hand. When his calloused one took hers briefly, a tingle shot up her arm. She didn't understand what was going on.

"I'm honored," he said in a low, drawling voice, his eyes inspecting the length of her even though she remained seated.

Sex personified.

"Thank you, Mr. McFarland."

"Make it Cutler."

She nodded, feeling the flush deepen in her cheeks.

"I'll leave you two to get acquainted," Barbie said in her shrill voice, setting the glass of wine down before she strolled off.

Kaylee could cheerfully have strangled the model.

For the longest time neither said a word. Then someone came up to Cutler and tapped him on the shoulder. When he turned to speak to the man, Kaylee took the opportunity to give the cowboy the once-over. Up close, the front view fell short of the back one.

He ought to have been pretty-boy good-looking. But his features were too harsh for that. Even so, he oozed charisma and sex appeal. He was tall and thin with just the right amount of muscle. His black hair was streaked with silver and his blue eyes were surrounded by dark sooty lashes.

"Would you care to dance?"

Kaylee gave a start, worried she'd been caught staring. That fear actually took precedence over the fact that he hadn't noticed her cane. "No…no, thank you."

He shrugged. "Okay. Mind if I join you?"

"Of course not."

As if he read between the lines, a grin, more in keeping with a smirk, crept across Cutler's lips. He eased down in the chair in front of her and said, "I understand congratulations are in order. Sorry I wasn't here when you received the award."

"Thanks." Could he see her heart beating out of sync? She hoped not. That would be the final humiliation.

His lips twitched again. "Relax, Kaylee, I'm harmless."

Her eyes widened. "Excuse me?"

He chuckled. "It's obvious you wish I'd get lost."

Kaylee opened her mouth to deny his words, but when nothing came out, she tightened her lips.

His chuckle sounded like a low rumble.

Who was this man anyway? And where had he come from?

Once again he seemed to read her mind. "It's my job to read people. If not, I wouldn't be a very good district attorney."

Her eyes widened again. "Sorry, I didn't know."

"That smarts, since I'm running for reelection."

"Are you drumming up votes?" she asked bluntly.

"I like your style—direct and to the point."

"Is that a yes?"

He laughed. "I'm the best man for the job."

"How do I know that?"

His eyes drilled her, and his voice dropped a pitch. "You don't, but you will as soon as you get to know me better."

Kaylee sucked in her breath. Was he flirting with her? No, her imagination must be working overtime.

"Look, Mr. McFarland—"

"Cutler."

His gaze didn't waver and for a moment hers didn't either.

"Excuse me for interrupting, Kaylee, but I have some people I want you to meet."

The voice of the chamber president, Kevin Holmes, brought her back to reality with a jolt. Cutler suddenly stood and moved aside. Pulling her gaze off him, she forced a smile. "I'd be delighted to meet your friends."

"McFarland, you're welcome to remain," Kevin said. "In fact, I insist."

"Thanks, but I was just leaving," Cutler said. "I've taken up enough of Kaylee's time." Then he leaned down and, for her ears alone, he murmured, "I'll see you later."

Feeling shell-shocked, all she could do was watch him stride off.

He couldn't believe his eyes.

Yet he had no choice. What he was witnessing was a fact. He'd put his hand on the Bible and swear to it. His daughter was actually having a conversation with a good-looking man and seemingly enjoying it.

Hell, if the animated look on her face was anything to judge by, flirting would be closer to the truth. Edgar's pulse raced and his palms turned sweaty. He'd prayed for this day since his precious daughter had awakened in that hospital room so many years ago and was forced to face the cruelest of futures.

Kaylee had more than risen to the challenges that faced her. Tonight was testimony to that. He was so proud of her he felt his heart would burst.

The man Kaylee seemed interested in looked vaguely familiar; however, Edgar knew he'd never met him. More important, he wondered what his motives were. Those questions and more filled Edgar's head.

He straightened his slumping shoulders and moved slightly closer, allowing the partygoers to shield him so Kaylee wouldn't notice his hovering. Yet he remained out of her vision more for his own personal benefit than hers.

Just watching her happiness made him giddy.

Edgar moved a little to his left for a better look at the man. Or should he say cowboy? Edgar almost laughed out loud at the idea that his daughter would give someone in jeans and boots even a second glance, especially at a black tie function.

Then just as quickly as the flirtation began, it ended. The cowboy relinquished his seat to others.

"Damn," Edgar muttered under his breath.

He had to do something. But what? He couldn't force the man not to leave his daughter, for God's sake. Ah, all was not lost. Tomorrow was another day. A day to devise a plan.

That thought brought him more than comfort. It shot his excitement level off the charts.

Two

What an incredible morning.

Kaylee had risen early, much earlier than normal, and brewed a pot of coffee. With cup in hand, she had adjourned to the patio and sat in one of her padded wrought-iron chairs. That had been over an hour ago now, and she still hadn't the wherewithal to move.

That in itself was unusual. Even before she'd opened the agency she had been an early riser, energized whether she'd slept or not. She didn't want to miss one moment of any day, her subconscious continually whispering that sleep was a waste of precious time.

Kaylee inhaled the fresh scent in the air. It was as clean as the dew that covered the ground. Turning slightly, she got a whiff of the wisteria blossoms draped on a nearby bush. She breathed even deeper. The fragrance was heavensent, like none other. Her gaze drifted to the rosebush on the other side. Although she couldn't smell it, she knew she only had to press her nose against one of the blooms and its sweetness would also swamp her senses.

Her small backyard was lovely, but then she'd worked hard to make it so—she and the nursery, that is. She couldn't keep her yard in this shape by herself, although she would've loved nothing better. Her taxing career, not to mention her physical limitations, made that impossible. She did what she could when she could, which helped keep her in shape.

She had bought this old home in West University Place, an upscale but older section of the city, even though her dad had discouraged her from making such a bold and aggressive move. He thought it would be too much for her to keep up, but she hadn't listened. Though he was her best ally and cheerleader, he never let her forget that she was handicapped, a fact that could fester if she let it.

He had wanted her to continue to live in the house with him where she had grown up. But she had desperately wanted her own space. She needed to stake her independence in order to keep her sanity. After all, she was handicapped, not dysfunctional.

Edgar now admitted that Kaylee had proved him wrong once again. He was so proud of her, of what she had accomplished and was continuing to achieve. Her father wasn't her only avid supporter. Her godfather, Drew Rush, her dad's longtime friend and employer, had always encouraged her to push the envelope, so to speak.

Without his monetary help and his endorsements, Benton Modeling Agency wouldn't be in existence today. While she might not have a husband, she certainly had two strong men in her life for whom she was grateful.

Suddenly a bird chirped loudly in a nearby tree. Kaylee listened to his melodious music, and smiled. In that same tree two squirrels were playing tag. She concentrated on them until they jumped to another limb and disappeared into the lush foliage of the live oak tree.

Lifting her head, she searched for a puff of clouds. Nary a one was visible. The sky was azure blue and the sun was well on its way to full strength.

This was a great way to start a morning.

Soon, though, she was going to have to stop lollygagging, dress and get to the office. But not just now. She guessed it was only around seven-thirty, which gave her plenty of time to continue down this path of indulgence and still not be late.

She smiled again. She could be late if she wanted, she reminded herself. After all, she was the boss. For a second that thought made Kaylee giddy. She still couldn't believe she'd been honored in such a fantastic way. She had enjoyed every minute of it, too, even though she had been exhausted when she'd crawled into bed around midnight.

She couldn't complain. Life was good right now, and Kaylee had learned early to treasure such moments. After nearly losing her life at such a young age, nothing had ever been the same and she never wasted one precious moment.

That thinking gave her all the more reason not to waste one second contemplating a particular man. Her heart did a sudden somersault as she admitted to herself that she had thought about that cowboy off and on all night.

Unsettling?

Absolutely.

Crazy?

Absolutely.

A waste of time?

Absolutely.

Lethal.

Absolutely.

So why couldn't she get him off her mind?

She couldn't answer that. All she knew was that she didn't want to think about any man, not in *that* context, anyway. But then Cutler McFarland wasn't just any man.

Under no circumstances could she label him average. After meeting him, she thought he would be better suited to have been born in the early eighteen hundreds. She could see him with a holster and gun strapped to his waist and thigh, defending justice at all cost.

That picture forced a chuckle from Kaylee's lips; but she saw no humor in her thoughts. She was just setting herself up for trouble and heartache, neither of which she could afford. Only since her agency had taken off had she felt like a whole woman, as if she wasn't different from the average female walking the streets.

Now was not the time to let a man, especially a man's man, the kind she could never have, undermine her happiness.

When she had first looked at her scarred stomach, the result of a trek across jagged glass, she had been repulsed. But over the years, and after several plastic surgeries, she could now bear the sight. But she couldn't stand the thought of a man seeing it. She'd built an impenetrable wall that hadn't failed her until she'd noticed Cutler McFarland's great tush.

The fact that he appeared taken with her hadn't helped any. Still, the minute he noticed her leg, she knew she'd see pity replace interest. She couldn't handle that. So any further thoughts of that cowboy were taboo.

"You can dodge this bullet, Kaylee Benton," she said to

the tiny wren who perched on a sagging wisteria limb. Only something that small could light on such a flimsy place and be safe, she thought with inane desperation.

Her verbal warning did no good. Her mind settled back on Cutler and wouldn't let go. Had he been as attracted to her as she had been to him? His gaze had held a special gleam, one she had never noticed in a man's eye, though she was certainly no expert on men. Relationships had never been in the cards for her, nor could she have explored any had they been. She'd been too busy trying to put her body and soul back together and trying to craft a life for herself outside the handicapped world.

She hated the word *handicapped,* but she despised the new socially correct "special needs" term even more. She didn't want to think of herself as special in any way. Or needy. She just wanted to be thought of as *normal.*

Unfortunately, that often became impossible, even for her.

When she got tired and her leg refused to function, she had to depend on her leg brace. That was when she noticed the pitying glances. They gagged her now just as they had so many years ago.

Suddenly Kaylee found herself traveling back in time to that fateful day when she had awakened from surgery to find her dad sitting beside her bed, his face twisted and drenched with tears.

"Daddy, where am I?" she remembered asking in a weak, trembling voice.

"In the hospital, baby."

"Why?"

"There's been an accident," he choked out. "Don't you remember?"

She thought for a moment, then said, "No. What happened?"

"You just got out of surgery."

"Is that why I hurt so badly?"

"Are you in pain?"

"My leg—"

"I'll call the nurse." He punched the button on the side of the bed.

"How bad am I injured?"

"Oh, God, baby—" Edgar's voice broke and he couldn't go on.

"Tell me, Daddy."

He must have heard the panic in her voice, because he blurted out the words that changed her forever. "You had a wreck and hurt yourself real bad."

"Mom? Mom was with me, wasn't she?" When he didn't answer, Kaylee went on, her voice in the shrill range. "Wasn't she?"

"Yes, baby."

"Where is she now? Why isn't she here with me?"

Edgar put his head down and sobbed.

"Daddy," she cried, placing a hand on his head and burying it in his hair. "Where's Mom?"

"She can't be here, baby," he sobbed.

"Why not?"

"She…she didn't make it."

At first those horrible words didn't penetrate, so she asked, "What do you mean?"

"She's…she's dead, baby. Your mother died on impact."

"No!" Kaylee let out a wail that sounded like a wounded animal's cry.

Edgar raised himself just enough to fold her in his arms, his chest absorbing the brunt of her sobs.

"I want my mother," she cried over and over. "I want my mother. I want my mother...."

It was fresh tears falling on her arm that brought Kaylee back to reality. She raised her head and struggled to swallow the huge lump lodged in her throat. Dear Lord, she hadn't taken that stroll down memory lane in years. But whenever she did, it racked her body and soul, rendering her useless for hours, days, even weeks.

This time was no exception. She felt spent, utterly drained and so depressed that she wanted to curl into a fetal position in the closet and say to hell with the world and everyone in it.

She wouldn't do that. Pity parties where she was the only one in attendance were another part of her past that no longer existed, but she knew that hadn't always been the case. Once she had gotten over the shock of her mother's death, she'd had to deal with another shock—her broken body.

And guilt. Even though the accident hadn't technically been her fault—the other driver had been charged—she had nonetheless borne the responsibility of causing her mother's death.

That, combined with the fact she would never be a vibrant sixteen-year- old turning cartwheels and dancing at will, had turned her into a monster, especially after her daddy had told her that she might not walk again and would definitely suffer permanent scarring on the lower half of her body.

Kaylee didn't realize she was no longer alone until she turned and saw her father standing behind the French doors watching her. Knowing it was too late to mask her tears, she motioned for him to join her.

Once he was outside, he walked over and silently pulled her into his arms.

"I'm so glad to see you, Daddy," she whispered, clinging to him as tightly as she had done so many times in the past.

"You're still my baby and you can always count on me."

Three

Cutler's desk was piled high with files and folders.

He looked at them, feeling a knot form in the pit of his stomach. If he didn't get off his ass things were going to start unraveling. He couldn't afford that. Not in an election year.

Not in any year. His high standard of ethics wouldn't allow it.

As he peered at his calendar, a sigh split Cutler's lips. Two major cases were on the trial docket, cases that even his top assistant wasn't up to prosecuting. That responsibility fell squarely on his shoulders.

Both were controversial, with the potential to explode, and that was precisely why he had to be perfectly prepared. Losing was not something that interested him. When he walked into a courtroom, he expected to walk out a winner. He would accept nothing less.

Cutler glanced at his watch. He and Angel were due to meet as soon as he made it to the office. Too bad he hadn't told his prime investigator to meet him early, but he knew Angel wasn't in the best of moods first thing in the morning. Besides, it was barely seven and all his staff worked more nights than not. Ergo, he needed to cut them some slack. That was hard, because he required very little sleep.

Coffee could take most of the credit for that, Cutler reminded himself. Thinking of coffee made him realize he hadn't taken advantage of the pot he'd brewed minutes after he'd walked into the office. He'd had several cups at home, but those didn't count. He was just getting started.

Moments later, back from the kitchenette, mug in hand, Cutler sat behind his desk. The paperwork hadn't lessened any, he noticed with a smirk. After sipping on the hot liquid, he leaned back in his chair, lifted his arms above his head and stretched.

Man, he was tired. No sleep and long hours were telling on him, something he couldn't let happen. He had to be razor sharp mentally because he knew a shark was circling, a shark that was after his blood.

During his tenure as district attorney, Cutler had made more than his share of enemies, one of whom, his current opponent, Winston Gilmore, was a high-profile attorney from an old established family with big mouths and big dollars. Gilmore was known to be abrasive, self-confident and into mudslinging.

No matter.

Cutler was more than ready to take him on. He had earned a reputation for his own brand of hard-ass volatility. He'd been accused of being so self-assured he wouldn't listen to others. His own head of Major Crimes, Mike Snelling, had told him that to his face. He couldn't argue with him.

He liked to think that he merely approached everything

with the grit and determination that eventually brought justice to all. For that Cutler would make no apologies regardless of whether he was reelected. He'd be devastated if he wasn't, but no one would ever know, not even his mother.

He'd started out as a cop before attending law school, then had spent several years practicing criminal law, and his determination had catapulted him to the office of district attorney.

If he lost this election, Cutler knew he could always go back to practicing law, but he didn't want to do that. He had grown to respect, if not actually enjoy, his job and he wanted desperately to hold on to it. According to his mother, he'd sacrificed a home and family for the people, which was only partly true.

Although he'd been with a lot of women, he'd never found one with whom he thought he could spend the rest of his life. That included his present significant other, Julia Freeman. He cared about her as a friend, though he wasn't positive that was her perception of their relationship despite his candor on the subject. When he needed a woman on his arm for social purposes, he chose Julia.

It would take a special woman to put up with him, and he knew it. Until last night he hadn't met anyone he felt the desire to sleep with.

Kaylee Benton had set his heart racing, and he was still thinking about her.

He hadn't had that reaction to a female in ages. But there was something about Kaylee that had intrigued him from the moment his blue eyes had locked with her large brown ones.

He was used to appraising stares from the opposite sex, and he was aware that he was thought of as a player in the singles arena. But there was something different about Kaylee and her eyes. She had touched him on a deeper level.

Had he detected sadness reflected in her expression when they had met face-to-face? Whatever melancholy she might have been feeling, Cutler immediately recognized one classy lady, someone more striking than drop-dead gorgeous, in both looks and personality.

Perhaps it was the dimple in her right cheek that had revved his engine. Perhaps it was her body, although he hadn't seen her standing. His instinct assured him that wouldn't be necessary. She was nipped in all the right places. And for someone with such a lithe figure, she was amply endowed.

In his opinion, she would light up a runway more than any of the models who worked for her, and he assumed she had been a model herself. Her unblemished skin, high cheekbones and shoulder-length golden-brown hair were dazzling features.

Down, boy, he warned himself. Now was not the time to get seriously involved with a woman, not when his life was already on maximum overload. On the other hand, maybe a relationship was exactly what he needed to take the edge off his overstressed mind and body.

For a moment he considered turning to the computer and running a background check on her.

Nah.

If she was a woman he wanted to know better, even on a short-term basis, *and she was,* then it was better to slowly unwrap the package and savor its contents.

"You got a moment?"

Startled at the unexpected interruption, Cutler barely managed not to show his surprise. And disgust. He'd rather start his day biting into a wormy apple than cross paths with this man.

Mike Snelling, head of Major Crimes Division, was a royal pain in the ass, and had been from day one of Cutler's term in office. He and Mike had crossed swords from the start, and he didn't see that changing. Whatever Cutler said, Mike would argue the opposite.

Yet he'd have to give the devil his due. Snelling was damn competent and when push came to shove, Cutler could depend on him. That was why he curbed the urge to deck him every time he opened his mouth.

"What's up?" Cutler finally asked, trying to keep his voice even.

Mike, who was short and round with ears that protruded far too much, ambled toward one of the vacant chairs in front of the massive desk, sat down and took a deep breath. That short trek had clearly winded him. Cutler wanted to point that out, but that would be like tossing a lighted cigarette butt on a puddle of gasoline.

"I just wanted to make sure you know what you're doing," Snelling said without mincing words.

What a pompous prick. "I'm not even going to respond to that."

"I'm referring to Judge Jenkins," Snelling pressed.

"I know that."

"My advice is to back off."

Cutler squinted his eyes. "I don't recall asking for your advice."

"I know you two butt heads in court like angry bulls," Snelling went on as though Cutler hadn't spoken. "Everyone knows that, but to blatantly open an investigation against him is preposterous, if not suicidal."

"Thanks for that assessment."

"Just because he's overturned several of your cases doesn't give you the right to go for his jugular. There's such a thing as evidence."

Cutler narrowed his eyes and strengthened his voice. "I'm not going to take that as an insult, Snelling. Not this time, anyway."

Snelling flushed, but didn't make a comeback. Good call, Cutler thought.

Following a terse silence, Snelling asked, "Give me something tangible to work with."

"What I have is suspicion. It's your job to get the evidence."

This time it was Snelling who looked as if he'd bitten into a worm. "I'm listening."

"Angel and I have noticed a pattern in Jenkins's dismissals. Not just mine, either, though mine were slam dunks for sure."

"You're saying he's taking bribes."

"That's my guess."

"How?"

"Several of the dismissals were good-looking women...." Cutler purposely let his voice fade.

Snelling looked shocked. "Are you saying he's trading dismissals for sex?"

"Maybe, maybe not. What I am saying is that the bastard has something going, and I aim to find out what it is."

"He's a powerful man, Cutler, one who has the power to knock your dick in the dirt with one hand tied behind him."

"That thought ought to make *your* day."

"I don't know why I try to reason with you." Snelling's tone was testy.

"Look, I'm going to get the judge, one way or the other." Cutler's features were grim. "Your job is to help me."

"As head of Major Crimes, I think you're making a big mistake."

"You're entitled to your opinion."

"He's going to sink you, cost you the election," Snelling stressed.

"Then so be it." Cutler clenched his jaw. "A man's gotta do what he's gotta do."

"Maybe I should come back later."

Talk about timing. Cutler could cheerfully have gotten up and hugged Angel Martinez's neck for opening the door enough to get his head through it. "Come on in. Mike was just leaving."

"You haven't heard the last of this, McFarland," Snelling said, stomping to the door, then slamming it behind him.

"Why don't you two put on gloves, climb in a ring and get at it?"

Cutler grinned for a second. "Not a bad idea."

Angel just shook his head as he made his way farther into the room. He was dark haired and white skinned. His name was the only thing that labeled him Mexican-American. Still, he was proud of his heritage even though he'd never set foot in Mexico, having been born and reared in Houston.

He was good-looking, a truly decent guy and a competent investigator. Cutler didn't know what he would do without him. Angel's calm demeanor and sound advice had saved his ass on many occasions.

"So what's got Snelling up in arms this time?"

"The judge."

"He thinks we can't nail him."

Cutler noticed that Angel made a plain statement of fact. "You agree?"

"Does it matter?"

"Yep."

A short silence.

"Let me put it this way," Angel said. "When you make up your mind to get someone, judge or not, my money's on you."

"I was hoping you'd say that."

Angel snorted. "As if you ever doubted."

"I never take anything or anyone for granted. You should know that."

"If Major Crimes can get the evidence on Jenkins, then I can prosecute." Angel paused, then changed the subject. "From the looks of your desk, we're drowning."

"I couldn't have put it better myself."

"So let's get started."

Cutler opened the first file and groaned. When he would've chucked it aside, Angel shook his head. "No choosing favorites. We have to take them as they come. Let's hear it."

Cutler blew out his breath. "It's the Sessions case."

Angel visibly winced. "It's cases like this one that make me want to take this job and shove it. How any woman can drown her three kids in the bathtub is more than my mind can comprehend."

"Me, too. In fact, I could vomit right about now."

"To make matters worse, she'll probably get off on an insanity plea." Angel paused. "You know her husband's hired Arthur Beaumont."

"No, dammit, I didn't."

"If anyone can get her off, it's that double-dealin' son of a bitch."

"That's not going to happen," Cutler said, a violent edge to his voice. "Not as long as I'm upright and breathing, that is."

"Then we'd best put our heads together and plan our strategy."

For the next hour they made significant progress depleting the stack. Once Angel left, Cutler helped himself to another cup of coffee, went over some files with his secretary and then buried himself in more files.

The growl of his stomach told him the day was more than half gone. Pushing away from his desk, Cutler rubbed the back of his shoulders, trying to get rid of the burning sensation in his muscles.

He needed a break, but he needed to continue to work, as well. He was surprised that Julia hadn't called him, asking him over for dinner. He wouldn't go anyway. Dinner with her didn't appeal to him.

Without weighing the consequences of his actions, he reached for the phone and called his favorite florist. Then he dialed Information. "Benton Modeling Agency, please."

Four

"Yes, Christy."

"Uh, there's a man on the line—"

"If it's not important, I don't want to talk," Kaylee said in a more abrupt tone than she'd intended. But her mind was on the twenty or so beauty shots scattered across her desk, and she wasn't in the mood to be interrupted. It was her fault, however, for not informing Christy Deason of that. She was the assistant who manned the lobby desk.

"I'm not sure." Christy's tone was hesitant.

Kaylee sighed, curbing her building irritation. "What does that mean?"

"He said it was personal."

Kaylee's hand froze around the receiver while her heart raced.

"He has a great voice, that's for sure."

"What?"

"Uh, sorry, Kaylee, I didn't mean—"

"It's okay, Christy. Put him through." Why not? Her circuits were already frazzled. Besides, her caller could be any number of business associates she dealt with on a daily basis.

"This is Kaylee."

"Good morning."

At the sound of *his* vibrant, sexy voice, her hand once again turned rigid around the receiver. "How are you?" Somehow she managed to get that normal-sounding question out without sounding like an idiot. At least, she hoped so.

"I'm good."

He chuckled then. Through the line the chuckle sounded low and intimate. No doubt she was headed down a slippery slope. If she didn't stop that slide, she was headed for big trouble.

"My, but we're so formal," he said into the beating silence.

She picked up on the note of humor in his tone along with an imagined smile. "What can I do for you, Mr. Mc-Farland?" Hopefully her tone had the right amount of distant politeness without sounding offensive.

"Cutler. Remember?"

"All right, Cutler."

"I believe the question was what can I do for you?"

"That's right."

"It's simple. Have dinner with me."

His unexpected invitation took her so aback that for a second Kaylee was at a loss for words. She hadn't had much time to wonder why he was calling, but dinner would never have occurred to her no matter how much advance notice she'd had.

"Are you there?"

"I'm here," she responded, desperately trying to regain a semblance of control. In her mind's eye she could picture him looking relaxed, sitting at his desk, his boots resting on the edge of it.

Like a cobra ready to strike.

"So, how 'bout it?" he pressed.

Kaylee jerked herself back to the moment at hand. "No can do, but thanks anyway."

A significant pause. "Maybe another time."

"Maybe," Kaylee said, hearing the slight tremor in her voice.

Another pause.

"I'll hold you to that."

The next thing she knew she was holding the receiver with the dial tone assaulting her ears. Feeling as if she'd just gotten off a roller coaster, Kaylee slowly hung up the phone, then sat unmoving, waiting for her stomach to settle. Had she heard him right? Had he actually asked her out?

Absolutely. But why her, when he could have any woman he wanted? Even though she'd had no confirmation that he was a ladies' man, her instinct told her that he was. For all she knew, he might even be a married one, though she didn't think so. It would be so easy to find out details about him, but she didn't want to. Cutler McFarland was not for her and she was not for him.

While his invitation was flattering, if not the stuff dreams were made of, she couldn't allow herself the luxury of even considering such a move.

Once he learned her limitations, he would lose interest.

That had happened during her senior year in college. She had met a guy at a friend's birthday party. Even after he'd seen her in her brace, he had kept after her to go out with him. Because he'd made her feel good about herself for the first time since the accident, she had thrown caution to the wind and acquiesced.

Their relationship had been great. In the beginning. Only after their friendship blossomed into something more did things turn sour. She hated thinking about the crushing moment she'd prayed to die, aching to be released from the torment that raged inside her.

They had been in his car one evening at twilight, headed to another party, when Kenny Johnson had pulled off the road into a secluded area, grabbed her and kissed her. Shock had been her first reaction, and she had stiffened like a piece of wood in his arms.

"Hey, baby, relax and enjoy," he whispered against her lips. "I've been wanting to do this a long time."

"Oh, Kenny, I don't know. I…I don't know—"

"Sure you do," he countered passionately, kissing her hard while thrusting his tongue into her mouth. "You want me as much as I want you."

He was right; she wanted him. She wanted to learn more about that crazy feeling that made her head spin and her body melt. So she went limp in his arms and returned his kisses with a passion that had both shaken and frightened her.

She'd heard her friends talk about making out, about what they did with their boyfriends, but because she'd never had one, she had been ignorant. When given the opportunity to change all that, to be accepted by her peers, she wasn't about to snub the invitation.

It was when he began fumbling with the buttons on her blouse that panic had nibbled around the edges of her subconscious. "I don't think—"

"Shh," he said in a scolding tone. "It's okay, baby. You

and me are going to have a little fun. I promise you're going to love it, too."

With his mouth still devouring hers, Kenny finished unbuttoning her blouse and unzipping her jeans. She had been so taken with the feel of his mouth and the fact that someone actually wanted her that it was a long moment before she realized he was no longer holding her, that he had pushed her to arm's length.

It was then that she stared at him through wide, dazed eyes, and saw the look of horror on his face.

With a muted cry Kaylee recoiled, but couldn't stop herself from looking down, seeing her body through his eyes.

Nausea replaced her panic, rendering her useless. Finally, though, she found the wherewithal to cover herself and back as far away from him as she could possibly get.

"God, what happened to you?" he asked, continuing to look at her as if she were a freak out of a circus sideshow.

Her heart, already mangled, twisted to the breaking point. Yet from somewhere deep inside, she pulled together the broken strings of her pride and said with amazing strength, "Please take me home."

"I didn't—"

"Don't...don't say anything. It doesn't matter. Believe me, I understand." Her voice was barely audible. "I just want to go home."

Kenny hadn't argued. Once she'd struggled out of the car and reached the sanctuary of the apartment she shared with two other girls, she had locked her bedroom door, lain across the bed and sobbed until her entire body jerked with fatigue.

Then she got angry, angry at God for letting the accident happen, and angry at herself for being such a stupid idiot. She rolled off the bed, picked up the first item in view and tossed it across the room. The shattering sound of glass brought her back to her senses, revealing that she had broken the one picture of her mother and daddy that she most treasured.

Crying out loud, she had dropped to her knees, wrapped her arms around her upper torso and rocked back and forth until sleep had mercifully overtaken her.

The following morning she had awakened to a numbness that had stayed with her for weeks. She had existed in a zombielike state. But she had finally made a promise to herself never to let her guard down ever again. She would never subject herself to that kind of pain and humiliation.

To date, she had kept her word.

But she had to admit that Cutler's phone call had made a tiny dent in her shield of steel. Dredging up that awful memory had, however, served as a wake-up call.

She had to keep her vow uppermost in her mind or she would sink back into that black hole from which she might never recover. She wasn't about to let that happen. She had worked too hard, gone through too much hell to get where she was today. There wasn't a man in this universe for whom it was worth sacrificing her peace of mind.

Not even a hunk like Cutler McFarland.

"Good morning."

"Hey, Sandy, come on in." Her assistant couldn't have chosen a better time to make her appearance. The past was just that, Kaylee reminded herself. She didn't need to keep dragging it out of storage and rehashing it—for more reasons than one, the most pressing one being her work.

"I knew you'd want to see me first thing, so here I am."

"And none too soon either. Even though I've culled this stack of shots, I need your critical and clinical eye."

"You got it. But before we get started, I think you might need to have a heart-to-heart with Jessica and Gwen. Maybe Barbie, too."

"Oh, dear, what's going on now?"

"Same old, same old."

Sandy made no apology for her choice of words, but then Kaylee didn't expect her to. Her frankness was part of her winsome personality.

"I hate to come to you with this, but they don't seem to listen to me anymore," Sandy went on. "I had to get away from them before I lost my cool and said something I'd regret."

"I'll take care of it," Kaylee said, steel in her tone. "You're right, that petty jealousy between those three has gone on long enough. With the Neiman Marcus and the Medical Alliance shows close on the horizon, I need to nip this in the bud right now."

"They may even refuse to work together."

"If they so much as hint at such at thing, none of them will work the shows."

Sandy grinned. "Lady, did I ever tell you I like your style?"

"You're full of it, too." Kaylee grinned, then frowned. "Before you and I get down to the nitty-gritty, go get the three rebels and send them in."

Sandy's eyebrows went up. "Now?"

"Nothing like the present to kick some butt."

Five

"Gwen, I'm counting on you to tell me what's going on."

The model lifted her head with a defiant jut to her chin. Kaylee clenched her jaw to keep from coming on too strong in the beginning. She didn't want to start World War Three unless it proved necessary.

She had called the models into her office one by one. Gwen was the last. So far, she'd struck out. Jessica and Barbie had refused to divulge what had triggered the rift. Hopefully she would have more luck with Gwen, who was more even tempered than the other two.

"I'm waiting," Kaylee finally said.

"What did the others say?"

"That's something I'm not prepared to share."

Gwen blew out a breath, then tightened her protruding lower lip.

Of all the models who worked for the agency on a steady basis, this young lady had the most potential. Not only was she gorgeous—with perfect features that enhanced her alabaster skin, big dark eyes and coal-black hair—she had the body to match the face. Unlike the majority of her cohorts, she didn't have to starve herself in order to remain thin as a stick. It was in her genes. She was a natural. At five foot ten, Gwen seemed to float down the runway or jump off the pages of a magazine.

"I don't have anything to say." No mistaking the mutiny in her voice and features.

"So that's the way you want to play?"

"Are you going to fire me?"

Gwen's question shocked Kaylee. Letting any of them go at this point had not crossed her mind. Dealing with temperamental girls and their heightened egos was a big part of her job. While she would like to throttle them when they acted like spoiled brats, she chose to curb that urge and opt for the diplomatic approach. That had always worked.

Until today.

Something was definitely going on, something more serious than the petty jealousies that often triggered these outbursts. The girls were three of her top models, and with two important style shows only weeks away, her strategy had to produce results. If none of the three was willing to talk, then she, with Sandy's help, would have to go in the back door, which was not her first preference. It was her policy to be honest and direct with her girls. She always wanted them to know where they stood with her. She expected the same courtesy from them and for the most part, they complied.

"Is that what you want?" Kaylee finally asked. "For me to fire you, that is?"

"Of course not." Gwen's response was emphatic, though spots of color surged in her cheeks.

A warning bell clanged in Kaylee's head, but again she had no evidence, concrete or otherwise, to give her concern a bona fide name.

"Is that all you have to say?"

Gwen nodded.

Kaylee chose her words carefully. "You've made your choice, and I'll respect it. Having said that, I want to remind you that choices have consequences."

Kaylee paused hopefully to let that statement soak in. "And the consequences are not always pleasant."

Gwen lowered her head, but not before Kaylee glimpsed a moistening on her thick eyelashes. Suddenly she felt the urge to get up and give the girl a comforting hug. But that would show a weakness she couldn't allow if she didn't want this situation to blow up in her face.

"Can I go now?"

"You may. But I'll tell you what I told the others. I won't put up with any behavior that blights this agency or its reputation."

When Gwen stood, her face turned chalk-white, and another alarm went off silently inside Kaylee's head.

"Is that clear?"

"Yes, ma'am."

"My suggestion is that the three of you go for pizza—"

Gwen gasped. "Did you say what I think you said?"

It was all Kaylee could do to keep a straight face. "If you're referring to the word pizza, yes."

"You're telling me that we can have pizza?"

"If that's what it takes to settle this mess between you three, then I'll even spring for it."

Gwen's features broke into a smile, but for only a second. Her solemn, troubled look quickly returned, and she shifted her gaze.

Kaylee smothered a sigh before motioning toward the door. "Go on, get out of here and get back to work."

"Yes, ma'am," Gwen muttered, then fled as if her backside was on fire.

Feeling as if all the energy had been sucked out of her, Kaylee stayed put. Her leg was also throbbing, which meant she should've strapped on her brace before leaving that morning.

But she hadn't. On purpose. Some days she simply couldn't deal with that piece of steel, and today was one of them. Kaylee's conversation with Gwen, or rather the lack of one, had frustrated her, a rare condition since most of the time she could reason through any problem.

She considered herself to be one tough cookie who could overcome any obstacle thrown in her path. From age sixteen on, she had borne more than most, but it had given her character depth and strength, both traits she needed to run a successful business, though it still wasn't as prosperous as she wanted it to be.

Only when she reimbursed her godfather and mentor, Drew Rush, for the money he had lent her to start the agency would she feel completely successful. Although he hadn't been sure this business would take off in Houston, he'd told her to go for it, that he would back her 100 percent.

If the agency continued on its present course, Kaylee would have Drew paid off sooner rather than later. Diversity was the key to her success, or so she'd been told by a friend at the Ford Modeling Agency in New York. She had visited with Emily Austin many times before making the decision to open her agency.

Emily's advice had been to lean heavily toward the commercial side of the business rather than the live fashion side, though Kaylee was proud that her models did fashion as well, catering to the large upscale stores in the city such as Neiman Marcus, Saks Fifth Avenue and Macy's.

Yet her agency's focus was on jobs for clients who promoted household items, vehicles of all sizes and shapes, hardware, baby goods, cosmetics and the many essentials people used daily.

Print modeling, which catered to catalogs, high-fashion magazines, billboards and so on was gaining popularity and momentum in her agency, and as a result, Kaylee had gotten nationwide recognition.

"How did it go?"

Shaking her head, Kaylee smiled, then gestured for Sandy to come in and sit down. "It didn't."

"Ah, so they took the Fifth."

"That's about the size of it, even though I spoke to them separately."

"Good move," Sandy said, sitting down, then neatly arranging a stack of folders on her lap. "Too bad it didn't work."

"None of the three would budge." Kaylee shook her head. "I just don't get it."

"Neither do I."

A silence ensued during which Kaylee absently rubbed her quad on the bad leg, feeling a bit of relief in that sore muscle. She longed to be home soaking in a hot tub of water with bubbles up to her neck.

Suddenly the image of Cutler McFarland joining her, *naked*, popped into her mind.

Where had that come from?

Feeling her face turn crimson, Kaylee ducked her head before Sandy noticed anything amiss.

"So how do you want to play this?" Sandy asked.

"I'm open for suggestions."

Sandy shrugged. "Continue to ignore it."

"That's what I'm leaning toward, but—" Kaylee broke off, her mind getting ahead of her words.

"But what?" Sandy pressed.

"What if it, whatever this is, continues to simmer until it blows up?"

"Then we're screwed."

"My thought exactly."

"So tell me what you want me to do," Sandy said. "If anything."

Kaylee thought for another long moment. "Talk to the other girls, see if any of them knows what's going on."

"Do you think they'll rat?"

"No," Kaylee said, "but it's worth a try, especially since this group seems to be so competitive."

"If that fails?" Sandy left her sentence open-ended.

"We'll have to go to plan B?"

Sandy leaned her head sideways. "And that is?"

"Let's just say I'll know when the time comes."

Sandy gave the thumbs-up sign. "Works for me."

"Meanwhile, just keep your eyes and ears open." Kaylee's features turned grim. "If they have done anything to hurt this agency's reputation, then I won't hesitate to give them their walking papers."

* * *

Cutler took another sip of his coffee, then looked at his watch. He should've already been in his office preparing for his first court appearance of the day. He was dead tired and had needed some down time, so he'd indulged himself and was out on the balcony of his River Oaks highrise apartment with his feet propped up, a full cup of freshly dripped coffee in hand.

He deserved this moment of respite, didn't he?

Not when he had more to do than was possible to get done, he told himself with a smirk. He'd been in tight situations before—in fact, he performed better when he was under the gun. But with the upcoming election, fast turning nasty, and his high-profile caseload, he felt as if his insides were in a meat grinder.

Even sitting there with a bee buzzing around his head, he couldn't unwind. He figured that if he didn't win a second term, perhaps he could get used to lollygagging, but he knew with a deepening smirk that would never happen. He had far too much energy. Hyperactive had been his mother's term for his inability to stop moving.

Mary McFarland, unlike her son, had the patience of Job. He bet he'd almost driven her over the edge more times than she would care to count. Not only had he always been on the move, both physically and mentally, but he'd been inquisitive and had always demanded answers. He never stopped until he had them.

And he'd been argumentative to boot.

"Son, you've definitely chosen the right career," his mother had told him in her firm but sweet voice. "You'll make a perfect attorney."

He had his doubts about the perfect part, but he'd done his best. For the most part, he had never been sorry he'd chosen his profession, although dealing with scum on a daily basis worked on him, especially lately when he had to deal with postpartum women who murdered their kids. Those kinds of cases cut him to the core. Even so, he had to push his personal disgust aside and see that justice was served.

And that was what he intended to do, no matter how repugnant or controversial. He'd nail the "haves" as quickly as he would the "have nots." Class, gender, finances or the lack thereof made not one whit of difference to him. If someone broke the law, he wouldn't stop prosecuting until they paid.

Such hard-line tactics had made him a lot of enemies.

It had gained him a few friends, too, or at least he liked to think that. Time, and the election, would prove that one way or the other. In the meantime he'd best attack the stack of folders on top of his desk.

He had just drained his cup when his cell phone rang. After checking the name on the caller ID, he frowned but flipped the lid anyway. "Morning, Julia."

"Are you at the office?"

"Nope."

"Are you serious?"

"Yep."

A short silence ensued, followed by a sigh as if his one-syllable answers irritated her. "Is something wrong?"

"No. I'm just moving slow."

Julia laughed. "That's a first."

"Actually, I'm on my way out the door," he said, even though that wasn't quite the truth.

"I just wanted to remind you about dinner tonight. Remember, I've asked several other couples to join us."

He winced, having forgotten. "I don't know, Julia. I—"

"Don't do this to me, Cutler. Just bear in mind these particular friends can help you politically. They all have deep pockets. Besides, you promised."

He doubted that, but he must've made a commitment of sorts. Damn, but that was the last thing he wanted to do, the last place he wanted to go. "How 'bout I call you later in the day?"

"All right, but call me on my cell. I'll be out of the office showing houses all day." Julia paused, then added with emphasis, "I'm counting on you not to let me down."

"Later, okay? I gotta run."

Once his cell was back in his pocket, Cutler picked up his cup and stared at the empty bottom. He tried to come up with a viable excuse to skip tonight even though his conscience pricked him. He'd much rather be working, which was not a good sign.

When it came to women, he needed to be more social. The old adage was true: all work and no play made for a dull guy. He didn't think he was in the dull arena yet, but he was getting close despite Julia's efforts to the contrary. Maybe he should bow out of that relationship, take a breather, so as not to give her hope that wasn't there.

If the invitation had come from Kaylee Benton, he wouldn't have hesitated to jump at her beck and call. He had never met a woman he wanted immediately. But he wanted Kaylee. That was an emotion he hadn't felt in several years. She had stirred the banked-down fire in his loins, made him hungry for a woman's touch, *made him hungry to be inside her.*

He'd never married, much to his mother's disappointment. Since he was an only child, she had no one else to look to for grandchildren. While he'd rather do most anything than disappoint her, he simply hadn't been able to make that commitment. When a woman interfered with his job, he cut her loose.

Kaylee seemed much the same. A match made in heaven. A smile crossed Cutler's lips. She had looked so soft, so delicate, so much a woman, and he desperately wanted to get to know her better. He sensed she felt the same way, although she had turned down his invitation to dinner.

He wasn't giving up, though. He wouldn't have tagged her as a woman who played coy, but he couldn't rule that out. Not yet, anyway. Whatever obstacle held her back, he'd bet it had something to do with those sad eyes, and he wanted to overcome it.

The bottom line was he wanted her and he intended to have her.

His cell phone rang again. "Damn," he muttered as he stood. Without looking at the caller ID, he said, "McFarland."

"Son?"

"Hi, Dad, what's up?"

"It's your mother."

It wasn't so much what Trevor said, but the tone he used. Hair stood up on the back of Cutler's neck. "What about her?"

"She's sick. I need to call the doctor, only she won't let me."

Swallowing his panic, Cutler said, "Call the damn doctor. I'm on my way."

Six

Drew Rush stared at the blonde's creamy white rear exposed to his view.

"Cover yourself," he said in a harsh tone.

Jill Jay rolled over and stared at him through wide, wary eyes. "You're not coming back to bed?"

"Did you hear what I said?"

Her wariness turned to fear, and she bolted upright. "Uh, sorry."

"If you do like you're told, you never have to be sorry." Though he never raised his voice, it sounded chilling even to his own ears. "How many times do I have to tell you that?" A cold smile accompanied that question.

Her lower lip shook. "No more. I promise."

"I hope not. Get your clothes on and get out."

She scrambled off the bed and within ten minutes was gone, leaving him to ready himself for a long and hopefully profitable day. While he'd had a good time with Jill, he didn't care if he ever saw her again.

His stable was too full of women to ride the same horse

more than once. Variety was what kept him young and pumped, despite his sixty-plus years. He didn't feel old, and he never wanted to act it. He didn't have to use Viagra, a fact that made him feel like a real stud since so many of his cronies talked about using the drug. They bragged about how wonderful it was, but Drew just saw it as a weakness that was abhorrent.

He had it made with women, just as he did in every other aspect of his life. He was one fortunate bastard who had no one to thank but himself.

Drew was still patting himself on the back when he entered his office some thirty minutes later. Edgar Benton was waiting for him.

"How long have you been here?"

Edgar's normally pale face showed no reaction. "Not long. Just thought I'd hang around to see if you have some last-minute instructions."

"I think we covered everything yesterday," Drew replied in a slightly irritated tone.

A flush replaced Edgar's paleness as if he realized he'd goofed. "Sorry. Just wanted to make sure I covered all the basics."

"I want to see you the minute you get back."

"You're the boss."

"You got that right."

The color in Edgar's face deepened, but he didn't reply. Drew wondered what he was thinking, but it didn't matter. Edgar could roll with any punch he was dealt, which was to his credit.

Drew looked at his longtime employee, thinking Edgar appeared much older than his fifty-eight years with his thinning dark hair, his slightly stooped shoulders and to-bacco-stained teeth from long years of smoking. Even though he no long indulged in those stank sticks, his teeth would never recover.

"How's our girl?" Drew asked when Edgar still didn't show any signs of leaving.

"Real good." Edgar smiled, eliminating the sadness in his eyes, a sadness that was visible even through the thick lenses of his glasses. The same sadness was usually mir-rored in Kaylee's eyes.

"That was a hell of a party the chamber threw for her the other night," Drew said. "She more than deserved it."

Edgar's smile grew. "You bet she did. I appreciate your coming. That meant a lot to her and to me."

"What made you think I wouldn't?"

"With your schedule, who knows?"

Drew snorted. "I'm not too busy for my godchild."

"I'll never be able to repay you for your kindness to her."

"Yeah, you will. Just continue to be loyal to me, no mat-ter what."

Edgar looked disconcerted. "Don't worry about that. I'll never let you down."

"Good. I'll see you when you get back."

Edgar nodded, then ambled out the door.

Drew pushed back in his chair and stared out the window of his top-floor complex in southwest Houston. He had pur-chased this high-rise office complex, which was within spit-ting distance of the Galleria, right after he made his first million, and the building had since tripled in value. He could've sold it and made several more million on that deal alone. But he had no intention of ever dumping this property.

Sitting atop this building and having his office cover the entire top floor made him feel important, made him forget his humble beginnings and the bitter fact that he had grown up with none of life's amenities, thanks to a mother who whored for a living.

AIDS ended up killing her—her just deserts, he'd told himself without guilt. As for his father, he had no idea who he was, and he didn't care. He'd been on his own since he was ten years old, and he'd done just fine.

He was a rich man. He could go, do and buy anything he wanted. And he wanted a lot. If someone told him he couldn't have anything on his "wish list," he got it somehow.

If the word *no* had been part of his vocabulary he wouldn't own a thriving corporation or command the respect he did now. He might not have a pedigree, but he had money, and that went a long way in his society.

A confident chuckle erupted from his lips as a feeling of power surged through him. Yep, he was sitting atop the world, staring down at the poor blokes below.

"You must've gotten some good nooky last night."

Drew grinned as he motioned for his closest business adviser to enter. Glen Yates was a big man, in stature and weight, with a bushy gray mustache that hid his upper lip. If Drew trusted anyone, which he didn't, it would be Glen. Like Edgar, he was always at his beck and call and eager to please.

But then, he paid his lackeys well. Hence, they were loyal and behaved in a servile manner.

"As a matter of fact, I did," Drew said at last, shoving his feet off the desk and swinging around in his chair.

Glen's mustache grew with his grin. "Can't beat it."

"You ought to try it sometime."

"Who says I don't?"

Drew shrugged, suddenly tired of this inane conversation. He made it a point never to let anyone penetrate his hard shell and glimpse what lurked underneath. To do so would make him vulnerable, make him susceptible to emotions he didn't want to feel. His motto was screw before getting screwed. He'd lived and prospered by that code for too long now to change.

"What's on tap for today?" Glen asked, breaking the silence.

"I've sent Edgar after the files on the Magnolia Creosote Plant."

"Ah, so you are going after them?"

"You don't think that's a smart move?" Drew didn't really care what Glen thought; he'd already made up his mind. Yet it was advantageous to know what someone else was thinking. Different opinions often came in handy.

Glen pulled on his mustache. "I didn't say that, boss. You told me yourself they're pretty solvent."

"Not so solvent they can withstand a smear campaign."

Especially not from him. Gobbling up small, floundering companies was how he'd made his millions. The fact that he'd ruined their good names beforehand didn't enter into the equation. He chalked that up to sound business practices.

Glen's face crinkled in a grin. "That company would definitely be a feather in your cap, if you can get it, that is."

"Do you doubt my ability?" Drew's tone was hard.

"Absolutely not."

"When Edgar gets back with the information, I want you

two to get together and give me the bottom line particulars. We'll proceed as usual. I'll devise the plan, then give you the green light to go forward."

"I have some info on the paper mill deal."

"I was hoping you'd say that. I like those who try to make me happy."

"The family is going at it tooth and nail."

"Ah, now that *is* good news," Drew said, his juices starting to flow as vigorously as they had this morning when he'd humped Jill. "I take it my offer has them divided."

"Yep. They're squabbling like hounds over a bone."

"If they don't take my dirt-cheap offer," Drew said, "then I'm going for the jugular by putting the EPA on them for dumping waste. When I plan my exact strategy, I'll keep their backbiting in mind," he added, his anticipation growing with each second.

"Meanwhile, I'll keep working on our present takeovers."

"No problems so far with this latest group, right?"

"Right."

"That's what I like to hear."

"I'll be in touch."

Drew turned his attention to the buzz from his secretary.

"Sir, Miss Benton's on line one."

He reached for the phone. "Kaylee, my dear, good morning."

"I don't know what I'm going to do with you," she said, coming directly to the point, an asset he admired.

He chuckled. "I don't know what you're talking about."

"Oh, please."

"No, really, I'm serious."

Silence reigned for a moment, during which he could

sense her concentration. "I wish I could believe you. But since I don't, I thank you." She paused. "One more time."

"Okay, thank me," he said with another chuckle. "But again, I can't take the credit."

"You didn't send me this huge bouquet of flowers?"

He heard the surprise in her voice, and for a moment rage filled Drew, not because she'd received the flowers, but because he hadn't sent them. He rarely ever made a mistake like that. Following her honor, he should have sent her a congratulatory bouquet.

If he had a soft spot in that hard core of his, it was for Kaylee. He'd never had the nesting urge. A home and family were responsibilities he hadn't wanted. He was much too self-absorbed for that. But if he *had* wanted a daughter, he would want her to be just like Kaylee.

He had known her since she was a youngster, had met her right after Edgar started working for him. She had captivated him then and still did. He would do anything for her.

As long as she adhered to and played by his rules, that is.

To date she had, and he didn't see that ever changing. She was indebted to him in more ways than one and he aimed to make sure that didn't change.

"No, honey, I didn't."

"But…" Her voice faded.

"Sounds to me like you've got an admirer?"

"Perhaps Daddy…" Again her voice faded.

Drew knew better than that, and apparently so did she. Sending flowers to his daughter on any occasion would never have occurred to Edgar. His mind simply didn't work that way, even though he adored the ground Kaylee walked on.

"Well, anyway," she said, filling the silence, "they're absolutely breathtaking."

"And well deserved, my dear."

"Thanks, Drew. But I was so sure they came from you."

"You holding out on me, sweetheart?"

She laughed. "I have no idea who sent them, but it's no secret admirer, for sure."

"I guess that remains to be seen."

"Look, when are we going to have lunch together?" she asked, blatantly changing the subject.

"I'll call you in a day or so, and we'll set it up. Meanwhile, enjoy your flowers. And enjoy the fact that I'm proud of you."

"Thanks, Uncle Drew. I wouldn't be where I am without you."

He certainly didn't want her ever to forget that. "Be sweet." With that he hung up and stared into space. He didn't know if he was happy with the thought of Kaylee having a secret admirer or not.

Somehow, he didn't think so.

Seven

"Have you called 911, Dad?"

Trevor McFarland walked quickly toward Cutler, a pained expression on his face. "No, but I did call the doctor."

Cutler was definitely his mother's son, having none of his dad's physical characteristics. Trevor was shorter than both him and Mary by several inches. He wore his light hair in a flattop. His skin was weathered from having spent years in the sun as a building contractor, even though he was now semiretired.

Father and son weren't alike in personalities either. Trevor was far more sober, except when he laughed. Then his pleasure came from deep in his belly, and in that, he and Cutler were alike. Trevor adored Mary and Cutler had always thought they had a good, solid marriage.

Having them as an example, he often wondered why he couldn't make a similar commitment.

"What did he say?" Cutler asked with impatience when Trevor didn't convey anything more.

"Only that he's on his way."

Cutler quickly went to his mother's bedside and stared down at her. Fear wrapped its tentacles around his heart. Was she breathing? For a second he couldn't move. When he saw her chest rise and fall relief assailed him.

"She's asleep, son."

Cutler faced Trevor. "What happened?"

"Same thing. She just had a dizzy spell and passed out."

"Those 'spells' are happening far too often."

"I know."

"Steven needs to do something," Cutler said more to himself than to his dad.

Steven Hughes was not only Mary's physician but a member of her church and a longtime friend. Mary trusted him without hesitation. Although he had a reputation for being a crackerjack heart specialist, Cutler had urged Mary to seek a second opinion, something that hadn't gone over well in the McFarland household. To date, Mary had opted not to take his advice.

Maybe now that would change.

"Steven didn't think the hospital was necessary," Trevor said. "I…we have to trust he knows best."

Cutler was about to disagree, but knew now was not the time. Whether or not his mother sought a second opinion was not Trevor's choice. He released a sigh and said, "One of these days she's going to fall and break something."

"I know." Trevor's eyes remained troubled. "But you know how stubborn she is. Or at least you should. You inherited the same trait."

Cutler ignored that latter comment, and continued to watch his mother. Where the hell was the doctor? He couldn't believe she wasn't on her way to the E.R., but for now he had no choice but to trust the doctor.

"Since you're with her, I'm going downstairs and wait for Steven."

Cutler nodded, easing into the chair that Trevor had pulled up to the bed. Though he was wired to the max, Cutler forced himself to remain seated. Reaching out, he took his mother's hand in his and held it, feeling his heart constrict.

She had to pull through. The alternative was *not* even a consideration. Mary had always been and would always be his best friend and ally. Even though he had a good relationship with his dad, his mother was the mainstay in his life. He couldn't conceive of her not being there for him.

Under the circumstances, however, he realized that kind of thinking was unrealistic. She had been diagnosed with a weak heart muscle that surgery could not correct. Only medication would help, and she already took plenty of that.

From the outset, Dr. Hughes had told them that Mary could live to be an old woman or she could die at any moment. If she took care of herself, he'd added, her chances of survival were much better, of course.

Cutler almost snorted out loud at the thought of his mother taking care of herself. She took care of others. She was a pastor of a fairly large community church, and her entire existence centered around helping others. That was what made her the special person she was.

Yet that devotion to her fellow man could very well bring about her demise, which grieved him because he didn't see her ever changing. Mary appeared to be the picture of health. A tall woman, rawboned in stature with a flair for the dramatic, she carried herself as though she was proud of her height.

He had her blue eyes and her hair.

She wasn't pretty; like his, her features were too strong for that. Yet she was never ignored in a crowd because of her powerful presence.

"Mom, can you hear me?"

Cutler held her hand tighter when she didn't respond. That's when he felt a gentle squeeze, though she still didn't open her eyes. But she knew he was there and that was what counted.

"Mom, you gotta stop pulling these stunts," he said. "I can't have you lying in bed, especially not in an election year."

Suddenly Mary's eyes popped open and she gave him a weak smile. "You selfish brat, you."

He laughed outright, feeling as though the weight of the world had been lifted from his shoulders. "How do you feel?"

"Like I've been beaten with a wet rope. Other than that I feel just fine."

"Sure you do."

Mary struggled to sit up.

He clamped a hand on her arm. "Whoa, let's not get too feisty."

"I'm okay."

"Mom, you passed out."

An irritated look crossed her face. "Well, I'm okay now."

"Did anyone ever tell you what a stubborn broad you are?"

Mary slapped him on the hand. "Don't talk to your mother like that."

They both grinned, then he leaned over and gave her a

hug as he eased her back down on the bed. "Stay put. Steven is on his way."

"Oh, for heaven's sake, I don't need him."

"Really? You can't keep on like this. Something's gotta give."

"If you'll help me sit up…"

Cutler shook his head. "Help? If I have to assist you, then you're far from okay."

"Get out of the way, then, and I'll get up on my own."

"One of these days—"

Ignoring him, she struggled upright, then gave him a triumphant look. "Goes to show you can't keep a good woman down."

Cutler turned as the doctor, followed by his father, made their way into the room. Steven was of medium height with red curly hair and a ruddy complexion.

Moving aside, Cutler let Steven have access to his mother, but watched ever so carefully while he examined her.

"Bottom line?" Cutler asked without preamble once Steven had stepped away from the bed.

"She's been overdoing it."

All eyes riveted on Mary, who looked both irritated and unrepentant.

Cutler would cheerfully have throttled her if it would have done any good. "How 'bout we chain her to the bed, Doc?" he said, staring at his mother through narrowed eyes.

Mary swung onto the side of the bed. "Just because you're grown, young man, doesn't mean you can back talk your mother."

Cutler spread his hands, then stared pointedly at the doctor.

Steven didn't shuck his responsibility. "Mary, I'm not going to preach to you. I'm going to leave that to you." He smiled.

Mary gave him one of her looks.

"What I'm not going to leave you is the choice to obey or disobey."

Cutler watched Mary jut her chin as though prepared to fight.

"You're wasting your time giving me one of your quelling glares. I'm immune. I'm changing your medication and I expect you to rest one hour or longer every day." He glanced at Cutler, then Trevor. "I'm depending on you guys to see that she complies."

"That's not going to happen," Mary said with force.

Trevor crossed to the bed, peered down at his wife and said, "Oh, yes, it is, sweetheart."

"Thanks, Dad," Cutler said, throwing his mother a grin. "You can count on me to do my part."

Mary glared at all three before a slow smile softened her features. "All right. I'll try it your way and see what happens."

"Praise God," Cutler muttered, rolling his eyes.

"Son, don't drag the Lord into this."

Though his mother's tone was prim, Cutler heard the humor edging it. Confident that this crisis had passed, he walked over and kissed Mary on the cheek. "I'll talk to you later. Meanwhile, behave yourself or else."

Had he been in the audience the entire time?

Kaylee tried not to panic, but she couldn't help it. Cutler McFarland was the last person she expected to see at this luncheon.

Thank God the show was almost over. If she had noticed him earlier, she would've been much more shaken.

She shouldn't have been surprised that he was there, especially since a style show was part of the planned activities for the annual Medical Alliance luncheon. This was the first time men had been invited, which was no problem for her agency when it came to putting on the show, as she had almost as many male models as females. In fact, she'd been delighted with the change in plans, although it had been a challenge for both her and her staff.

The thought of Cutler McFarland sitting through a display of the latest fashions, however, seemed laughable given his relaxed attire, but Kaylee didn't feel like laughing. In fact, she wished she was anywhere but about to step up to the podium in a matter of minutes. And of all days, she'd had to wear her brace, because when she'd awakened that morning her leg had refused to cooperate. She had thought about nursing her pride and wearing a long skirt in order to help camouflage her handicap, but in the end she hadn't.

Her limp was part of her, and people could either accept her as she was or not. Most of the time that bravado worked.

But not today.

Seeing Cutler suddenly brought all her insecurities to the surface, making her sick to her stomach, which in turn made her furious with herself. What did she care what he or anyone else thought? Hadn't she gotten over her concerns regarding other people's reactions to her years ago? Why was she so bent out of shape wondering what this man would think?

"And now let's welcome Miss Kaylee Benton."

Kaylee froze.

"Hey, get the lead out, girl," Sandy whispered from behind, swatting her on the rear.

Kaylee turned and faced her. "Why don't you go instead?"

Sandy looked at her as if she'd lost her mind. "Is something going on I don't know about?"

Kaylee shook herself mentally, then said, "Forget I said that. I'm fine."

"If you're sure," Sandy responded in a tone that said she wasn't at all sure.

After taking several deep breaths, Kaylee plastered a smile on her face and slowly made her way onstage, praying that she reached her destination without mishap.

She did, though when she reached the podium she clung to the sides until her knuckles almost cracked under the pressure.

"Let's give this lady another round of applause," the master of ceremonies added with a wide grin.

While they clapped and whistled, Kaylee looked into the audience. Her gaze landed on Cutler. For what seemed like an interminable length of time but was actually only seconds, their eyes met.

Then he turned his back and walked out.

Eight

Edgar felt her eyes on him long before she shared her thoughts.

"You've really been preoccupied lately," Rebecca Goolsby said. "Have I done something to offend you?"

"Of course not, honey."

He stared at the woman sitting across from him at the Starbucks coffee shop near the Galleria. They had been an "item" for a while now, and he was quite taken with her. She wasn't beautiful; she really wasn't even pretty.

Her face was too square and her eyes were too far apart. But she had a sweetness and grace about her that had captured his heart. And her smile—how could he forget that? He couldn't. When Rebecca smiled, it lit up her face and everything around it, which reminded him of Kaylee. She was blessed with that same gift.

Rebecca was the first woman he'd cared about since his wife died, and that had been a lifetime ago, or so it seemed. Kaylee had always been enough.

He couldn't say when that had changed or even if it had.

His daughter and her needs would always come first. He'd made that promise the day of the accident. But apparently time had dulled the pain and hurt enough so that he could now move forward.

While a relationship with a woman hadn't been on his mind, Rebecca had simply snuck in the back door of his heart without his knowing it.

He had met her at one of Drew's parties. She worked for a brokerage firm with whom his boss had done business. When Drew introduced them they had clicked right away. She was easy to be with, didn't make demands, didn't push. Most of all, she didn't seem to resent his devotion to Kaylee.

"Was my question out of line?"

He forced his attention back to Rebecca. "You know better than that."

"Do I?"

Edgar smiled, then reached across the table, took her hand and squeezed it. "You can ask me anything you want."

"Only, you reserve the right not to answer." She tempered her bluntness with a smile. "Right?"

He smiled back. "Right. But not this time. I was thinking about Kaylee."

"Aren't you always?" she said without rancor.

His smile spread into a grin. "Not always. You have a tendency to interfere."

"Good," she said with obvious pleasure. "Somehow I sense you're concerned. Has something happened I don't know about?"

"Possibly."

"Really?"

Edgar ran a hand over his thinning hair and squinted his eyes. "And it's a good thing, too, though I'm making it sound the opposite." He paused. "Or at least I think it is."

"Now you've really got me curious. What on earth is going on?"

"I think she's interested in a man."

Rebecca's gray eyes widened. "Why, that's wonderful. If the feeling's mutual, that is."

"Ah, that's the kicker."

"How about you start at the beginning and fill in all the blanks."

Edgar told her about Kaylee's encounter with the cowboy at the chamber function. "She didn't know I was watching, of course."

"Oh, honey, I think that's wonderful, but just because she seemed interested doesn't mean she really is."

He was taken aback and didn't bother to hide it. "What's that supposed to mean?"

Rebecca squeezed his hand again. "It means that Kaylee might've been charmed for the moment and that's all."

"You didn't see her face," Edgar responded, an obstinate set to his jaw.

"You're right, I didn't, which means I'm not qualified to make that call."

"I didn't mean to snap at you."

"You didn't." Rebecca paused and narrowed her eyes on him. "Where are you going with this? I know you have something up your sleeve."

"I have to figure out a way to get the two of them together."

"Who is he? Do you know?"

"When I first saw him, a niggling in the back of my

mind told me I should know him. But for the life of me, I couldn't place him."

"Not then, maybe," Rebecca said, harboring a smile, "but I bet you can now."

"You bet right. His name is Cutler McFarland."

Rebecca's eyes widened. "The district attorney?"

"One and the same."

"Wow."

"That's what I thought."

"So tell me about him."

"He's not married. Right now that's the most important thing."

"Which you think gives you a green light to play matchmaker."

Edgar leveled his gaze on her. "And you don't?"

"That's not—" She stopped midsentence and flashed him a sweet smile. "Tell me how I can help."

"You look shell-shocked, boss lady."

Kaylee shook her head to clear it, realizing Sandy had walked into the room and was staring at her out of puzzled eyes.

"What up?" Sandy asked when Kaylee didn't respond right off.

"You're not going to believe who I just talked to."

"Mmm, that sounds interesting, especially since you're still wearing that dazed look. So ante up. Who was it?"

Kaylee could barely contain her excitement. "Emily Austin."

Sandy looked puzzled. "But you've talked to Emily before."

"I know." Kaylee's grin consumed her features.

Sandy gestured with a hand. "You're not making sense, girl. Tell me what she wanted."

"She wants to fly down and meet with us."

"And…" Sandy coaxed.

"I'm trying to keep a lid on my excitement, only you're not helping."

"Tell me what you're trying to keep a lid on before I pee up one leg and down the other waiting."

Kaylee rolled her eyes. "You're crazy."

"Details. Give me the details."

"One of the French houses—she didn't say which one—wants to do a show here. They hired Ford to spearhead it. Ergo, she wants our expertise and our models."

"Oh, my gosh."

"I know. It's mind-boggling, isn't it?"

"The purpose of the visit is to hash out the details."

Kaylee blew out a breath. "I assume so."

"What a coup."

"I can't help but wonder what made her tap us."

Sandy made an unladylike snort. "You know the answer to that—we're damn good. *You're* damn good."

"Sometimes I have my doubts, especially when I can't seem to corral my girls."

The fire went out of Sandy's eyes. "I hate to put a damper on things, but now that you mention the girls—"

"Don't tell me there's been another uprising."

"Not yet, but it's brewing. I still don't know what the hell is going on, but it's *ongoing,* whatever it is."

"Undercurrents, huh?"

"Oh, yeah. Big time."

"Damn," Kaylee muttered under her breath.

"But until one of them cracks, we won't know."

"If they mess up this deal with Ford, I'm going to personally strangle them. But I think they know that."

"You'll have to get behind me," Sandy said through tight lips.

"Maybe by the time Emily gets here, whatever's ailing them will be resolved."

"I wish I could bet my booty on that."

"Just keep me informed, okay?"

Sandy nodded.

"Do you have time to go over this mountain of photos?" Kaylee asked, switching the subject. "I feel like tossing them, but I'm afraid I might miss the next Cindy Crawford."

"All the more reason to take a look-see."

For the longest time they sorted through hundreds of photos from aspiring models. While the task appeared daunting, it wasn't, as it took an expert only a split second to know whether the young face had potential or not.

"Sorry if I'm interrupting."

Both women were so mired in the job at hand, they hadn't realized they were no longer alone. But when Kaylee heard that low, sexy voice, her stomach bottomed out.

What was he doing here?

How had he gotten past the reception desk? Apparently Christy had stepped away to the restroom.

Sandy was the first to acknowledge Cutler, looking him over from head to toe. "May we help you?"

"Hope so," he drawled, his gaze concentrated on Kaylee.

She managed to pull her scattered wits about her enough to properly introduce them.

Although Kaylee could see that curiosity was eating at her, Sandy held herself in check and peered at her watch. "Oops, I have a meeting. I'll check in later."

Once her assistant walked out, an awkward silence descended.

"Surprised to see me." A flat statement.

Kaylee couldn't bring herself to look Cutler in the eye for fear of what she would see there. Yesterday's incident when he had deliberately turned and walked away as though repulsed by her lameness was too fresh in her mind.

She couldn't bear to see that look, nor did she want to think about it. Why should she care what he thought?

Only, she did.

As though he could read her mind, he said, "Look at me, Kaylee." A beat passed. "Please."

Unwittingly she responded to the husky note in his voice and turned and faced him, but not before she lifted her chin a notch. That was when she noticed he had closed the distance between them. He was so close now that the clean smell of his cologne penetrated her senses.

Heady stuff.

Thank goodness an iron will and long years of keeping her emotions in check came to her rescue. She didn't so much as move a muscle. She merely stood her ground.

"Why didn't you tell me?"

"Tell you what?" She knew he could see through her stall tactic, but she didn't care.

"Did you think I wouldn't find out?"

"I didn't think about it one way or the other."

"Liar," he whispered, his eyes delving deep into hers.

Kaylee's breath stuck in her throat and for a moment she was indeed rattled.

"So how 'bout the truth?"

"Actually it's none of your business," she said without taking her eyes off him.

"What if I chose to make it my business?"

"Why would you do a fool thing like that?"

"Maybe because I find you damned attractive."

"I don't believe that."

"Give me a chance and I'll prove it."

Her heart was going haywire. "How?"

"Have lunch with me."

"I don't think so."

"Chicken."

Her head bowed back. "It's going to take more than lunch to convince me."

"If that's a challenge, then I'm more than up to it."

"You have no idea what you're getting into."

"Did anyone ever tell you you talk too much?"

"Yes, but—"

His lips stopped her flow of words.

Nine

It was a hard but passionless kiss.

Yet when Cutler pulled his lips away, she couldn't utter a word. She was too stunned. She couldn't even think about addressing anything else she felt. Not now, not with him still standing *much too close*.

She glared at him. "Why did you do that?" She wouldn't have him feeling sorry for her.

"It was the only way I could figure out to shut you up." He paused. "And I wanted to kiss you."

His tone deepened and sent chills down her spine. That made her even madder. If he was going to kiss her, she wanted it to be because he felt passion.

"That wasn't fair."

His lips twitched. "I know."

"Which says you don't play by the rules." She heard the unsteady edge to her voice, increasing her anger.

"My rules, maybe."

His lips then spread into a full-fledged smile, which sent her further down that slippery slope.

"Come on, let's get out of here."

"I never said I'd go to lunch with you."

He paused, his hand on her arm, once again staring into her eyes. "You never said you wouldn't either."

She knew she'd regret what she was about to do. Nonetheless, she nodded and preceded him out the door.

"I like to see a woman eat."

"Then you're not disappointed."

Cutler smiled. "You got that right."

Kaylee diverted her gaze in order to keep from staring into the depths of his incredible blue eyes. Already she suspected they saw far too much. Her soul was private, and she aimed to keep it that way, no matter how attracted she was to him.

"I thought you'd enjoy this place, and I was right."

"My steak was cooked to perfection."

"Mine, too. But then it's hard to beat pasta and steak as a combo."

Kaylee took a breath, then pushed her plate aside. He followed suit, and immediately their waiter appeared and whisked their plates away.

"How 'bout another glass of wine?" Cutler asked.

"I'll have a cup of decaf coffee instead."

When silence fell between them, Kaylee perused the restaurant. It specialized in Italian cuisine, which was one of her favorites. They were seated in what she suspected was the garden room with soft music and live plants surrounding them.

Kaylee tried to relax, to enjoy the company of a sexy, charismatic man, something she had only dreamed about.

He was dressed in a white mock turtleneck and black jeans that perfectly outlined his hard body.

Maybe that was one of the reasons she couldn't relax. He looked big, broad and sexy. And he smelled good, too. All were powerful aphrodisiacs.

The fact that she'd agreed to share lunch with him and the kiss they had shared were too much for her unadventuresome mind to handle.

"You're awfully quiet," Cutler said in an almost musing tone.

"Sorry."

One side of his mouth quirked. "No need to apologize."

"Why did you ask me to lunch?" Once she'd asked the blunt question, Kaylee regretted it. But there was no way to retract her words.

He didn't answer right away. Instead, he stared at her with a strange glint in his eyes. "Why not?"

"That's just like a politician to answer a question with a question."

He chuckled.

"I asked first."

He thought for another long second, then said, "Why can't you accept the fact that I wanted to be with you?"

"Ah, another question." Kaylee forced a smile. "We're not making much progress."

"Sure we are. We're talking."

"That we are," she responded, watching his mouth take on a sensual curve. She averted her gaze.

"Kaylee, look at me."

His husky voice did nothing to calm her frayed nerves. She had to get a grip on herself or she wouldn't make it through the remainder of the meal without making a complete fool of herself. Their conversation was getting far too personal, thanks to her.

"Kaylee," he repeated.

She responded to the soft steel in his tone.

"What?"

"You're a lovely woman with all the right stuff. You have to know that."

For a moment she was mesmerized by his long brown fingers as they toyed with the stem of his now empty wineglass. She concentrated on the splattering of wiry black hair on his wrists.

He was a man's man and the sense of suffocation she felt at his nearness almost overwhelmed her. She'd never had this kind of strong reaction to anyone, but then when it came to the opposite sex, she'd had only one close encounter and that was with Kenny, who in the scheme of things didn't count.

So why should she be so drawn to a man she could never have?

"You're wrong," she said at last. "I don't have any of the right stuff."

"Someone sure did a number on you."

Kaylee blinked. "What makes you think that?"

He ignored her question. "I'd like to get my hands on the bastard."

This time she was taken aback and didn't bother to hide the fact. "You don't know anything about me."

"I know that much," he said flatly.

She felt color flood her face, but she didn't deny it because it was, after all, the truth.

"I'd like to change the subject, if you don't mind."

"Fine, but first, know that I'm here with you, right now, because I want to be."

Kaylee fought the urge to get up and get away from him. She didn't like his being sweet to her. She didn't want to feel this unwelcome attraction toward any man, especially *Cutler.*

She looked away one more time. "Tell me about your reelection chances."

A smile tugged at his lips. "Okay, you win. For now, that is."

"Thanks," she said with a tinge of sarcasm.

His smile stretched into a grin, then disappeared. "My reelection bid. I'd say there's a chance I might be defeated."

"Surely not."

"Winston Gilmore's a formidable opponent."

"Still, it's awfully hard to beat an incumbent."

"Not if you've chalked up a lot of enemies."

"Is there a reason for that?"

Cutler shrugged. "I've been told I'm too hardheaded and hard-assed."

She smiled. "At least you admit it."

"Oh, I know my shortcomings, all right, only—"

"You're not willing to do anything about them."

"Ah, you've already got me pegged."

His smile again sent her pulse racing. "Not hardly."

He let that slide. "I'm due to try several controversial cases, any of which could sink my ship."

"Even if you win them."

"Either way, I'm going to piss someone off."

She blew out a breath. "So how do you de-stress?"

"My ranch. Whenever I get the chance, I hightail it there and hole up. Takes the starch out every time."

"Somehow that doesn't surprise me—the ranch, that is."

"I betcha the boots were a dead giveaway."

"You think so," she said in a teasing tone.

Cutler laughed outright and then sobered, with the exception of the gleam in his eyes that was centered on her, and her pulse quickened even more. He was flirting with her, and she was flirting back. But how could she not? His magnetism could incite a riot in a nunnery.

"So how do you chill?"

"I don't."

"That's not true."

"Oh?"

"You're chilling now."

"You don't know that."

"Wanna bet?"

Kaylee pursed her lips, which drew another laugh from him.

"Gotcha, right?"

She didn't bother to respond, cautioning herself to pause and take note of the dangerous game she was playing. She had no intention of becoming a casualty of this man.

"Mind if I ask you something?"

"I have a feeling I should say no."

"Feel free."

She sighed openly. "What is it?"

"How long have you been like this?"

"And how is that?"

His eyes delved with laserlike intensity. "Crippled."

Ordinarily the use of that word flew all over her, even

if it was the truth and even if she'd goaded him into saying it. But coming from him, said in such a nonchalant manner, it was not in the least offensive.

"Since I was sixteen."

"That's a hell of a long time."

"That it is."

"I'd like to know what happened, but if you don't want to share—"

"Some other time, perhaps."

"That'll work." He paused. "Are you ready to get out of here?"

"Let's go."

Cutler paused again, his gaze locking with hers. The expression in his eyes made her feel hot and breathless and more than a little alarmed.

"Come on," he said huskily.

She was about to get into the car when it happened. She misstepped, losing her balance.

Just as the pavement rose to meet her, Cutler cried, "I've got you, Kaylee!"

Ten

"**W**ant me to come back later?"

Edgar had responded to Drew's "Come on in" before he realized his boss wasn't alone. Glen Yates, whom Edgar didn't particularly like, occupied one of the plush chairs in front of Drew's massive desk.

Pointing to the chair next to Glen's, Drew said, "Take the load off. We need to know how the mill project is going, anyway."

Edgar nodded at Glen before he made himself comfortable, propping one foot across his knee.

"You were saying." Drew refocused on Glen.

"From what I've been able to gather, boss, the company hasn't been dumping waste illegally."

"Would you swear to that on the Bible?" Drew asked.

Glen was silent for a moment, pulling on one corner of his mustache. "Nope. I couldn't go that far."

Drew responded with a smile. "Then we're good to go."

"Meaning that if we contact the EPA and hint that

dumping may be taking place, then the company's goose is cooked."

Drew's smile ripened. "Just the mere hint of scandal, and the rest is history, as they say."

"Their stock will plummet," Edgar put in, "and you'll get the mill for nothing."

Drew looked at him with a cocksure grin. "And the beat goes on."

"And on," Glen added with gleeful sarcasm.

Edgar had planned on keeping his mouth shut, but it hadn't worked out that way. What his boss was up to with these small family-owned businesses turned his stomach. On the other hand, Drew did a lot of good in the community, making it difficult to figure him out.

To date, the good seemed to outweigh the bad, which helped ease Edgar's conscience. While he didn't always agree with how Drew conducted his business enterprises, he wasn't fit to judge him.

Edgar owed Drew too much to lambaste him for his *modus operandi*. He had been a godsend to Kaylee, and that had earned Drew his complete loyalty.

"What's going on with the creosote plant?"

"Nothing definitive yet," Edgar said. "I'm still gathering data. I'll let you know."

"That'll work."

Glen uncoiled his hefty body and stood. "If that's all, boss, I'll be about my rat killing."

"Check in later," Drew demanded.

"Will do."

Once Edgar and Drew were alone, Edgar came straight to the point. "Do you know Cutler McFarland?"

"The D.A.?"

"Yep."

"Sure I know him, though not well. However, I have contributed to his campaign. Not a great sum, but respectable." Drew's eyes narrowed. "Why the interest in McFarland?"

"You're probably going to think I've lost it, and maybe I have, but—" Edgar broke off, struggling to find the right words to say what was on his mind without coming off sounding like a complete imbecile.

"What the hell, Edgar? Spit it out."

Drew wasn't one who enjoyed small talk. For Drew, time was money.

"Be patient with me," Edgar said, clearing his throat. "I'll get to my point shortly."

Drew gave him an irritated look, but didn't argue.

"Is he an okay guy?"

"As far as I know." Drew stood, then added in a contrary tone, "But I'm really not qualified to make that call."

"He came to the chamber party and spent some time with Kaylee."

Drew's brows shot up. "Oh?"

"Kaylee seemed to really like him."

"Did she tell you that?"

"No."

"Didn't think so."

"But I saw how she reacted to him."

"Edgar—"

"Hear me out, okay?" No matter the outcome, he was doggedly determined to have his say.

Drew fiddled with his pen. "I'm listening, though not very patiently."

"It appeared they were actually flirting with each other."

Drew looked astonished. "Kaylee, flirting?"

"I know. I was stunned, too." Edgar paused, then stumbled on. "But the more I observed, from afar I might add, I became convinced there was chemistry between those two."

"That's great."

"That's my feeling, too, only Kaylee won't admit to that or do anything about it."

"Which is her call, right?"

Edgar ignored Drew's unveiled sarcasm. "Yes, but—"

"Hey, get a grip, man. You can't go masterminding your daughter's love life behind her back. That's ludicrous. More to the point, she would have a conniption fit."

Edgar felt his face sting, but he wasn't about to back down. "If I can do anything that will help Kaylee have the things she wants, like a home and family, then I'm prepared to do it."

"You're crazy," Drew muttered. "Give the girl credit for having some sense."

"Tell me you wouldn't like to see her married."

"Of course I'd like that. Hell, I'd love to buy her a house with a white picket fence around it and see her have two point three children—the American dream, right? But we both know that's not in the cards for her."

"I refuse to think that."

"I love her, too, you know. But again, that's her choice whether to get involved with a man or not."

"At least McFarland's not married. I just wonder if he has someone special."

Drew snorted. "Did you hear what I just said?"

Edgar pursed his lips.

An expletive shot out of Drew's mouth. "I don't know whether McFarland's married or not and frankly I don't give a damn. I do know that every time I see him socially, he has a different woman on his arm."

"Which means he just hasn't found the right one."

"You're close to pissing me off, Edgar. Leave Kaylee and her love life be. Trust me, if you don't, you'll end up regretting it."

"I thought you'd be more supportive." Edgar found himself hard-pressed to keep the bitterness out of his tone.

Edgar stood, though not on steady legs. They felt like putty, but he didn't let on. "I'll certainly give your advice some thought."

"I suggest you do."

"But I'm making no promises," Edgar added on a firm note.

"Don't say I didn't warn you."

Edgar made his way of out the office, his shoulders stooped and his heart heavy.

The fact that he couldn't stay focused was not good. Cutler had come to the office early once again to clear some of the debris off his desk before the office came alive. So far, he'd made little progress. Instead of concentrating on his important day in court, his mind kept drifting to Kaylee.

Their time together had been both delightful and disastrous. He blamed himself for the latter, though he couldn't exactly say why. Maybe it was because he made her nervous, even though that wasn't blatantly apparent. But he knew women. Underneath her confident facade he'd sensed Kaylee was definitely not in her comfort zone.

Still, that wouldn't have made her lose her balance and stumble, something he bet she didn't do often. But on second thought, how would he know? He hadn't been in her company enough to know anything personal about her, especially when it came to her damaged leg.

A deep sigh escaped Cutler, and he rubbed the back of his neck in frustration. Looking back on the incident turned his stomach inside out.

He had reached her just in time. If he'd been a second later, Kaylee would have gone down. "I've got you," he'd muttered, grasping her forearm. "Easy does it."

Once she was upright, she closed her eyes and breathed deeply. Then she unexpectedly sagged against him. He didn't know what he'd expected, but not that. When her body made contact with his, he'd felt a surprising jolt, almost like an electrical shock. He went hard instantly before creating a safe distance between them, though he kept a tight hold on her arm.

"Thanks for helping," she said at last, keeping her gaze averted.

He knew she was humiliated, if not mortified, but her voice held strength and just the right amount of dignity. What a class act, he thought, even in the midst of adversity. He wanted to express that to her, but for some reason he didn't, sensing she might take it the wrong way.

"No problem," he muttered, guiding her toward the vehicle and into it.

Once he was behind the wheel, she faced him and said, "I don't make a habit of that."

"Didn't think you did."

"But sometimes my leg seems to have a mind of its own. And most of the time that's not good."

"You don't owe me an explanation," he said, keeping his voice light and even, trying desperately to put her at ease. Whether he pulled that off or not remained to be seen. He didn't want this fiasco to be a deal breaker. He wanted to see her again. She intrigued the hell out of him.

He wouldn't go so far as to say he was smitten, but he was close. And while that scared the hell out of him, too, it also excited him.

"I know I don't owe you an explanation, but—" Kaylee's voice broke off.

He glanced sideways and saw that she had clamped down on her lower lip as though struggling to get her thoughts out. He'd give anything to have been holding her arm, sparing her this embarrassment.

"No buts attached, okay?"

"Now you see why I don't—" Again she broke off.

"I want to see you again." He hadn't planned on saying that. The words just tumbled out of his mouth.

Kaylee stared at him wide-eyed. "What?"

"You heard me," he muttered.

"I don't think that's a good idea."

"Would you have said that if you hadn't stumbled?" He saw no point in soft-pedaling the truth. He'd always called a spade a spade; if he had judged her right, so had she.

"Yes," she said.

He chuckled. "I hate to call you a liar again, but I'm going to."

"You're awfully sure of yourself, aren't you?"

The irritation was clear in her voice, but instead of giving offense, it further amused him. "I'll admit you've thrown me a bit of a curve."

"Somehow that doesn't bring me comfort."

Although her tone bordered on stiffness, he heard a touch of humor, which gave him hope. In fact, his chuckle deepened.

She cut him a look, then smiled. Moments later they were at her office. Before he could move, she had the door open and was out. "Thanks for lunch."

"I'll be in touch."

Her response had been to turn her back on him, then make her way inside. He hadn't driven off until he could no longer see her. He just wished he could stop seeing her now, in his mind. To see her was to think about her, making him want to grab the phone and call her. But he knew that type of heavy-handedness wouldn't work with her.

If he wanted a relationship of any kind, he had to tread softly. When it came to men, she was as skittish as a newborn colt. The kiss had proved that. If she was afraid of him and his motives, he wouldn't get to first base with her.

That was why he had kissed her with far more distance than he wanted. He'd wanted to harden the contact with his tongue. But he'd dared not for fear of irreversible consequences. But he'd definitely craved more.

It had been years since he'd found a woman who actually tasted good. And she'd tasted damned good. And smelled good, too. And felt good. She hadn't been immune to him either. He'd felt a flicker of response, even if she might not admit it.

He had no intention of letting the spark between them die, if for no other reason than to remove that sadness from her eyes. With that thought, Cutler placed his hand on the receiver just as he heard the beep on his speaker phone.

"You're due in court. Now."

He released a sigh, thinking his secretary's blunt reminder had kept him from making the wrong move. He grabbed his briefcase and walked out.

Eleven

"Emily, I can't tell you how much I appreciate this opportunity."

Kaylee meant it, too. In fact, she was finding it hard to contain her excitement. She would have loved to dance around the room, shouting the Hallelujah Chorus. But since she couldn't, she'd have to be content with shouting it silently.

Her meeting with Emily had just come to an end and Emily was leaving shortly to board the plane back to New York. Kaylee couldn't have asked for a more productive afternoon. The tall, curvy brunette—an ex-model—had both a keen sense of business and a winning personality.

"Hey, it's me—us—who's thanking you," Emily said after making her way to the door. There she turned and extended her hand.

Kaylee clasped it with a smile. "We'll get to work right away on our end."

"Again, our agency has every confidence in yours. That's why we handpicked you."

"I still find that amazing."

"Don't. You've built quite a reputation for yourself, and after spending time here, I can see why. You have great girls, and you run a tight ship."

"I try. But I couldn't do it without Sandy and the others."

"Give my regards to your assistant, and tell her I'm looking forward to working with her, as well."

"I'll tell her. Meanwhile, you take care. And thanks again."

Emily smiled, then walked out. Immediately Kaylee sagged against the closed door, feeling as if all her energy had been zapped. Throughout the session with Emily she'd been uptight, wanting everything to go perfectly. And for the most part, it had.

Benton Agency had gotten the big contract and the big bucks that went along with it. What a coup, as Sandy had said. What a responsibility. The amount of work required to put on a show of this magnitude was mind-boggling. Versace was the top name in the fashion industry, and Kaylee still couldn't believe she was going to get to work with such a prestigious house.

But again, the responsibility was awesome. Yet she was more than up to the challenge. For years she'd hoped for a break like this. No way was she going to blow it. She would put her mind and heart wholeheartedly into the project, letting nothing else interfere.

And that included Cutler McFarland.

Kaylee let out a groan as she made her way back to her desk and eased into her chair. She didn't want to think about him and what had happened at the restaurant. Unfortunately, that was all she had thought about.

Even now Kaylee felt a surge of color flood her face. In

the back of her mind she knew the potential to fall was there. She wondered if in all her success she'd grown overconfident.

Which was not smart.

Actually, what wasn't smart was to have gone to lunch with Cutler. She had known better, but she hadn't listened to her head. Instead, she'd gone with her heart and paid the price, reminding herself again that choices have consequences. In this particular case her consequence was humiliation.

She blinked back unwanted tears, hating it when she felt sorry for herself. She wished things were different, wished she was whole in body and soul. But she wasn't. No matter how hard she tried or how hard she pretended otherwise, she *was* different.

Damn him for making her feel this way. Damn him for making her feel bad about herself. Damn him for making her care.

About him.

Her attraction to Cutler had seemingly come out of nowhere, leaving her clueless as to how to handle these raw emotions.

Yesterday it had taken every ounce of willpower she possessed to gather her dignity and drag herself away from him, fearing she would see pity in his eyes.

Distancing herself had been hard, especially when a shaft of desire had shot through every pore of her slender frame. No matter how much she tried to rationalize her reaction, she knew her body craved to know his touch, feel his hands on her flesh.

That scared the wits out of her.

She tried to calm down, telling herself she wouldn't see him again and risk pain for which she had no antidote. She had to remain focused and keep her mind on her business and the chance of a lifetime the Versace show offered her company.

She could do that. After all, concentration was her strong suit. Besides, while Cutler didn't seem bothered that she'd almost fallen flat on her face, that didn't mean he was smitten with her or that he wanted to make love to her.

Kaylee's breath caught at the thought of intimacy with him. She felt as if she was bleeding on the inside, and knew she had to stop such forbidden thoughts from assailing her. If only she had more expertise in this arena, she was certain she'd know what to do.

The whole experience left her feeling as vulnerable as she'd felt for years following the accident. It was an emotion she had come to despise, and still did. She wouldn't let herself sink into that black hole again. She had worked too hard, overcome too much, to let that happen.

Armed with new resolve, Kaylee shrugged off her doldrums, got up, walked down the hall to the lounge and poured herself a fresh cup of coffee. In a few minutes she had appointments with several prospective new clients, one of whom had recently purchased both a television station and a large automobile dealership. If she convinced him of her agency's ability to handle both accounts simultaneously, her company would reap another tremendous financial reward. She'd been working on her sales pitch for weeks and was eager to present her ideas.

She was headed back to her office when she heard screaming. For a second Kaylee froze, feeling a frisson of fear stand her hair on end.

"What on earth," she muttered, realizing the commotion was coming from one of the dressing rooms.

She was halfway there when the door opened and a model stuck her head around the corner and cried, "Kaylee, come quick."

Cursing her uncooperative leg, Kaylee upped her pace as much as she dared, yesterday's fiasco a vivid reminder of her limitations.

Still, she moved faster than she should have as the screams became shriller. By the time she crossed the threshold and saw what was going on, rage filled her.

Two models were locked together on the floor involved in a free-for-all. At first she couldn't tell who they were. After moving closer, she identified them. Barbie and Jessica.

"Stop it!" Kaylee cried. "Stop it right now."

She might as well have been talking to herself for all the attention they paid her.

"You bitch!" Barbie spat, clawing at Jessica's eyes.

Jessica grabbed a handful of Barbie's long hair and yanked. "It takes one to know one!"

Barbie took another swipe at Jessica, landing a blow on her neck.

Kaylee winced, while the other girls simply watched the spectacle in silence, terror mirrored in their faces.

"What can we do?" Gwen asked, a frantic note in her voice. "Do you want us to try and separate them?"

"Not on your life," Kaylee said in a terse whisper. "Two in a catfight is enough."

"Surely *you're* not thinking about stepping in?"

"Absolutely not."

"But we have to do something, don't we?" Gwen asked amidst the continued screaming and punching.

Kaylee looked at her; then her gaze perused the others before dipping back to the floor where the two were still fighting. "As a matter of fact, we don't have to do anything."

"What?" Candy Crenshaw screeched. "But…but one of them is going to get hurt."

"That's the price they'll have to pay, isn't it?" Kaylee said, hearing the steel in her voice.

"Jeez, Louise, what's going on?"

Sandy appeared in the doorway, her mouth agape. "Am I seeing what I think I'm seeing?"

Kaylee nodded. "That you are."

"Want me to do anything?"

"No, I don't."

Sandy grinned. "Okay, I get you."

"Girls," Kaylee said, "out of here. And I don't have to remind you to keep your mouths shut about this incident. What goes on under this roof is no one else's business. If I find you've betrayed that confidence, you'll be fired."

Once the room was cleared except for the two still grappling on the floor, Kaylee and Sandy watched the girls continue to slap and hiss at one another.

Barbie already had a black eye and Jessica had a welt on one cheek.

"Let's go, Sandy," she finally said, disgust making her sick to her stomach.

"What are we going to do?"

"I have no choice but to give them their walking papers."

"God, Kaylee, if we lose them now, we're up the creek

without a paddle, especially with the Versace deal in the works."

Kaylee frowned. "What do you suggest—that I let them get by with that kind of behavior?"

"No, but…"

"But what?"

Sandy merely shook her head. "I don't know. I'm just as confounded about this as you are. As we've said all along, something foul is in the air, but I'll be damned if I can figure out what it is."

"If word gets out, we're in deep trouble. We don't need our competition portraying our girls as vicious princesses who can't get along on an assignment."

"All the more reason why I think we should try and get to the bottom of this rather than dump them out to hit the streets. Of all our models, those two have the biggest mouths."

Kaylee didn't say anything. Sandy was right. Yet her anger far exceeded any rational thought. She shouldn't make a hasty decision that she would live to regret, she cautioned herself.

"Okay. I'll sleep on it."

"Meanwhile, I guess I'd better check and see if either one has any hair left."

"I'm thinking about their faces," Kaylee said in a glum tone.

"They won't be able to work the Neiman show, which makes me want to strangle them." She paused and blew out a forlorn sigh. "Hopefully, they'll be ready for the Versace shindig, though they might look more like clowns than models."

Kaylee knew Sandy was making an attempt at humor, but she found nothing to laugh about.

Her well-ordered life was rapidly careening out of control.

Twelve

Winston Gilmore took a sip of his drink, then swirled the liquid around in the glass before indulging himself again.

He was a man of average height and build with a set of pearly whites that he considered his best asset, especially when it came to the press. Dressing to perfection enhanced his desired image as a self-confident, good-looking man who would do his constituents proud if he were elected to the office of district attorney.

"So do you think we've got him running scared?"

Winston sighed deeply, then pursed his lips while staring at his campaign manager, Harvey Eddison, a tall, bald man with big ears and large lips. Homely was the only way to describe him. But what Harvey lacked in looks, he made up for in brains. He was smart and aggressively organized, just the kind of person Winston needed to spearhead his campaign to replace Cutler McFarland as D.A.

He had agreed to meet Harvey for lunch at a small restaurant near Winston's law firm. He wished he could've given his manager more time, but he had a heavy court schedule.

"I'd like to think he's panicked," Winston finally said, "but with McFarland you never know. He holds his cards close to his chest."

"Maybe his personal card, but not his business one," Harvey pointed out. "His record is an open book, which is what we're going to use to hammer him."

"Don't underestimate him, Harvey. Underneath that cowboy persona is a tough hombre, no pun intended."

"Trust me, I know. I've done my homework on our present D.A." Harvey scratched one of his ears, then took a drink of his Scotch. "Still, I believe we've made a dent in his credibility with our television blitz."

Winston finished his wine, then motioned to the waiter for a refill. "Not to mention the controversial cases he's trying," he pointed out once his glass was replenished. "He's up to his ass in alligators with at least two of them. Maybe more."

"The woman who nixed her kids, who's now claiming insanity, could eat his lunch. Murdered kids is a topic hotter than a branding iron."

"I can't argue with that."

"During the trial we'll make him look as bad as we can."

Winston nodded. "The defrocked priest who instigated the murder of that abortion-clinic doctor is probably next on his agenda. That case will give us extra ammo to shoot at him."

Harvey nodded in agreement. "We just have to have our guns loaded, ready to move in for the kill."

Winston's eyes narrowed. "It's time for that cocky bastard to go."

"You never told me why you have your stinger out for McFarland. Did he by chance sleep with your wife?"

Winston clenched his jaw and cursed.

Harvey held up his hand in a defensive gesture. "Hey, that was meant to be a joke. Don't tell me it isn't."

"He and Jan were an item once," Winston admitted through tight lips. "But that has no bearing on this election. Let's just say I want his job and leave it at that."

"Works for me," Harvey responded with ease. "What we need to do is hit him where he's weak."

"Right."

"Which means digging the skeletons out of his closet and exposing them."

"Suppose he doesn't have any."

Harvey snorted. "Everyone has secrets. Some are easier to find than others, but again, everyone has something to hide."

"I did hear something interesting." Winston gazed around the premises, then leaned forward.

"I'm listening," Harvey said, also leaning in.

"It concerns Judge Jenkins."

"Oh?"

"McFarland has it out for him."

"How crazy is that?" Harvey's tone was incredulous.

"Exactly. If he crosses Jenkins, he'll wipe the floor with McFarland."

"So I guess I should find out what that's all about."

Winston smiled. "I don't particularly like Jenkins myself. He's given me more than one headache in court, but I'm not crazy enough to take him on. He takes no prisoners."

"So if McFarland crosses him, Jenkins could knock him off for us."

"That's what I'm hoping for, but I'm not going to put

all my eggs in the judge's basket. Not to beat a dead horse, but McFarland's a slick operator and won't go down without a fight."

"No problem. We'll just be smarter and tougher. I've bested far better men than a wannabe cowboy. Don't worry, come election time, he'll be out on his ear."

Winston lifted his glass and grinned. Harvey did likewise.

"To victory," Winston said.

Their glasses clinked before they drained them.

Cutler stared out the French doors onto the opulent grounds that stretched as far as the eye could see. His old-time friend and backer Salem Caskey was one rich dude.

Several years ago Salem had purchased one of the largest and oldest homes in upscale River Oaks and had it completely renovated. Cutler rarely gave a second thought to where people lived, or how they lived, for that matter, because he didn't care.

But this place was overwhelming with its huge columns, high ceiling-to-floor windows and the magnificent, artwork adorning the walls. He couldn't forget the huge indoor lap pool that Salem used every day to soothe his crippling arthritis.

"May I get you something to drink while you wait?"

Cutler swung around and smiled at Lupe, the housekeeper. "Got any hot tea cakes?"

Lupe's black eyes lit up. "Just took them out of the oven."

"Will you marry me?"

Lupe giggled. "Do you want some now or had you rather take a batch home?"

"Home, if you don't mind."

"I'll have them ready," she said, then moved aside as Salem made his entrance.

Despite his gnarled hands and slightly humped shoulders, he was a large, robust man who kept himself fit. Though in his seventies, he still had a full head of black hair with no gray, thanks to his Native American heritage.

"Sorry, but she's already taken."

Lupe fluttered her hand as if embarrassed, though she was obviously pleased with all the attention she was getting. "Nice to see you again, Mr. Cutler."

"Same here," Cutler said with a wink, then watched as the housekeeper walked out.

"Bourbon and Coke?" Salem asked, crossing to the bar.

Cutler peered at his watch. "Don't normally drink until after five."

"It's five o'clock somewhere."

"According to the country-western song, you're right." Cutler grinned. "I'll take a beer."

"Beer it is."

Once they were seated across from each other, drinks in hand, Salem didn't waste any time sampling his Scotch. Cutler did likewise with his beer, and they sipped in silence. Cutler relished the moment, feeling his insides uncoil for the first time in a long while. He couldn't remember when he and Salem hadn't been friends, though that friendship had been tested a few months back when Salem's only son had gotten into trouble.

Thank God their friendship had weathered that storm and remained intact. He didn't think he could win the election without Salem's money and backing. There was no thinking about it; he *couldn't* win. Cutler was convinced this summons to the mansion was to seal Salem's commitment.

"I think you should hear it straight from the horse's mouth," Salem said, following a discreet belch.

"I can't thank you enough for your support, Salem."

"Only, I'm not supporting you."

At first Cutler thought his ears had deceived him. But then he met Salem's eyes head-on and knew better. They were as cold as a block of ice. Cutler's stomach hollowed. He had to hand it to himself, though; he forced his voice and his manner to remain calm and even. "Why's that?"

"I think you know."

"Nathan." A flat statement of fact.

"That's right." Salem's tone was harsh. "You took my only son away from me."

"I didn't have a choice, and you know that. He broke the law."

"You had him committed, for God's sake, to that house of horrors."

"The place wasn't my call, Salem. It was the judge's, and you know that, too."

"But you prosecuted him, damn you. Need I remind you of that?"

"He was using *and* dealing."

"You could've cut a deal."

"Don't you mean *another* deal?" Cutler asked, his voice sharper than he intended. But he'd just had the rug jerked out from under him, and it went against his nature not to defend himself. "As it was, I went so far out on that limb, it nearly broke off."

"You're simply making excuses, Cutler. Covering your

own ass. You could've kept Nathan out of that place, only you chose not to."

"So you're punishing me by withdrawing your support?"

"That's about the size of it. You might as well know this, too. I'm going to see that Gilmore whips your ass."

"I bet he's jumping over the moon." Cutler's voice now dripped with unsuppressed sarcasm.

"He doesn't know yet."

Cutler stood. "Well, he's one lucky man."

"Is that all you have to say?"

"What else is there?"

"You could say you're sorry for shitting on me then rubbing it in."

"You know me better than that, Salem. I did Nathan a favor. I might even have saved his life. I thought you of all people would understand that."

"Well, you thought wrong. My son is all I have. You ruined his life and mine."

"It's too bad you feel that way."

"Get out of my house, Cutler. You're no longer welcome here."

Cutler stared at his old friend long and hard and then said, "Have a nice life, Salem."

Kaylee rubbed her leg, feeling the effects of the pruning she'd given her flowers on the patio. Weatherwise it had been a glorious Saturday afternoon. It had rained during the wee hours of the morning, and all the greenery smelled and looked lush. She'd been outside all morning, opting not to go into the office.

She had just sat down and taken a sip of lemonade when

the first tweak of pain hit. Grimacing, she massaged the sore spot with more vigor and determination. She should go inside and take something to relax the muscle, but she didn't want to move. She'd just endure until she had to get up.

Thank goodness she'd been pain free while her dad was there. It upset him terribly to see her suffer. No matter how much she hurt around him, she never let on. Besides, the discipline was good for her, as well. Her leg would never get any better. Hence she had to ignore the pain or give in to it. She chose the former.

Even so, she wasn't sure she'd pulled the wool over Edgar's eyes. When it came to her and her needs, he was much too intuitive.

This morning had been a good example of that when he'd asked with blunt intent if she'd seen Cutler McFarland since the party.

Clearly taken aback, she had taken several seconds before answering. "What makes you ask that?"

He shrugged as though his question was no big deal. She knew better.

"I was just curious, that's all. So, have you?"

"Don't you know that curiosity often killed the cat?" she said in a teasing voice, hoping he'd get the message.

He didn't.

"You two seemed to have hit it off."

"Were you spying on me, Dad?" She kept that teasing tone, though she was miffed that he'd even mentioned Cutler.

Edgar flushed. "Of course not. I just happened to see you talking to him."

"And that's all it was, a conversation," she said with emphasis. She had no idea where his mind was headed, but just in case it wasn't in her best interests, she'd nip things in the bud right now.

"He seemed to like you."

"I like him, too. In fact, I've seen him a few times, but—"

"Hey, that's great." Edgar's eyes and face glowed. "That means there's a relationship in the making, because you don't *see* men. He seemed to like you."

She laughed without humor. "Oh, please, Dad, stop trying to play the matchmaker."

His flush deepened. "You know—"

She held up her hand, shushing him. "We've been down this road before. I'm not interested in traveling it again. Let's change the subject, okay?"

He grinned sheepishly. "You win."

Edgar hadn't stayed long after that, and Kaylee had thought he seemed agitated. Something was bothering him, but since she didn't allow him to pry into her business, she had to respect his privacy, as well. When he was ready to confide in her, he would. Not only was he her father, he was also her best friend.

She didn't know when she realized she was no longer alone. Maybe it was the scent—*his scent.* When she turned her head, her brown eyes met his blue ones.

Following several beats of shocked silence, she asked, "What are you doing here?"

Thirteen

"Isn't that obvious?"

His words sounded husky as he regarded her with intense, unreadable eyes.

"No, it's not obvious." She tried to override the quarrelsome note in her voice but failed.

A smile tugged at his lips. "Okay. I came to see you. How's that?"

"You frightened me." He hadn't, not in the way she had intimated, but it was something to say until she could collect herself. She knew she was not at her best. She wore an apricot tank top and white capri pants that clung to her skin due to the high humidity. Her hair was damp and pulled back in a ponytail, and she had on very little makeup.

While the temperature itself was low, the moisture in the air made breathing close to impossible.

Or was it Cutler's presence that affected her breathing?

"Are you pissed off?" he asked, a glint of humor in his eyes as he leaned his head to one side.

"Shouldn't I be?"

"Depends."

He looked good, dressed in worn, faded jeans and a white shirt that earlier might have been crispy, but was now wrinkled and clinging to his body. His hair was slightly unkempt, lending him an air of masculine primitiveness that produced a coil of heat inside her.

Kaylee intentionally averted her gaze before he could read her thoughts.

"Do you want me to go?"

His blunt question drew her eyes back to him, making her once again conscious of his height and the broadness of his shoulders. What was so special about this man?

Chemistry.

She couldn't continue to deny it. The treacherous intimacy that hummed like an undercurrent beneath all their conversations was alive and real. She felt it and knew he did, too.

"Kaylee?"

"Now that you're here, you might as well stay."

Another smile tugged at his mouth. "I'll watch you work."

"Work?"

"Yeah. Weren't you playing in the dirt?"

Her hands were stained black from the soil and she felt the sweat run between her breasts. Thank goodness she'd put on a bra. Some Saturdays she didn't. Still, she sensed her nipples were erect in reaction to him. She figured she looked as messy as she felt.

"As a matter of fact, I was."

"Then don't let me stop you."

"You know better than that," she said in a snappy tone.

He shrugged with a grin.

"Would you care for a glass of lemonade? Fresh squeezed."

"Would I ever."

Kaylee gestured toward a wrought-iron chair. "Have a seat. I'll be right back."

"Need any help?"

She didn't bother to answer or turn around, though she was conscious of his eyes following her. She couldn't help but wonder what he was thinking as he watched her drag her leg. Suddenly she felt like bursting into tears, which made her furious at herself. Collecting herself, she decided she would serve him his lemonade, find out what he really wanted, then send him on his way.

End of story.

She added several cranberry-iced tea cakes from her favorite bakery beside the pitcher of lemonade. Not so much for him as for herself. Realizing she had skipped lunch, she felt hunger gnaw at her.

"Thanks," he said, having sat down with his long legs stretched out in front him. "Ah, cookies, too."

"I'm hungry," she said by way of explanation.

As though she was as transparent as glass, he chuckled. "You really are pissed off."

"Stop saying that. I let you stay, didn't I?"

"Begrudgingly."

"All right," she said with a reluctant grin. "I'll admit you surprised me."

"Surprised myself, actually."

Kaylee raised her eyebrows.

"I just got sucker punched in the gut and while I was

nursing my wounds, I found myself in your driveway. Go figure." He took a drink of his lemonade and stared at her over the rim.

When he looked at her with those deep blue eyes, her pulse leaped with excitement. "Is what happened something you want to talk about?"

"Are you in a listening mood?"

Careful, Kaylee, you're getting in over your head. Keep your distance and you'll survive. Otherwise… "Sure. Go ahead and vent."

In order to maintain her nonchalant attitude, she reached for a tea cake and began munching on it. For some reason it tasted like sawdust. She was tempted to spit it out; instead, she chased it down with a drink of lemonade.

"A good friend—you might even say mentor—told me he was backing my opponent."

Kaylee's eyes widened. "No wonder you feel sucker punched."

She listened as he filled her in on the details about Salem and his son. When he finished, she asked, "At the time you had no idea he harbored such bitterness toward you?"

"Not really. Oh, we definitely had words after Nathan was picked up. But in the end, I thought Salem finally realized that I had done the boy a favor. If he hadn't gotten locked up, he'd be dead by now."

"I'm sorry, Cutler," she said for lack of anything else to say.

"Me, too. Besides having the rug pulled out from under me jobwise, I hate losing a good friend whose ear I bent more than once during controversial cases. He never failed to steer me in the right direction. In fact, today I had planned to talk to him about a couple of pending cases."

"Would one of them be the woman who killed her kids?"

"Yep. The other one is that abortion-clinic shooting masterminded by an ex-priest."

"I'm not familiar with that one."

"Both have the potential to sink my ship if they're not handled properly."

"You'll just have to trust yourself and go with your gut."

"Suppose my gut's wrong?"

"Why not cross that bridge when you get to it?"

"Good idea."

There was a long period of silence.

Cutler stood and peered down at her. "Are you game to take a ride?"

She frowned. "Where to?"

"I can't surprise you?"

"I don't think so."

"I have a ranch outside the city. When I'm uptight, bonding with nature usually works out the kinks."

Although he smiled, his eyes were now sober and his face strained. Losing his friend's support had really been a blow. She felt for him on that score, but she wasn't sure she wanted to get more personal with Cutler. She did and she didn't. Thinking about being alone with him in the woods was more tempting than she cared to admit. And more dangerous.

"So what's it going to be?"

"I shouldn't go."

"Do you have plans for the rest of the day?"

"No."

"Then I'd really like the company."

"You drive a hard bargain."

"So I'm told."

Trying to slow her hammering pulse, Kaylee forced herself not to look at him. "Should I change clothes?"

"Absolutely not. And don't worry, I have bug repellent."

"I hadn't even thought about that," she said with a spontaneous smile.

She heard his breath catch and felt his eyes on her, drawing hers like a magnet. For the longest time they stared at each other. It was only after she saw the raw desire jump into his eyes that she turned away.

"Are you ready?" he asked in a hoarse tone.

Without looking at him she said, "I need a minute."

"Take your time. I'll just help myself to another glass of lemonade. By the way, it's delicious."

She gave him a semblance of a smile. "Thanks. I won't be long."

"No problem," he responded, reaching for the pitcher.

She watched him a moment longer and then fled to her bedroom. Refusing to think about what she was about to do and the possible consequences, she refreshed her makeup, grabbed her purse and made her way back to the patio.

Cutler rose, his gaze roaming over her. Then he said in a husky voice, "Have I ever told you that you're beautiful?"

"No," she whispered around a suddenly dry mouth.

"Well, I'm telling you now," he said, his eyes delving deeper.

Take cover, Kaylee, she warned herself, while you still have the strength to do so. Yet she didn't make a move. Instead she stood there and gave in to the blood thundering through her veins with excitement and alarm.

She licked her lips. "I think we should go."

"I think you're right," he said, his voice still hoarse. "Come on."

The ranch was a spectacular spread. She hadn't known what to expect, but she hadn't thought it would be this large or grand. They had spoken very little on the way, though it hadn't been an uncomfortable silence despite the fact that she knew he remained troubled.

She'd let him set the agenda. If he'd wanted to talk, she'd been willing to listen. So far, he'd held his tongue.

After nearly two hours of driving, they arrived around six—a perfect time of the day. As they got out of his vehicle the air seemed cooler, or maybe it was because the wind had picked up, chasing the humidity away. Whatever the case, being outside was more than tolerable.

Cutler gestured toward the house, which appeared to be more like a cabin. Leaning heavily on her cane, she made her way up the steps, then inside.

"Are you okay?"

Her lips tightened. "I'm fine."

"Just checking," he said lightly, making his way ahead of her into a large area that was both a living and dining room.

Its high-beamed ceiling made it appear larger than it probably was, Kaylee noted, yet it didn't have a barnlike feel. Actually, it had its own brand of cozy charm with the dark green leather furniture softened by plump, colorful pillows and a couple of chenille throws. Bookcases filled with books and other memorabilia lined both sides of the fireplace.

"You like?" he asked, walking to the glass door that opened onto a screened porch that she guessed ran the length of the house.

"What's not to like? It's wonderful."

"I have about five hundred acres in all with a full-time foreman who takes care of it, mainly working the cattle."

"When your job gets to you, you head here."

"As fast as I can."

She smiled. "And what a place to unwind. The view's awesome."

And it was. Rolling green hills dotted with huge trees filled her vision. In the distance she could see a lake, its water sparkling like diamonds wherever the sun touched. Beyond that, cattle grazed, adding fuel to their already fat bellies.

"The view's what sold me on the place. And the fact that I can get here without too much hassle."

"I'd like to take a walk," Kaylee said once they were on the porch.

"Are you sure?"

"At least to that first fence. Beyond that might be too much."

"It's your call."

By the time they reached the split-rail fence, her leg was throbbing. Yet she had no intention of complaining, nor did she regret the venture. The beauty surrounding her was worth the sacrifice.

If only Cutler wasn't standing so close. Out of the corner of her eye she stared at his profile. The wind had mussed his hair and his jaw was dark with end-of-the-day stubble. As much as she wanted to dismiss the potent attraction between them, she couldn't.

He turned suddenly and held her gaze. "Kaylee."

An unnamed fear lumped in her stomach as his cool fingers slid around her neck. But there was nothing cool about his mouth when it sank onto hers. It was hot with yearning. She melted into him.

Fourteen

Cutler's hands pressed into her back as the kiss deepened. Kaylee wanted to jerk away, but she couldn't bear to sever the contact between them, especially when his tongue lashed against hers time after time.

If his first kiss had sparked a fire inside her, this one set it roaring. Yet it was sweet, and he tasted so good.

"God, you taste good," he whispered against her lips.

"I was thinking the same thing about you."

He sank his mouth back onto hers, nibbling, then sucking on her lower lip before deepening the kiss even further.

Passion. She didn't want to feel that. She didn't want to feel anything. It was easier that way. But she had no willpower where he was concerned, and she returned his kisses with a feverish hunger that shocked her.

"Kaylee," he murmured, his voice thick, his breath hot.

"What?"

"Just Kaylee." His lips meshed with hers again—slow, intimate, unhurried.

The rational side of her continued to fight, to cling to

all the values she knew were so critical in holding on to her life's equilibrium. Yet another side of her was as hungry for him as he seemed to be for her. She felt her muscles contract deep inside as her hands wandered down and over the hard cheeks of his buttocks. So perfect, so satisfying to her touch.

He was real, substantial and vibrantly alive and he made her feel that way, too.

She was alive.

It was wonderful.

He moaned, then choked out, "Do you have any idea what you're doing to me?"

"This is crazy," she whispered.

"I know."

"That's why it needs to stop," she breathed against his lips, before finding the strength to push out of his arms.

Once they were apart, they simply looked at each other, their chests heaving, as though stunned by what had just happened.

"I won't apologize." His voice was brusque.

"Did I ask for an apology?"

"No."

Kaylee looked away, fearful of betraying herself, fearful she would reveal how attracted she was to him, though she suspected he already knew.

She no longer recognized herself, and that scared her.

"Kaylee, don't shut me out."

Ignoring him, she lifted her head toward the sky, feeling the breeze blow on her hot face. She breathed deeply until she felt some of her panic subside.

"Cutler, I—"

"Let's go back to the cabin," he interrupted, touching her arm and urging her forward.

She stood her ground. "I don't think so."

"I wasn't planning on taking up where we left off," he said with a note of passionate belligerence. "Unless you wanted me to, that is."

Her chin quivered. "You should take me home."

"We have to talk."

"There's nothing to talk about."

"I beg to differ." His voice was thick.

Stop it! she wanted to scream. Caring about him was foolish, stupid and dangerous.

"I'm tired," she said, then hated herself for using her handicap as an excuse. She had never done that before.

A white line encircled his mouth. "You win this time, Kaylee. But mark it down—you haven't seen the last of me."

A heavy silence fell between them.

"I don't want to argue with you." Especially now, she told herself, not when she was emotionally wrung out and distraught. And not when a jackhammer was having a field day inside her head.

Cutler's gaze turned molten. "Good, because you wouldn't win."

He had always wanted to own a bank, and damn if he hadn't finally found one in which he actually owned a small percentage of stock, giving him a leg up. He just needed more information on its solvency before making a decision.

"Is that everything, Mr. Rush?"

Drew peered at his secretary, Mandy White, a plain and

withdrawn young woman who had worked for him for several years now. She was as loyal an employee as he'd ever had, yet he didn't know one personal thing about her, except that she wasn't married. He'd often wondered if she was gay; though it wouldn't have mattered.

Now, though, as he looked at her from his hospital bed in the top-floor suite, he suddenly wondered how she would react if he uncoiled that bun at the nape of her neck, pulled off her glasses and kissed those thin lips.

He suspected she'd go ape-shit.

For a second he was tempted to try his luck. He was as horny as hell, having been cooped up in this room for three days now. His fool doctor had told him it was time for a full physical and he wanted him admitted to do it. At first Drew had said an emphatic no, but then Dr. Swanson had reminded him that he was a prime candidate for a stroke, given his family history.

Drew had finally given in. Now, though, he was champing at the bit to get out. To date, Swanson showed no signs of letting that happen.

"Mr. Rush, are you all right?"

He shook his head, then said in an irritated tone, "Damn straight I am."

"You were so quiet, I thought—"

"Well, you thought wrong."

Pink cheeked, Mandy rose. "Since we've covered everything on my list, I'm headed back to the office. I'll be available."

"Just keep in touch."

After the door closed behind her, the phone rang. It was Kaylee. That soothed his ruffled feathers.

"Hey, girl, how are you?"

"I should be asking you that."

"Hell, I'm great."

"I hope so. I about had Dad's head on a platter because he didn't tell me you were in the hospital. I want to come see you."

"Don't you dare come anywhere near here. If I need you, I'll let you know."

"You promise?"

"Sure, honey. You just take care of your business and yourself. Do *you* need anything?"

"More hours in the day."

He chuckled. "Can't help you out there. Now, if it's money—"

"Whoa. I'm not taking another penny from you until my debt is paid in full."

"I don't want my money back."

"That's nonnegotiable."

He chuckled again.

"I love you, Uncle Drew."

"I love you, too, honey. Now, guess who just walked in the door?"

"Dad?"

"Yep."

"Good. I'll talk to you soon. You take care."

"Will do."

By the time the receiver was back on the hook, Edgar was sitting in the chair that Mandy had just vacated. "She raked me over the coals for not telling her you were here."

"I'm glad you didn't tell her. She doesn't need to be bothered with me."

"You know better than that. She's crazy about you."

Drew smiled.

"Any news on any of your tests?" Edgar asked.

"Haven't seen Swanson yet."

"I was hoping you'd get out today."

"Discharged or not, I'm getting ready to bolt."

"Best not do that," Edgar said in his easy drawl.

Drew snorted, then said, "I'm assuming you've got something on the creosote plant."

"They were investigated a couple of years ago by the EPA."

Drew straightened in the bed, all senses on full alert. "Did anything come of that investigation?"

"Not that I could uncover. The company was either exonerated or let off the hook."

"Keep digging, but it sounds like they're going to be an easy takeover."

"That it does. Anything else I can do for you?"

"As a matter of fact, there is."

"Shoot."

"I need some papers out of my safe at home." He then told him what folders to get.

Edgar stood. "I'll be on my way as soon as you give me the combination."

"Commit it to memory. I don't write that kind of stuff down."

After Edgar had left the room, Drew made a mental note to call a locksmith and have the combination changed.

Camilla let him in and then disappeared.

Edgar trod softly as he entered the opulent study in

Drew's palatial home nestled in the middle of twenty acres. Though he'd been inside countless times and made to feel welcome, he still felt as if he wasn't good enough to be there.

Perhaps it was because he preferred the simple life, as he was an unassuming man whose main goal was to see that his daughter had the best life could offer. One of the ways he could make that happen was to keep Drew Rush happy.

Apparently he did, or he wouldn't have trusted him to open his safe.

The bank papers Drew wanted were exactly where they were supposed to be. But in pulling them out, he dislodged another folder, or rather a packet. Later, Edgar couldn't say what made him look at it. When he read the words "Termination of Parental Rights" scrolled across the envelope, his curiosity rose to the occasion.

What did that mean?

With his heart thundering in his chest, Edgar unhooked the tab and pulled out a sheet of paper. Attached was a copy of a birth certificate. After perusing both documents, Edgar eased down into the nearest chair, shaking as if he'd just been kicked in the gut.

"Oh, my God," he whispered, his eyes on the ceiling. "Oh, my God."

Fifteen

"Mom, I'm sorry I've neglected you lately."

Mary McFarland smiled, then lifted her cheek. "A kiss will do wonders toward forgiveness."

Cutler grinned, then complied, adding a hug as well.

"You're for sure off my list now."

Miracle of miracles, Cutler had actually gotten out of court early, and had been able to swing by his mother's church to visit her. Since her flare-up, he hadn't seen her. He'd talked to her on the phone, but that wasn't the same. He needed to see with his own eyes that she was doing okay.

And she was. In fact, she looked great, dressed in a pale pink linen suit that accented her dark hair and features. Color was in her cheeks, too, a good sign that this last bout with her heart was behind her.

He knew, though, that she wasn't without problems that would occur again. A weak heart muscle could not be repaired. So each day he had with her, he treasured as a blessing.

"How about some coffee, son?"

"I'm floating as it is, but you talked me into it."

Mary grinned and started to get up from behind her desk.

"Keep your seat. You don't have to wait on me."

"Okay. You know where it is. Help yourself."

In a minute he walked from the kitchenette back into her small office with two cups of coffee. "I don't like to drink alone."

She smiled. "Me, either."

While they drank in silence, Cutler's eyes perused his mother's home away from home. He could understand why she loved being here. Mary's domain at the rear of the community church overlooked a garden that was ablaze with flowers. Nestled among them was a gazebo filled with wrought-iron furniture.

A large picture window behind Mary's desk allowed her to turn at will and gaze at that beauty. Cutler knew she sometimes took members of her congregation there to counsel them.

The church members as a whole seemed to adore Mary and were proud their minister was female. Even though Cutler wasn't a regular attendee, much to his mother's chagrin, he knew she had the right stuff behind the pulpit.

"So what's going on?" Mary asked, setting her cup down and eyeing him through warm eyes.

"I'm up to my neck in alligators," Cutler said without preamble.

Mary raised an eyebrow. "And that's different?"

"Nah. But lately there seem to be even more of them in the pond demanding their pound of flesh."

"Ouch."

Cutler smiled ruefully. "I'm not hearing a whole lot of sympathy."

"That's because my sympathy is limited." Mary grinned, then her face turned serious. "You know how I feel about you pushing yourself so hard. One of these days, you're going to crash and burn." She paused. "And I might not be around to shovel up the ashes."

Although she said those last words in a nonchalant and light tone, Cutler knew she was dead serious, causing his own heart to lurch. When she talked like that, it unnerved the hell out of him. He couldn't imagine his mother not being a meaningful and viable part of his life.

"I wish you wouldn't say things like that."

She gave him a puzzled look. "Like what?"

"About your not being around."

"Oh, honey," Mary said with another smile, "we both know I could go anytime, but then so could you. Anyone, for that matter."

"True, but—" Cutler broke off, taking a sip of his coffee.

"Back to you," Mary said, changing the subject. "How's your campaign going?"

"It's not. I just haven't had time to do much politicking."

"Back to your workload and your cases, especially the one about the woman who drowned her children." Mary paused with a sigh. "I can't imagine a woman's mind being that tortured. To make matters worse, the media seem to thrive on that kind of heartache."

"I just got out of voir dire on the Sessions case before I came here."

"You mean you actually picked a jury that could be unbiased?"

Cutler grimaced. "Unbiased? That remains to be seen, but I have my doubts."

"Gail Sessions has to be insane to have killed her own children, son." Mary paused and regarded him thoughtfully. "Only, you don't see it that way, do you?"

"Nope. I think she knew exactly what she was doing, and I aim to go for the jugular."

"That could hurt you in the polls with women. Post-partum depression is a serious medical problem."

"I recognize that, but that's not the issue."

Mary sighed. "I'm not going to argue with you." A twinkle suddenly appeared in her eyes. "Besides, I know I wouldn't win."

"Oh, I'm not so sure about that," Cutler responded in a teasing tone. "I've been on the other end of your sharp wit and tongue."

"Why, Cutler McFarland, that's not a very nice thing to say about your mother the preacher."

He laughed. "Not even if it's the truth, Reverend Mc-Farland?"

"It's so good to see you laugh," Mary said on another serious note. "But you still look so tired."

"I'm weary to the bone, but I can't give in or up."

"Will the other case be as draining? The one concerning that abortion-clinic shooting?"

"Yep, and just as time-consuming. Plus all the others in between. As to when I'm going to find time to stump on my behalf, that remains to be seen. If I don't do my job, I'll get beaten for sure." Cutler paused and took several sips of coffee, then added, "To make matters worse, Salem

Caskey jerked the rug out from under me." He repeated their conversation in detail.

"Oh, son, I'm so sorry. You and Salem have been friends forever."

"He thinks I duped him with his kid. I've tried to think of how I might make him see the light, but so far I've come up empty-handed."

"Do you want my advice?"

"Always."

"Leave him be. If he ever sees Nathan for what he is, it won't be because of anything you've said or done."

"I know you're right," Cutler said, "but dammit, I hate to think of our friendship going down the drain because of a dopehead."

"That dopehead happens to be his son," Mary responded in a soft, chastising tone.

"I hope I'd have enough sense not to excuse my kid."

"Is something going on I don't know about?" A quizzical grin toyed with her lips.

Cutler was taken aback. While he was thinking of a suitable comeback, Kaylee's face jumped to the front of his mind. If marriage had been in the cards for him, which it wasn't, she was the type of woman he'd look for. Just thinking about her now, and those hot kisses they had exchanged, recharged his groin.

At this time in his life, however, even the thought of making that kind of commitment scared him. Sex was one thing—a very pleasant thing—but marriage was a different matter.

Suddenly Cutler grinned unabashedly. "Sorry, no grandchildren in the offing."

"Too bad. I thought maybe you and Julia—"

"That's never going to happen. She's a friend and that's all."

"Promise me you won't grow old alone."

"Aw, Mom, we've been down this road too many times to count. I can't make a promise like that. Hell, I just don't see myself as marriage material." Cutler grinned with a wink. "At forty, I know my biological clock is ticking, which means I should probably get off dead center."

Mary laughed outright. "You can poke fun if you like. But that's not a bad idea. Keep your age in mind."

"Will do," Cutler quipped, peering at his watch, then lunging to his feet. "I gotta be in court ASAP." He leaned over and gave Mary another peck on the cheek. "I'll call you later."

"Get some rest," she said to his back.

He merely waved his hand and kept on going.

"So how was Jenkins's pulse today?"

"Elevated. I was late. Need I say more?"

Angel whistled. "Dumb move."

Cutler shot his investigator a look. "I was with my mother."

"Still a dumb move."

"You've made your point." Cutler didn't bother to contain his sarcasm.

Angel grinned, unaffected. "Hope so."

"Speaking of the judge, got anything for me? I haven't talked to Snelling. I think he's avoiding me."

"No shit." Angel eased back in his chair and narrowed his eyes. "He's not avoiding me, though."

"You two been talking, huh?"

"Yep. About your favorite judge, too."

"Now you've got my attention."

"And what I have to say is going to make your day."

Cutler's tired brain sprang back to life, and his gaze turned piercing. "Let's hear it."

"You have an appointment tomorrow with a Ben Andrews."

"Am I supposed to know him?"

"He's one of those cases the good judge dismissed."

"Go on."

"It's his sister who's the key here. She allegedly knows Jenkins well, according to her brother, that is."

"Oh, baby, this is really getting good."

"Ben said when his sister returned from a date with the judge, she was all beat up."

"Where's the sister?"

"At this point she's unwilling to come forward, so brother's speaking on her behalf."

"What you're saying is that Jenkins slapped her around?"

"That's what I'm saying."

"I want to talk to the girl."

"Sure you do, but you gotta go through brother first."

"I'll hear what he has to say, but—"

"Hold your 'buts' for later," Angel said. "In the meantime, just be grateful. This is the first anyone's been willing to suggest that Jenkins trades dismissals for sexual favors."

"You're right. And that's a start."

Angel looked at his watch. "I've got an appointment. I'll holler later."

Cutler didn't move for the longest time after Angel left, though he should have grabbed the folder off the top of his file. What the hell? Who was to say he couldn't close up shop early? He should use the time to meet with his campaign adviser, Rory Dunlap, to discuss strategy against Winston Gilmore.

Thinking about his opponent made him realize they would meet that evening at a bar association shindig. Cutler would rather have had a root canal than go, but he didn't really have any choice. Functions were part of his job. He'd given Julia the heads-up several weeks ago. He'd much rather have taken Kaylee, but it was too late to back out on Julia now.

Besides, he doubted if Kaylee would've gone for a lot of different reasons. Cutler's thoughts turned pensive. Kaylee was a puzzle to him. No doubt there was chemistry between them. He knew she felt it, too. He also knew she didn't like that attraction, that it made her uncomfortable.

He made her uncomfortable. *Men* made her uncomfortable.

In that arena of her life, she had no confidence. But God, she was lovely to look at, lovely to touch. Just thinking about her made him hard. All the more reason to run like hell, he told himself. Anyway, she wasn't the kind of woman he could have casual sex with, no strings attached. He suspected if he had a taste of her body, he wouldn't want to haul.

That was the problem. He'd told her he wasn't letting her off the hook. Maybe he should, for his own self-preservation. He didn't want any emotional entanglements. He just wasn't ready. As he had told his mother, maybe he never would be.

"Excuse me."

Startled, Cutler lifted his head. A strange man stood in his doorway. "Yes?" he asked in a guarded tone, wondering how he'd gotten past reception.

As if the tall, gangly man could read his thoughts, he said, "I waited until your receptionist was away from the desk."

An alarm went off inside Cutler. Was he some crazy off the street who had an ax to grind against him? More than likely. Any minute now, Cutler expected to see a gun pointed at his head. He braced himself.

"What do you want?" Cutler asked when the stranger remained stationary and quiet, almost embarrassed.

"A minute of your time."

"I was about to leave," Cutler said pointedly.

"I'm sorry to delay you."

He didn't sound at all sorry. "Look, Mr.——"

"Benton. Edgar Benton."

Cutler felt his mouth go slack. "Are you related to Kaylee Benton?"

"She's my daughter."

Relief washed through Cutler, then he tensed again. "Has something happened to her?"

"No, she's fine. But I appreciate your concern."

Cutler frowned, growing more puzzled by the second. "What can I do for you, Mr. Benton?"

"Call me Edgar."

Cutler nodded.

"Mind if I sit down?"

Cutler felt he had no choice but to say yes. "Of course not."

"Thanks."

A silence fell over the room before Edgar finally broke it. "I guess there's no way to say this but to say it."

Cutler's frown deepened. "I'm listening."

Another silence.

Edgar cleared his throat. "I think it's in your best interests to marry my daughter."

Sixteen

Cutler was dumbfounded as he tried to process what Edgar Benton had just said. No one in this day and time, at least not in this country, arranged a marriage, for chrissake.

"Surely I didn't hear you right."

"You heard me, all right," Edgar said with confidence. "But if you want me to repeat what I said, I'll be glad to."

"What I want is for you to leave."

"Only way you're going to get rid of me is to physically toss me out on my ear."

Not a bad idea, Cutler thought. And for a second he was tempted to do just that. However, common sense prevailed, and with as much cool as he could muster, he asked, "Does Kaylee know you're here?"

A flush tinted Edgar's face. "No."

"Didn't think so."

"That doesn't change anything." Edgar's tone was tinged with belligerence.

"Look, Mr. Benton…"

"My request is nonnegotiable."

Cutler felt his temper rise. He couldn't believe he was even party to this weird conversation. He shoved a hand through his hair before narrowing his eyes back on his unwelcome guest. "You gotta be daft, man."

"You'll see things differently when you hear me out."

"The only reason you're not out the door is because of Kaylee."

"That's what I was counting on," Edgar responded without so much as a blink.

Cutler had to hand it to the man—he had balls. "Spit it out," he said, not bothering to hide his frustration.

Edgar nodded. "I have information that will bring harm to your family, especially your mother, and it could, in fact, cost her her pastorate." He paused significantly. "If you don't comply, that is."

"No one threatens me, Benton, and gets away with it. If you keep on spitting out this nonsense, Kaylee or not, you're out of here."

Edgar didn't so much as move a muscle. Instead, he went on in his same calm, methodical voice, "You told me to spit it out. That's what I'm trying to do."

In spite of efforts not to be taken in by anything this man said, curiosity had gotten the better of Cutler. Hell, he'd indulged Benton this far; he might as well hear him out. If he could hang on to his temper for that long, that is.

"Get on with it." Cutler bit out the words tersely.

"Trevor is not your real father."

Cutler snorted. "Is that cockamamie story the best you can do?"

"It's the truth."

"You're full of shit, too."

Edgar remained stoic, adding more fuel to Cutler's now raging temper. But two could play this game. He could be as stoic and emotionless as anyone, especially when it suited his purpose. It definitely suited his purpose.

"I have proof."

"You're a damned liar."

"I don't lie." It was obvious from Edgar's tone that he took umbrage at that personal attack.

"Says you." Cutler's tone was hard with impatience. "But that's not how I see it. And right now I'm the one who counts."

"I told you I have proof."

"Okay, let's say you do, or you think you do. Just how are you privy to such information?" Cutler made a point of sounding insulting, suddenly tired of letting this man jerk his chain.

"I stumbled on it by accident."

"Sure you did."

"You can insult me all you want to," Edgar said in that same tone. "But it's not going to change the facts."

"Ah, the facts, as you know them to be."

Edgar's chin tipped. "That's right. And whether you want to admit it or not, I'm the one holding all the cards."

An expletive exploded through Cutler's lips before he smiled a humorless smile. "For now, I'll play your silly little game and ask the question that you're dying to answer. So who is my *real* father?" That last sentence came out a smirk.

"Drew Rush."

Cutler's jaw literally dropped, rendering him totally speechless.

"He's your birth father."

This time shock kept Cutler from saying anything. He simply sat there, reeling. The Drew Rush he knew? The businessman who had a reputation for sticking his nose in every pie in town? That couldn't be; it was just a crock of crap. Cutler didn't know where Benton's information had come from, nor did he care. All he cared about was shutting him up and getting him out of his sight.

Although he didn't know the man personally, the thought of Rush's blood running through his veins was so off the wall he couldn't begin to grasp it.

"To repeat myself," Edgar said into the hostile silence, "I have the proof to back up my words. Documented proof, no less."

Cutler felt his own blood thunder through his body with such force that he had to fight down the urge to attack. He ached to knock the breath out of the old man so he'd know just how it felt to be sucker punched in the belly. But again he refrained from resorting to violence, partly because his gut told him there might be some truth to what the old man was saying.

No one could make up a story like that.

"Unless you marry Kaylee, I'll go public with that information."

Cutler's stomach roiled, and for a moment he feared he might puke. "I'll see you in hell first."

Edgar didn't back down. He jutted his chin another notch. "I may very well end up there, but not until my daughter's taken care of."

"And you think marrying me will do that?"

"I know she cares about you."

Cutler shook his head to clear it, thinking he was losing his grip altogether. He had to be, to sit there and discuss anything so preposterous. "Did she tell you that?"

"No."

"Did she tell somebody and they told you?"

"No. Not that I know of, anyway."

"Then how the hell can you speak for your daughter?"

"Because she won't speak for herself."

"Maybe that's because she doesn't want to."

"I won't argue with that."

"So what you're saying is that she's not a party to this scheme?"

"No."

"If she knew, she'd have your head on a platter, right?"

Edgar stiffened. "Right."

"Have you no shame, man?"

"You can insult me all you want, but it's not going to make me back down."

Cutler rubbed his forehead, his head threatening to explode like an overripe watermelon in the hot sun. "I can't believe I'm listening to this growing mound of horseshit."

Edgar flushed. "You're not making this any easier on yourself."

Cutler would've laughed at this man's logic had it not been such a waste of effort. This man was nuts. And he, Cutler, was nuttier for continuing to indulge him.

"I'll keep what I know to myself." Edgar's voice dropped an octave. "All you have to do in return is convince my daughter you love her and want to marry her."

"Oh, is that all, now?" Cutler's laugh was harsh and bitter.

"I know you care about your mother."

"What the hell does that have to do with anything?"

"Plenty."

Cutler's lips thinned and his nostrils flared. "Listen, you bastard, you leave my family out of this. More to the point, leave them the hell alone."

"Only if you cooperate can I promise to do that."

"What the hell makes you think I could convince Kaylee to marry me even if I believed what you told me?"

"Because you're a very persuasive man, especially when it comes to women."

Cutler's patience had snapped. "Get out of here, Benton, while you still have some of your dignity left. I promise I'll forget all about this conversation."

"You're the one lying. You have no intention of forgetting about what I've told you. You won't leave a stone unturned until *you've* uncovered the truth. Only, you won't find it, unless I tell you."

Cutler waved a hand in disgust, frankly out of options as to how to deal with this deranged man.

"Drew Rush terminated his parental rights shortly after you were born. I have copies of those papers, plus a birth certificate." Edgar paused. "*Your* birth certificate."

Hot bile shot up the back of Cutler's throat, almost gagging him. He had to swivel his chair around and take several deep sucking breaths or he would have lost it.

That scoundrel Drew Rush and his mother together?

Screwing?

With him the end product of that liaison?

This couldn't be happening. He was having a horrific nightmare from which he'd soon awaken. Cutler closed his eyes, but when he opened them again, Edgar Benton was still there, staring at him with those unrepentant eyes. The only difference was that he was now standing.

"I'll let you see the papers, but only if you agree to my request."

"Don't you mean blackmail?" Cutler bit out harshly.

"That's not the way I see it."

Suddenly Cutler stood as well and closed the distance between them, his breathing becoming ragged. Edgar was tall, but Cutler was taller. He caught a momentary look of fear on the old man's face. Still, Edgar didn't so much as make a move to back away.

If rage hadn't had a stranglehold on Cutler, he might have admired the man for his tenacity and grit. He knew where Kaylee got her determination.

Kaylee.

"I think you'd best get your ass out of here before I do what I've wanted to do from the first." Cutler spat out the words. "I think you know what that is."

This time Edgar backed away. "I'll give you a week to make your decision. Otherwise, I'll make good on my promise. You can kiss your career goodbye right along with your mother's."

"I told you not to mention my family again. Do what you want to me, but don't mess with my mother, or you'll be sorry. And I don't make idle threats."

"I'm sure of that. But then, neither do I."

Cutler had reached his limit. His temper and fear overcame his gentlemanly professionalism. "Get the hell out of here. Now!"

"A week, Mr. McFarland. A week."

Cutler barely gave him time to get out the door before

he slammed it so hard that it shook some of the pictures on the wall. Then paralyzing fear rooted him to the spot.

His mother.

Granted, his career was important. Hell, it was his life. But his mother—she was even more important. Without her, his life wouldn't be worth a tinker's damn.

Cool it, McFarland, he told himself, though neither his breathing nor his fury would abate. No one had ever blindsided him and gotten away with it. He didn't intend to set a precedent now.

God. His stomach not only roiled but turned sour. The fact that his mother could have had him or any child out of wedlock was too impossible to fathom. Benton was a lying son of a bitch. That was all there was to it.

But he had the goods, or so he said. Cutler couldn't refute anything. Until he'd seen the evidence. Until then, he couldn't confront his mother.

Who was he kidding? He would never have the nerve to blatantly accuse Mary of anything even if he ever had proof.

On the other hand, what choice did he have? If what Edgar told him was not the truth, he knew that the merest hint of such a scandal could and would do irrevocable damage to his mother's hard-earned reputation.

Several other factors immediately clouded his mind. His mother's bad heart. The stress from a long-guarded secret coming to light could possibly trigger a fatal attack. She had worked hard at keeping her personal life private, and she'd never once given her congregation fodder to deem her unworthy to serve them. And last, but certainly not least, there was her pastorate.

Mary had jumped one hurdle after another to become a

minister. She had launched herself into a man's world with determination to succeed, and she had. She would wither up and die if she had to give that up, especially under such hideous circumstances.

Therefore it was paramount he protect his mother even if what Benton said was true. But he could feel terribly betrayed by the fact that Mary had kept this ugly truth from him, as she'd never given him the slightest reason to think that Trevor wasn't his father.

Why would she have done that to him?

The best way to find that answer was to get the lead out of his ass and go see her. Not now, he told himself again. He needed time to cool off, to collect his thoughts, to find out if what Benton said was indeed the truth.

Suddenly Cutler knew what he had to do. Trevor. Perhaps he was the key to unlock the past. He'd go to his father and talk to him. With his adrenaline flowing, Cutler grabbed his briefcase and left the office.

He didn't know how this would all fall out. But one thing he did know. No one was going to blackmail him into marriage.

While he couldn't throw his mother to the wolves, he refused to be coerced into marrying a woman he didn't love. Even if he did love her, he wouldn't necessarily marry her. Love wasn't always synonymous with marriage.

There would be another solution. He just hadn't thought of it yet.

With grim determination he jumped into his vehicle and spun off, his heart in bleeding pieces.

Seventeen

"Are you okay?"

"Do I look okay?" Edgar asked, slowly rising from the toilet where he'd just lost the contents of his stomach.

"No," Rebecca said bluntly, sympathy radiating from her eyes. "You're pale as a ghost and weak as a kitten."

"After I wash my face, I'll be fine."

"I'll be in the kitchen. A cup of peppermint tea will be waiting for you."

Edgar forced a smile. "Thanks. That sounds good."

"Hopefully it will settle your stomach."

Edgar blew out his breath, then leaned over the basin. Once he made his way into the kitchen and saw Rebecca, he realized how lucky he was to have her, especially now when he couldn't stand to be alone with himself or his thoughts.

While he still missed his wife, he couldn't imagine what she would look like now or how it would feel to touch her. Time had dulled those senses. At first he had resented that, but now he knew that helped him survive. He could now get out of bed every morning and function like something other than a robot.

Rebecca had definitely added a new and exciting dimension to his life. And though they didn't live together, she spent an occasional night at his house and vice versa. He had been so distraught last evening, he hadn't wanted her to leave.

"You're too thoughtful," he said in a slightly gruff voice as he pulled out the chair and joined her.

"Feeling better?"

"Much." He blew on the liquid, then took a sip, reveling in its warmth as it hit his stomach.

"You don't have a virus, do you?"

Though she put an obvious question mark at the end of her sentence, Edgar knew she had made a statement of fact. "No," he said honestly.

"I know you're terribly upset and I've tried not to pry."

"Only you are now." Edgar eased his bluntness with another forced smile.

"That's right, especially since you seem so on edge. Perhaps worried is a better word." Rebecca paused and sipped on her tea. "But I don't want to put you on the spot." A frown deepened the lines on her forehead.

He reached out and covered her hand with his, giving it a squeeze. "You're not prying, my dear. I don't want to hide things from you."

"Then don't. Is something going on at work that has you tied in knots?"

"Always, but right now it's not work I'm concerned about."

Rebecca held her silence waiting for him to continue.

Her ability to remain quiet was another gift he admired. She never prodded, though he knew she'd like to marry him. He'd sensed that, not so much by what she said, but what she hadn't said.

He wasn't ready for that giant step. Maybe he never would be. At this point in his life he was content to concentrate on Kaylee and his job. Both were the top priorities in his life, though he sure didn't want to lose Rebecca.

"If it's not work, then it's Kaylee."

Another statement of fact. "You hit the nail on the head."

"What did you do?"

His smile was genuine but brief. "Ah, you know me too well. It scares me."

This time she squeezed his hand, then winked. "Don't be scared. I'm harmless."

His smile returned, only to fade once again. "I took things into my own hands, Rebecca."

"Are you referring to Kaylee?"

He nodded.

"Like how?"

He groped for the right words, but couldn't find them.

"Does she know what you're up to?"

"Absolutely not."

Rebecca looked taken aback. "But she will, won't she?"

"Sooner than later."

"What did you do, Edgar?"

"I went to see Cutler McFarland."

"And?"

"And told him I wanted him to marry my daughter."

As expected, Rebecca gave him an incredulous look.

But when she opened her mouth, nothing came out, so she slammed it back shut.

"So I'm an old fool who can't mind his own business." He heard the belligerence in his voice, but didn't care. He made no apologies. "I just couldn't let this opportunity pass."

"No wonder you're feeling sick."

"Still, I wouldn't do anything different."

"I guess that's a good thing. Second-guessing yourself certainly isn't."

He set his jaw. "I'm convinced I did the right thing."

"What did you say to him?"

"I had something to bargain with, something to hold over his head. However it's not something I'm prepared to share."

Until he knew what Cutler was going to do, he had no intention of revealing the contents of that safe to anyone. When Drew learned what had gone down—well, Edgar couldn't imagine how that would play out. He'd probably lose his job and Drew's friendship.

When crossed, Drew was hard and unforgiving. He had worked hard all these years in order to avoid Drew's bad side for fear of the repercussions. But now, even though the consequences of his actions might be dire, he didn't care. Making Kaylee happy was all that mattered.

He was prepared to live with the consequences.

Rebecca's expression didn't change, though he could almost see her mind working. "Do you think he'll comply?"

"Yes, I do."

"You must have some powerful ammo."

"I do." Edgar held her gaze for a long moment. "Thank you for not telling me I'm nuts."

"You're far from nuts, though I will say your method is a bit unorthodox, to say the least."

"And I haven't pulled it off yet."

"Kaylee's the one I suspect will want your head on a platter."

"It's imperative that she never know."

"She won't hear it from me. Besides, I don't know any of the details and that's the way I want it."

"You're a special person, Rebecca Goolsby. I'm lucky to have you in my life."

"It's going to be all right, Edgar. What you did came from the heart."

"We'll see. Even though I have no regrets, like I said, I know I'm taking a big gamble by interfering in the lives of two strong-minded and competent individuals."

"Let's hope the gamble pays off and you get what you want."

"Correction. It's not what I want. It's all about Kaylee."

Rebecca leaned over and kissed him. "She's a very lucky young woman to have a father who cares so deeply."

"She deserves to have what other women have," he said fiercely.

"But only if that's what she truly wants."

That was as close to a rebuke as Rebecca came, which was okay. He hadn't asked for her approval. He could live with himself and that's what counted.

"She wants it, all right," he said with that same fierceness. "I'm convinced of that and always will be."

"So what's next?" Rebecca asked in a soft, nonaccusatory tone.

"Wait. The ball's in Cutler's court."

"Want some company while you wait?"

"You bet."

Edgar kissed her again, then clung to her, praying he'd done the right thing.

Kaylee's nerves were on edge.

Yet she thought she was managing to handle this present situation with as much calm professionalism as she could muster.

"It's imperative you tell me the truth."

"There's nothing to tell," Nicole Reed wailed. "I'm just prone to bruise easily. You're making too big a deal out it."

"I don't think so," Kaylee said in a firm tone. "With bruises up and down your arms, you're no good to the agency. Bottom line, young lady, you can't work."

Nicole tossed back a strand of her long red hair before saying, "I'll cover them up."

"Unfortunately, that won't be possible. The marks are just too visible on your fair skin."

"Can't I at least try?" Nicole wailed again, her eyes wide with anxiety, as if she realized for the first time that she was actually in trouble.

"Sure you can try, but it won't happen."

Nicole clenched her jaw, her anxiety changing to irritation.

"So how did you get them?" Kaylee asked. "You're not leaving until I know."

Nicole muttered something.

Kaylee suspected it was an expletive, which didn't have any influence on her whatsoever.

"I lost my balance in the apartment and fell."

"I don't believe you."

Nicole Reed lowered her head, easing her hand down one leg of her linen slacks as though trying to smooth out the wrinkles.

Kaylee blew out a sigh, then glanced over at Sandy, who was sitting on the same settee as the model. Sandy merely raised her eyebrows and shrugged her shoulders.

If Nicole didn't want to confide in her, there wasn't much she could do about it except contact her parents. In order to do that the situation had to be really drastic. So far, it hadn't reached that point.

"Nicole," Kaylee said, disrupting the silence, "I'm waiting. And not very patiently, I might add."

"Okay, I went surfing this weekend. That's how I got bruised. Me and Scott had trouble with our boards."

Kaylee didn't believe that for a minute either, but she refrained from saying so. At least the girl was talking, and that was a good thing. Maybe if she talked long enough, she might actually tell the truth.

"If that's the case, then why are you just now bruising?"

"I don't understand."

"You go surfing most every weekend, right?"

"Yes."

"So why now?" Kaylee pressed.

"The surf was rough and we took several tumbles."

Kaylee turned to Sandy and addressed her. "What's your opinion?"

"I think you should see a doctor, Nicole."

"A doctor?" Nicole's voice reached a high note. "That's crazy. I don't need to go to the doctor."

"I agree with Sandy," Kaylee countered calmly.

"Scott hasn't hurt me," Nicole said in a tight, defiant tone, "if that's what you're thinking."

"If he has or ever does, I'd hope you would tell us so we could help."

"May I go now?"

Kaylee suppressed her regret, knowing she'd run into a brick wall. The model wasn't prepared to give an inch. "Yes. As soon as we set the doctor's appointment, we'll let you know." Kaylee gave her a pointed look.

Nicole released a resigned sigh, then scurried out of the room.

Kaylee blew out a long breath, not realizing how uptight she'd been. Suddenly her insides felt like jelly, much the same as when Cutler had kissed her. Where had that thought come from?

Panicked, she stood, walked from behind her desk and joined Sandy on the settee. "So what's your take?"

"We've got another tiger by the tail."

"I agree."

"Do you think Scott's knocking her around?"

"Someone is. I'd bet this agency on it."

"So would I," Sandy said, rising. "I'll see that she gets to the doctor."

Kaylee frowned. "I wonder what's next?"

"Don't even go there." Sandy's mouth turned down. "At least the other three rebels are behaving."

Kaylee threw up her hands. "Only their wounds haven't healed, and now Nicole's out of commission."

"Thank heavens we've still got time before the shows, or we'd be in a heap of trouble."

"You're right," Kaylee said in a glum tone.

"Hey, don't get down about this, boss," Sandy said with a thumbs up. "Remember the Ford Agency tapped *us*. So we've got it together or they wouldn't have given us the time of day."

Kaylee smiled. "Thanks for the pep talk. I needed it."

"I'll check in later," Sandy said, exiting the room.

Kaylee sat back down to the sound of the buzzer. "Your dad's here."

"Great. Send him in."

Two seconds later Kaylee had her arms around Edgar and was giving him a bear hug. "Hi, Pops. What's up?"

"Do you have plans for lunch?"

"Nope."

"Do you have time to let your old man treat you?"

Kaylee pulled back and looked at him, sensing something was wrong. That was when she noticed the pallor of his skin. A flutter of panic went through her. "You don't look so good. Are you all right?"

A shadow crossed his face, but then he smiled. "I'm fine, sweetheart."

That smile should've reassured her, but it didn't. Still, she didn't push. He'd share in his own time. He always did.

Eighteen

"Hey, son, what a pleasant surprise."

"Hey, yourself," Cutler responded, suddenly unable to call him Dad, which was crazy. But then Edgar Benton had messed with his mind. Since yesterday, Cutler hadn't known whether he was coming or going. He had to get the poison inside him contained or he wouldn't be worth a damn to himself or anyone else.

He was furious that he'd listened to that pile of garbage, that he hadn't pitched Benton out on his ass. But when someone looked you in the eye and told you he had documented proof that another man was your father, that got your attention.

Still, Cutler hated what he was about to do. He dreaded even the thought of questioning his dad, whom he loved and he knew loved him.

"What brings you out to the site?" Trevor asked, removing his hard hat, a grin splayed across his weathered face.

Cutler didn't answer right away, his eyes scanning the building site, which was a federal housing project. Trevor's company had gotten the lucrative bid. When that had happened, the family had celebrated. The deal had brought Trevor out of retirement and back on the job.

"I wanted to see you."

"I'm not sure how I should take that," Trevor said with a teasing glint.

Cutler gave him a look.

Trevor laughed.

That laughter sounded so genuine, so normal, Cutler had to fight the urge to grab his dad and hug him, something he hadn't done in years—too many years, to be exact.

Yet Cutler jammed his hands into his pockets and simply stared at Trevor for another long moment. His father lived life to the fullest, laughing as hard as he worked.

Cutler had so often thought how fortunate he was to have such great parents. In light of this latest revelation, however, he knew he'd taken both of them for granted. Maybe not so much his mother, but definitely his dad. He didn't spend enough time with Trevor, and what time he did spend wasn't quality time.

That was just about to change. Once this mess was settled, he was going to get to know what made his dad tick.

"Hey, boy, what's on your mind?"

Cutler jerked himself back to the moment at hand and realized Trevor was staring at him with puzzled eyes. "Thought maybe I could buy you lunch."

Trevor was clearly taken aback by that request. Cutler flushed under his close scrutiny. "Are you okay?"

Cutler felt more color steal into his cheeks, though it wasn't noticeable, as the sun beating down on them was parboiling.

Trevor mopped his face, then said, "Come on, let's finish this conversation in my shack. Without anything on your head, your brain will fry."

"I think it's too late."

Trevor chuckled, then motioned with his right hand for Cutler to follow him.

Once they were inside the air-conditioned trailer, Cutler reached for his handkerchief and mopped his face. "Damn, but this heat's a killer today."

"It ain't the heat, son. It's the humidity."

"Today it's both. I'm soaking wet."

Trevor flexed a tanned, muscled arm and grinned. "Ought to do this for a living."

"I wouldn't have minded it."

"But I would. That's why I worked my butt off so you'd have an education."

"You might not have a degree, but you're educated."

"It's not the same," Trevor said in a staunch voice. "You're doing exactly what you were meant to do. You're a born lawyer who works for the people. And I'm real proud of that."

"Thanks, Dad." Cutler cleared his throat, then added, "So how 'bout lunch?"

"I haven't eaten, but I'm not fit to darken the doors of one of those fancy restaurants."

"You look fine. You name it and that's where we'll go."

"I got a better idea. Let's go to the house. Your mother made the best batch of chicken salad ever last night and there's more than half of it left. How does that sound?"

"You know the answer to that. I'd rather eat her chicken salad than a juicy sirloin."

"Hold on while I tell my foreman."

Thirty minutes later they were in the kitchen of his parents' home in west Houston. It was an older house that Trevor had remodeled before they moved in. Cutler loved coming there, rambling through the large, airy rooms that bore a hint of his mother's cologne.

While Trevor washed up, he'd rummaged through the fridge until he'd found the salad and a container full of chopped fruit. His mother had bought croissants for the salad, which made it even more delicious.

Too bad he wasn't hungry.

Still, he went through the pretense of getting the breakfast-room table ready, then sat down and stared into the backyard aglow with flowers. His mother liked to garden and spent as much time playing with her plants as she could, except when her heart wouldn't permit that kind of activity.

A deep sigh escaped Cutler as he rubbed the back of his tight neck. He actually felt as if he was carrying around a chunk of lead in his belly, it was so heavy. And his chest— hell, it felt as if an elephant was camped on it. Somehow, though, he had to get something down or he'd never hear the end of it.

Besides, he didn't know if he had the courage—maybe balls was the better word—even to bring up the subject of his parentage. With the sunlight streaming through the windows and the birds chirping outside, the world seemed so normal, so untainted.

His stomach rebelled, especially when he got a whiff of the chicken salad. What a freakin' nightmare. He still couldn't believe his life had just been turned upside down, that he was being blackmailed, for God's sake.

"You didn't have to wait for me."

"Sure I did," Cutler said, turning and watching his dad meander to the table, then sit down. "No fun eating alone."

"You didn't get us anything to drink," Trevor pointed out, pushing his chair away and getting up.

"Sorry."

"Your mother also made some peach tea. You want some?"

"That sounds good." Cutler made himself smile. "She really went all out last night. Something special going on?"

"Nah. She just felt like puttering in the kitchen. And I wasn't about to discourage her."

"No way. Any time she putters, that's a thumbs-up. Means she's feeling good."

"She is for now." A shadow fell across Trevor's face. "But we both know that won't last."

"True," Cutler said in the same sober tone.

A silence ensued while they made their sandwiches and took several bites. Somehow Cutler managed to swallow twice. The stuff tasted as if he'd bitten into a bucket of sand. He rinsed the food down with his iced tea. In fact, he turned that up and drained the glass.

When he set it back down, his dad had stopped eating and was staring at him, a curious gleam in his eyes.

Cutler forced himself not to avert his gaze.

"What's up?"

"What makes you think something's up?" Cutler asked, toying with his empty glass, stalling for time.

Trevor chuckled. "Because I know you. You don't have this kind of free time to lollygag during the day. Your schedule's way too tight."

"You're right, I don't."

"Are you in trouble?"

This time Cutler's smile was genuine. "You know me well."

Trevor merely laughed, but then he turned serious. "Tell me what I need to do."

"It's not about needing your help, Dad." Cutler paused, thinning his lips. "Actually, I do need your help, only not in the way you think."

Trevor gave Cutler one of *his* looks. "Whatever."

"I don't know quite how to begin." This time Cutler did avert his gaze.

"What the hell, son? I'm about to get worried. I don't recall ever seeing you in such a frame of mind."

"That's because you haven't."

"You don't have cancer, do you?"

Cutler blinked. "What?"

"I said, you don't have cancer, do you?"

"No, of course not."

"Thank God," Trevor said with obvious relief.

Cutler frowned. "What a thought."

"Well, in today's climate you never know. So if it's not your health, then it has to be your job."

"Dad, if you'll just listen, I'll tell you."

Trevor pushed his chair back from the table, taking his iced-tea glass with him. "I'm listening."

Cutler opened his mouth but nothing came out, which forced him to clear his throat.

"Boy, spit it out. Whatever's wrong, we can fix it. We always have."

"I'm not sure this is fixable," Cutler muttered more to himself than to Trevor.

"Everything's fixable, son, especially if you're on the right side of the law."

If only that were true, then he wouldn't mind relieving his soul of this tremendous burden. But he knew that once he spoke the words they could do irreparable damage.

But what choice did he have? None. He'd been backed into a corner and his nuts squeezed. That aside, he had to know the truth concerning his birth, if for no other reason than his own sanity.

"Dammit, son, you're trying my patience and making me say words your mother doesn't like." Trevor smiled, as though trying to relieve the sudden tension between them.

"Are you my real father?"

Trevor gasped, then turned as white as a sheet.

Oh, God, Cutler thought, his guts twisting in a knot that had no possibility of loosening. His father's face said it all; no words were necessary.

"Who…where—" Trevor spluttered, only to have those words choke off.

"Who told me?" Cutler's voice was harsh. "Was that what you wanted to ask?"

"No, I mean—" Again his words broke off as Trevor lunged out of his chair and went to the window, where he turned his back to Cutler.

"I'm not budging until you tell me the truth."

"Then you might as well count on staying here. What you're asking is impossible."

Red-hot anger flared inside Cutler, serving to dull the pain to a tolerable level. "You leave me no choice but to talk to Mother."

Trevor swung around, stark terror in his eyes. "Don't you dare say anything to her." He spat out the words.

Cutler reeled as if he'd been struck. If his dad had ever spoken to him in that vicious tone, he couldn't remember it. Trevor had always been the mild-mannered, easygoing one of the two. His mother had torn into his hide verbally too many times to count, but never Trevor.

"Let it go, son. Let it go."

"Somehow I don't think you have the right to call me son."

This time Trevor reeled, actually rocking back on his heels as though he'd been kicked in the teeth. What color had returned to his face drained out again. For a second Cutler feared he might have a stroke or a heart attack.

"I might not have sired you, but I damn sure raised you. That alone makes you my son. And don't you ever forget that."

Cutler wanted to puke. Damn Edgar Benton to hell for brutally kicking him in the teeth, then leaving him to clean up all the splattered blood.

"Did you know that Drew Rush was my biological father?" Cutler hadn't thought he could get those repugnant words past his lips, but somehow he had. He was desperate to know the truth and desperate not to. He felt as if he was being drawn and quartered.

"The answer to that question will go to the grave with me."

"Hiding from the past won't work anymore. The worms are out of the can."

"What's to keep you from putting them back in?"

"If this was happening to you, could you do that?"

"No," Trevor said with blunt honesty.

"Enough said."

"If your mother finds out you know, it'll kill her."

Cutler clenched his jaw.

"Tell me how you found out."

Cutler related his conversation with Edgar Benton. When he finished, the chicken salad was now hot bile in the back of his throat. Trevor appeared in the same shape, his features having turned from white to sickly gray.

"Do you think that bastard will follow through with his blackmail scheme?"

"Yes, I do."

Trevor closed the distance between them. "I've never asked anything of you, have I?"

"No."

"Well, I'm asking you now. I married Mary because I loved her so much, and wanted to protect her at all costs. Make whatever sacrifice you have to. For your mother's sake."

Nineteen

Kaylee couldn't get Cutler off her mind.

Maybe that was because her dad had grilled her about him while they had eaten lunch, especially after she'd eaten too much and then confided that Cutler had taken her to his ranch.

The worried look that had been on Edgar's face seemed to have miraculously disappeared. She had been astounded and said so. "You suddenly look all smug. What's going on in that mind of yours?"

Edgar appeared affronted. "Me? Why, nothing's going on with me."

"Yeah, right." Kaylee's tone brimmed with sarcasm.

"No, really, sweetheart. I'm just glad to see you having a relationship with a man."

"Hey, Dad, listen up. I'm *not* having a relationship."

"Call it what you want, but—".

"That's not happening."

He shrugged. "Whatever you say."

Kaylee scrutinized him with a smile. "Don't look so

glum. I know you have my best interests at heart, but I'm happy with my life just the way it is. You have to accept that and go on with your life apart from me."

"I have."

She made an unladylike snort. "Then why don't you ask Rebecca to marry you?"

Edgar gave her an incredulous look. "Whoa! I'm not ready for that."

"Why not?"

Edgar shifted as though he were on a hot seat. "Sounds like you're meddling to me."

"Ah, now you know how it feels."

He gave her a sheepish grin. "I deserved that, didn't I?"

"Most assuredly."

Edgar's grin faded. "I'm just so used to taking care of you. It's hard for me to remember that you're no longer a little girl who depends on me."

"Oh, Daddy, I still depend on you, only in a different way and for different reasons."

"I want so much more for you—a home and family. I think you want those, too, only you won't admit it."

"That's because it's not to be," Kaylee said with a sigh. "You're going to have to face that sooner or later. I have, and it makes life so much easier."

His features tightened. "I'm not sure I can do that."

She kissed him on the cheek, then said on a light note, "You have no choice."

"Your mother—"

"Shush." Kaylee placed a finger against his lips. "If Mom had lived, she would have had to face the same reality as you."

Edgar's features twisted with agony. "You're asking the impossible. Besides, Cutler McFarland seems to—"

"Dad, I don't want to talk about him." Irritated impatience colored her tone. "He's off-limits."

"I gotta go, anyway. But you haven't heard the last of Cutler McFarland, my dear." He kissed her on the cheek. "I'll talk to you later."

When he had walked out, she'd noticed his shoulders seemed to droop a bit more. If only he'd stop trying to micromanage her life, he would be so much better off. *She* would be so much better off.

Their conversation kept Cutler in the forefront of her mind, though she didn't want to think about that scoundrel, not for one second. A sudden pang of guilt struck her. He wasn't a scoundrel. He was just a man who liked women, who knew how to use his God-given talents to charm them.

His charm had certainly worked on her.

He seemed to have taken control of her subconscious, which went against her grain. If only he hadn't kissed her. The passion he'd evoked in her was like nothing she'd ever felt before. What she'd experienced with Kenny couldn't compare. When Cutler had touched her, her insides had gone into meltdown. God help her, she'd wanted a lot more than kisses. She'd wanted to feel him inside her.

"Stop it, Kaylee," she hissed, feeling her cheeks flame.

How could she think such thoughts when she knew they would never come to fruition? *Never.* She was deformed, for heaven's sake. She'd accepted that. Or so she'd thought.

What man in his right mind would want to take her to bed? Tears suddenly pricked Kaylee's eyes. She blinked furiously. She hated it when she got down on herself, when she let her handicap take precedence over her sound judgment.

Maybe a hot bath would settle her down. It had been another long, difficult day. She and Sandy had signed on two new models. She had met with two new clients. In between she'd put out several office fires.

And her leg was hurting like a bitch.

Another reason for the hot bath. It was the panacea she needed both mentally and physically. She had turned on the faucet and made her way back into the bedroom when she heard the doorbell. Frowning, she went back into the bathroom and turned off the water. That was when she peered at the clock and noticed the lateness of the hour. Her frown deepened. Who would be at her door at this time of night?

If an emergency had occurred with her dad or one of the models, surely she would've gotten a phone call. No one just showed up at the front door. Not unless it was someone up to no good. With that thought in mind, Kaylee decided to ignore her uninvited guest and go on about her business.

But the doorbell kept on ringing.

"Go away," she muttered, concluding that whoever was there was either leaning against the chime or had a finger glued to it. Either way, it was a nuisance she didn't need.

Her tired leg slowed her down, but she finally made it to the door. She was tempted to turn on the light, but decided against that. Instead, she squinted and looked through the peephole. The moon, combined with the street lamp, provided her with enough light to see her visitor.

Her breath caught.

Cutler.

What was he doing here?

Her heart raced out of sync and her mouth went dry. What should she do? Since she hadn't turned on the light, he had no way of knowing she was standing on the other side of the door. She could turn and make her way back to her room and he'd be none the wiser. As to when he would get the message that she either wasn't home or was ignoring him, she couldn't say.

Instead she clicked the dead bolt. The obnoxious noise instantly stopped. She jerked the door open. The sight of him took her breath away.

"This had better be good," she said in a terse tone, her eyes roaming over him as he leaned against the column on the porch. His hair was mussed as if he'd been shoveling his hands through it. His face had a black stubble on it. His tie was loosened from the top button on his shirt.

He looked exhausted, disheveled, angry.

And absolutely irresistible.

"That should be obvious," he said, moving slightly toward her.

It was then that she smelled his breath. It reeked with alcohol. Bourbon, to be exact. Her blood chilled.

"Are you going to ask me in?" he asked through a husky drawl.

Kaylee licked her dry lips. She saw his eyes drop to her mouth and stay there. "Are you drunk?" Her voice sounded thin.

"No."

"But you've been drinking."

Why she stated the obvious she didn't know. Perhaps it

was because she couldn't make up her mind what to do with him.

"What if I have?"

"All the more reason to go home."

"I don't want to go home." Cutler's voice was harsh.

She'd been right. He was angry. At her? But why? "Cutler, it's late."

His jaw tensed and there was a glint in his eye that she couldn't quite read. "So?"

"I don't want to argue with you."

"Then don't. Let me in."

"No."

"I had to see you," he rasped, leaning toward her.

"Cutler, I—"

He pulled her against him and pressed his lips to hers. The kiss was deep, devouring and breathtaking. His tongue, lashing hers, sent waves of heat through her. If he hadn't been holding her, she was sure her knees would have buckled.

"Please," he muttered between nibbles, "let me come in."

Minutes later he was sitting on her sofa with only lamplight softening the room. She perched on the other end, careful not to get within touching distance for fear of landing in his arms again. As it was, her heart hadn't rebounded from the kiss at the door.

"I'll make some coffee."

She stood. A hand reached out and circled her wrist. Swallowing hard, she peered down at him. "Let me go."

"I don't want any coffee."

"You need some."

"That's not at all what I need."

There was an angry tone in his voice as though he resented her and the fact that he was with her. Why *was* he there? It wasn't as if he had a gun to his head.

"Yes, it is." She jerked her arm out of his grasp and made her way into the kitchen. Leaning against the cabinet for support, she took several heaving breaths. Oh, God, she had to get rid of him before something happened she'd regret for the rest of her life. She'd get some coffee down him and then send him on his way. Tomorrow he probably wouldn't remember anything.

"You didn't have to do this," he said a few minutes later, reaching for the cup in her hand.

"Yes, I did."

He took a drink, then set it on the table beside him. "I'm making a habit of pissing you off, aren't I?"

"I'm thinking it's the other way around."

His beautiful mouth tightened. "What makes you say that?" His tone was brusque.

"Your attitude."

"And what's that?"

He shifted and when he did, it put him closer to her. She wished now she'd sat in the adjacent chair, rather than on the sofa. He was much too tempting to touch.

"One of anger. Even hostility."

His mouth stretched even thinner. "I shouldn't be here."

"I agree," she said softly, casting an uneasy glance at him from under thick lashes.

Kaylee didn't know which was more predominant—the anger or the passion radiating from his eyes. This man was driving her crazy.

Yet she continued to sit next to him as though he weren't as lethal as a coiled rattlesnake.

Groaning, he reached for her and once again lowered his lips to hers. As before, the kiss was uncontrolled. It was as if she could taste his raw desire.

"Damn you," he whispered, his tongue circling her mouth before his lips traveled down her neck, nibbling on her flesh.

She moaned, winding her hands in his hair, clinging to him. Even though she didn't understand what made him angry or why he was taking it out on her, it no longer mattered. His hard body pressing against hers was all that counted. It was what dreams were made of.

When he began untying the sash on her silk robe she felt the first stirring of panic. Yet she couldn't pull away. For the moment she was at his mercy.

"Kaylee."

"What?" she murmured, her hands still buried in his hair.

He licked his way down her neck to her chest. When he licked the tops of her breasts with his tongue, she felt her body cry out, especially when his moist, seeking lips made contact with her lace bra.

She could feel her blood pulsing through her. "Cutler?"

His answer was to suck her nipple through the lace. Heat pooled between her thighs.

"Let it happen," he whispered at the same time that he popped the hook on the front of her bra, exposing her breasts.

He sucked in his breath and pulled back. His eyes were filled with desire. "God, is the rest of you this beautiful?"

She froze. Then, using every ounce of strength she possessed, Kaylee pushed him away, yanked her robe closed and got up.

"What's going on, Kaylee?" he asked in a strangled tone. "I know you want me as much as I want you."

"Please, just go home." She couldn't look at him, and her voice was barely audible. "I'm going to bed. Alone."

She didn't know which was louder—his curses or the door slamming behind him.

Twenty

Drew was late.

Kaylee glanced impatiently at her watch and noticed that he wasn't really late. She was fifteen minutes early. She had agreed to meet him for lunch at this small deli, not because she wanted to but rather because she felt obligated.

Her conscience pricked. She ought to be ashamed for thinking that. Often Drew had been more of a lifeline for her than her dad, especially when it came to finances. She couldn't imagine her life without him in it.

When he'd called and told her it had been too long since he'd seen her, she'd known he wasn't taking no for an answer. If her godfather made up his mind about something, experience had taught her it would be futile to argue. Besides, having lunch with him might just help settle her nerves.

Her altercation last evening with Cutler had turned her inside out, and she had not recovered. She couldn't believe she had come so close to letting him undress her, which might have led to him making love to her.

Thank goodness she had come to her senses in time. Otherwise, she would have awakened with even more regrets. Regrets from which she wouldn't recover. At least she still had her pride and could look at herself in the mirror without wanting to curl up and die.

Kaylee closed her eyes and allowed a wave of despair to wash through her. How many times had she vowed not to let her emotions get involved in anything other than her work? Too many times to count. Yet there was a part of her that held on to the hope she would find the perfect man who wouldn't care that she was different.

She'd found a man, all right, only he was far from perfect.

Suddenly Kaylee fought against hopelessness, an invisible malignancy that threatened to overpower her. She had ached to have his body cover hers, to feel him push inside her.

She sucked air into her lungs, feeling as though she was suffocating. She decided to concentrate on the busy people around her. The deli was nearly filled to capacity, though she'd managed to get a table in a far corner. She'd ordered a glass of iced tea that she hadn't touched. Figuring Drew would want a glass of wine, she hadn't ordered him a beverage.

Now she wished she'd opted for something stronger. Maybe then she wouldn't feel so fractured, so vulnerable, so unable to cope with this sudden and unexpected bump in the emotional side of her life.

She wondered what Cutler was thinking this morning. About her? If so, it was probably not flattering. She couldn't figure out if his pinched features had been due to anger or agony.

"My, but you look like you've got the weight of the world on those beautiful shoulders."

The sound of Drew's voice drew her head up and around. She plastered a big smile on her face.

"Ah, now that's my girl." He leaned over and pecked her on the cheek. "Hi, sweetheart."

"Hi, Uncle Drew."

When he took a seat across from her it struck Kaylee, as it had many times before, that her godfather was a good-looking man. His olive skin, few wrinkles and piercing green eyes, made him extremely easy to look at.

"Been waiting long?" he asked, grinning.

"Long enough to get my tea. That's all."

"Sorry. I got tied up on the phone."

"No problem."

She watched as he motioned for the waitress, then re-focused on her. "Are you ready to order?"

"If you are."

He nodded. Kaylee chose a salad and he chose a sand-wich, along with a glass of Chardonnay. "Sure you don't want to scrap that tea and join me?"

"I'm tempted, but I'd better not. I have two meetings this afternoon, and I need all my faculties."

"Another time, then."

After the waitress scuttled off, he smiled, "My, but you look smashing."

"I do?" she asked in surprise.

"Your face is aglow."

Oh Lord, that wasn't good, especially when she felt more color invade it. "I guess I got too much sun," she said lamely.

Drew's eyebrows rose. "Wouldn't happen to be caused by a man."

Her mouth compressed. "Have you been talking to my dad?"

"What makes you think that?" he asked in an innocent tone, then took a sip of his wine.

Kaylee glared at him. He responded with a deep chuckle.

"Dad is driving me crazy."

"Then there's nothing between you and Cutler McFarland."

"Absolutely not," she snapped, then averted her gaze, not trusting her ability to fool him.

"I don't know whether to be sorry or glad."

She flung her head back around. "That's an odd thing to say."

"Just chalk it up to jealousy," he said, shifting his gaze.

For a moment Kaylee sensed a tenseness in the air. She also thought he had wanted to say something else, but was reluctant. Then deciding it was her own paranoia playing with her psyche, she said with a grin, "Jealousy doesn't suit you."

Drew laughed, in spite of the serious set of his features. "I'd love to see you in love, but only—"

"Please, Uncle Drew, don't say anything else."

He paid her no heed. "You could do worse than McFarland, you know."

"McFarland, as you call him, is not even in the picture."

"Methinks you protest too much."

"Ah, here's our food," she said, feeling as though she'd been handed a life jacket.

"Okay, sweetheart, I'll give you a break. So tell me, how's business?"

"Great," she said with relief. "If things keep going like they are, I'll soon be out of debt to you."

"I wish you wouldn't pay me another dime. As it is, I've got more money than I'll ever spend. When I'm gone, it'll all be yours, anyway."

Kaylee's eyes widened. "Why, I wouldn't think of not paying off my debt."

"Whatever makes you happy." Drew shrugged. "I'll just add it to your inheritance."

She grasped his hand and squeezed. "You're too good to me. I'll never be able to repay you."

"You already have by being the daughter I never had."

Kaylee felt her eyes mist. "I do love you."

"And I love you." He took another drink of his wine. "Even if you're stubborn as a mule."

Kaylee grinned, only to have the expression freeze on her face. Cutler stood just inside the door of the deli and was looking straight at her.

A few minutes ago he had been standing front and center in her mind, playing with her emotions. Now he stood before her in the flesh, his presence teasing her. Remembering how his hands had felt on her flesh, she wanted to get up and touch him.

She felt the heat of embarrassment flood her cheeks as his gaze probed her features, nearly seducing her on the spot. Then he turned his back and walked in the other direction.

"What's wrong, Kaylee?" Drew asked.

She jerked her head around as if it were on a leash.

"You look like you just saw a ghost," Drew said with a frown.

Kaylee prayed her voice wouldn't crack. "You're imagining things." Making herself smile, she added, "I'm fine."

He looked as if he wanted to argue, but he didn't. He

raised his glass. "Before we chow down, let's drink to success and friendship."

Thank God he hadn't pursued the subject. She couldn't have taken much more grilling. Kaylee raised her glass, clinked it against his and smiled.

Cutler shook Ben Andrews's hand.

"I appreciate you seeing me, Mr. McFarland. I just wish it hadn't been under such hideous circumstances."

"I'm the one who should thank you," Cutler responded, accompanying the thin, wiry man to the door.

"Did I give you enough to arrest the son of a bitch?"

Cutler sidestepped the question. "My office will keep you posted."

"Meanwhile, I'll let you know if I find out anything else," Ben said, his voice riddled with enthusiasm. "Judge or no judge, it don't give the man a right to whip up on a defenseless woman, then rape her."

"That goes without saying," Cutler responded with a foul taste in his mouth.

"I'll never forgive him for what he did to my sister. And I've told her never to go near that man again, but she don't always listen to me."

Cutler opened the door. "If you see Peggy with him, call the number on the card I gave you. Immediately."

Andrews nodded, jammed on his cap and walked out.

Once the door was shut behind him, Cutler again looked at the pictures spread on the glass. He'd seen abuse, but the beating this woman had taken was over the top.

If Judge Jenkins was indeed responsible for those injuries, in addition to rape as Andrews had claimed, then castration was too good for the bastard. But without the sister and ironclad proof that Jenkins was indeed responsible, his office couldn't make a move.

Shoving his hands through his hair, Cutler turned away from the disturbing evidence with a grimace. It had been a day from hell and he was bushed. Perhaps if he hadn't seen Kaylee at lunch in the company of none other than Drew Rush, he wouldn't feel the need to tear somebody's head off.

It had taken every ounce of professional willpower he could muster to get through the interview with Andrews.

He knew that Kaylee's father worked for Drew, but he wondered what kind of relationship Kaylee had with the man. Were they friends? He didn't want to think of the possibilities beyond friendship.

He took a shuddering breath. At the moment, Kaylee and Drew's relationship wasn't the issue. Only Drew was. Cutler couldn't bear the thought that Drew Rush was even related to him, much less his father. It had to be a lie. If not, the entire world as he knew it had truly gone mad.

No matter what Trevor said, the only way to find out the truth was to speak to his mother. And soon, too. Time was running out.

Cutler heard the knock on the door, but before he could say anything, Angel opened it and walked in. "How did it go with Andrews?"

"Interesting, to say the least."

"What did he say?"

"The photos speak for themselves. Take a look."

For several seconds silence fell over the room, then Angel glanced up, expletives flying from his lips.

"My sentiments exactly."

"Do you really think Jenkins is capable of this?"

Cutler scraped a hand across his stubble, his eyes narrowing on Angel, who was perched on one end of his desk. "My gut says he is."

"But without tangible evidence, we've got zilch."

"And Andrews can't provide that evidence," Cutler pointed out. "His info is secondhand hearsay."

"What's the sister's name?"

"Peggy Trent."

"Why didn't she come to you?" Angel asked.

"According to her brother, Jenkins threatened her if she opened her mouth."

"For starters, can we trust a man who seemed to crawl out of the woodwork to accuse the judge?"

"Of something I've suspected for a long time," Cutler added, then pushed his chair away from his desk, got up and walked to the window. "Yeah, we can."

"But this guy's no ex-con and this woman apparently isn't hooker material. The perps Jenkins lets off don't fit in those categories."

Cutler turned. "Who's to say Jenkins doesn't tap outside sources?"

"We can't. So how do you want me to handle this?"

Cutler remained by the window. "Let's put a tail on Jenkins."

"I'll get Snelling on it."

Cutler shook his head. "You take care of it."

Angel's dark brows shot up. "As in hire someone?"

"Whatever. It's your call."

"Consider it done," Angel said without hesitation.

"Now, onto something even more important."

"Lay it on me," Angel said.

"Drew Rush."

Angel narrowed his eyes. "What about him?"

Cutler was tempted to blurt out, *The son of a bitch just might be my father.* But he didn't. Now was not the time to share that private thought, especially since he didn't know if it was the truth. "You know who he is?" he asked.

"Sure do."

"How?" Cutler's tone was sharp.

Angel gave him a strange look before answering. "Actually he's under investigation."

Cutler's jaw went slack. "By this office?"

"Yep."

"What for?"

"Suspicion of illegal business practices."

Un-fucking-believable.

"What's with your interest in Rush?"

Cutler cleared his throat, but when he spoke, his voice still sounded hoarse. "I want to know everything there is to know about that man—good, bad, or ugly."

"Not a problem."

"Make it top priority."

"I should have something in a couple of days."

Cutler balled his fists, then said in a terse tone, "Make it this afternoon."

"Yes, I do."

"You must have some powerful enemo."

"I do." Edgar held her gaze for a long moment. "Thank

Twenty-One

"Cutler?"

"Yes." Caution kept him brief, as he didn't clearly recognize the voice on the other end of the line. He'd been about to walk out of his office when the phone had rung.

"It's Edgar Benton."

Dead silence.

"I hope I'm not bothering you."

"What do you want?" Cutler demanded in a frigid tone.

"Just checking to see if you've—"

Red-hot fury held Cutler speechless for a second before he said through clenched teeth, "Don't call me again, Benton."

"But—"

Cutler slammed the receiver down with Benton talking. He paused for a moment and took a deep settling breath. That bastard had a lot of nerve calling him. The bastard had a lot of nerve *period*.

Cutler felt totally out of control of his life. That grated

on his last nerve. The fact that he'd called his mother and told her he was coming over made matters worse.

Of course, she had no idea she was about to be slam-dunked. But he had no recourse. He was fighting for his sanity, and she was the only one who could fix what was broken.

Or not.

It was the "or not" that had him so worried. Normally he was cool and levelheaded under fire, but the bombshell Benton had dropped in his lap had messed him up badly. Whatever it took to straighten this shit out, he'd do it.

Except marry against his will, dammit.

He'd be the first to admit that he was attracted to Kaylee. He hadn't tried to hide anything. She was the one who had been the reluctant participant in their relationship.

But attraction and marriage were two different things.

No one was going to blackmail him into doing something he didn't want to do, even though the prospect of having Kaylee as an everyday part of his life definitely appealed to him. In a lot of ways. Not only was she attractive, but he was certain that underneath her cool facade there was a hot-blooded woman.

Thirty minutes later Cutler was smiling at his mother, who had just poured them a glass of peach iced tea and was now backed against the kitchen cabinet.

"I can't believe you're here," Mary said, leaning her head to one side.

"Ah, Mom, come on, give me a break. You act like I don't ever see you."

"Okay, I'll give the devil his due. Lately you've been much better about doing your duty."

"Hey, you're really giving me a hard time."

She grinned, then walked over and kissed him on the cheek. "Just teasing you a bit. That's all."

"You know, I could whine, too. You certainly don't hurt yourself coming to see me."

"Ouch." Mary smiled as she pinched his cheek.

"Just keeping you in line, Mother dear."

"Come on, let's go to my study." She paused. "Or had you rather sit in the breakfast nook?"

"The study's fine."

"I hope you'll stay for dinner. Your dad's picking up Chinese."

"We'll see. Right now I'm not at all hungry."

Cutler felt as if his insides were unraveling. Mary seemed to be feeling so well that he hated to karate chop her from behind.

But the die had been cast, giving him no alternative.

"Are you feeling okay?" Mary asked once they were seated in another bright and airy room, thanks to the French doors that opened into a small garden with flowers and a birdbath.

Now as sunlight danced on a crystal cross standing on her desk, Cutler looked at it as though mesmerized.

"Son, I asked you a question."

Cutler shook his head. "Sorry."

"Don't be sorry," Mary responded in her direct fashion. "Just answer me."

Cutler grinned. "You drive a hard bargain, woman."

"I try."

"I'm just tired."

"I think it's more than tired, but if you don't want to share, that's okay. I'm just glad to see you."

Cutler swallowed hard before reaching for his tea and taking a healthy sip. When he set the glass back down, his mother's eyes were settled on him. "Don't forget what a good listener I am."

"I know that, Mom."

"Then talk. Your dad won't be home for a while yet, so it's just you and me, kid."

Cutler knew she was making an attempt at humor to lighten the tension that hovered over the room. Even though she had no idea what had caused it, her maternal instinct sensed it. She knew something was wrong with her child and wanted to help.

But he'd rather have his heart ripped out than say what he had to say. His gut told him once the words left his mouth, their relationship would never be the same again, no matter what.

"Mom—"

She smiled a sweet smile. "That's me."

When he didn't smile back, hers faded. "My, but you *are* uptight. Maybe you need something stronger than tea. How about a beer or glass of wine?"

Cutler shook his head. "Tea's fine for now."

"Okay," she responded with raised eyebrows.

He made an awkward attempt to clear his throat. "Mom."

"What?" Her lips twitched.

"I need to talk to you about a subject you're not going to like." Cutler watched her closely. Although she frowned, her features weren't at all guarded. She looked as relaxed and unperturbed as ever.

"You can talk to me about anything. You know that."

"I hope you'll still feel that way after we're done."

Her frown deepened. "What's going on, son? Just spit it out. You know how I am about playing cat and mouse. Your father does that, and it drives me crazy."

Still Cutler hesitated, his gut twisted in a knot while sweat oozed out of him as if he'd just run a marathon. "Why didn't you tell me Trevor isn't my real father?"

Mary didn't so much as blink, much less flinch. She sat as tall and confident as ever. Cutler hadn't known what to expect, but it certainly wasn't this unemotional reaction. Either Benton was full of shit or his mother had nerves of steel.

"Mom," Cutler pressed gently, "I want an answer."

"That question doesn't warrant an answer." Her calm still didn't waver.

"So Trevor is my real dad?"

Mary looked him straight in the eye. "Absolutely."

"His name is listed on my birth certificate, right?"

Several drumbeats of silence.

"What's this all about, Cutler?"

Was he seeing the first chink in the armor? His insides twisted another notch. "The truth. Getting to the truth."

Mary stood and walked to the French doors. For the longest time Cutler stared at her back, feeling as if he'd been tossed in the ocean without a life jacket. Suddenly he didn't know if he was capable of continuing this charade. He was tempted to tell Benton to take his best shot and let the bullets fall where they may.

But what if his mother ended up in the line of fire and took a fatal hit?

If there was even the slightest chance of that, he couldn't take the risk.

"I'm not letting you off the hook." Cutler kept his tone

calm and soft. But God, he was struggling to temper his raw emotions. He didn't know how much longer he could keep a lid on them.

Mary swung around, her face totally devoid of color. To Cutler, she looked as if someone had cut her throat and left her to bleed. His fear heightened. "Mom, I—"

She held out her hand, stopping him midsentence. "I think you should go."

"I'm not budging." He hadn't meant to say that, to take such a hard stance. But under the circumstances, he saw no other way. The damage was done.

"Then I'll leave."

"Mom, please," he said in a pleading tone. "You owe me the truth."

"I don't owe you anything, Cutler," she countered in a chilled tone, "except love and respect. And you have both."

"It's not that simple. *Life's* not that simple."

"It is to me." Her eyes challenged him to deny that.

He couldn't. But whether she loved or respected him was not the issue here, and she knew it. Getting her to admit that, however, was another matter.

Hence Cutler fought hard to curb his mounting anger and frustration. He hadn't wanted to get into this kind of verbal slinging match with her. He'd chosen his words with the utmost care. But somehow his best intentions had fallen short, and he was at a loss as to what to say or do next.

A situation he detested. Especially with his beloved mother.

"I went to see Trevor."

Her face whitened even more. "He didn't tell you anything."

"No, he didn't."

"I'm getting tired. I should go to bed."

"Is Drew Rush my father?"

It happened so fast, he didn't have time to move. Mary's eyes rolled back in her head and she started to fold like an accordion.

"Mom!" he cried, catching her just before she hit the floor.

Kaylee was the only one left in the office. She had planned to go home much earlier, only it hadn't worked out that way. One project had led to another and before she knew it, twilight had replaced the sunlight.

Her body bore testimony to the long day. Her limp was much more pronounced than it had been in a long time. Still, she had managed to get some things that had been bugging her marked off her "to-do list."

Now, though, she was ready to call it a day after one last sweep of the dressing room to make sure no garments were left strewn on the floor. No matter how hard she or Sandy preached, there was always at least one slob in the group who just didn't get it.

Sure enough, the slob was in evidence this evening. Several outfits were piled on a chair in one corner. Knowing it was useless to get her blood pressure up over a problem that was ongoing, Kaylee merely walked over, grabbed the garments and made her way to the closet.

She was hanging up a pair of overalls when she noticed a bulge in one of the many pockets. Thinking it was a wadded-up tissue, Kaylee reached inside. Even then she didn't realize what she had in her hand until she pulled the item out.

"Oh, my God," she whispered, though not really believing what she was seeing.

Pills.

Nestled in the palm of her hand was a packet of what looked to be prescription drugs. If they had all been the same kind, she might not have thought anything about it. But they weren't. They were different colors, different shapes, different sizes.

A variety of drugs.

She felt her heart pound against her rib cage, further weakening her limbs. Before she lost her balance, Kaylee sat in the chair, feeling drained.

What did this mean? Were there more? Was this packet just the tip of the iceberg?

Unable or unwilling to answer those questions at this point, Kaylee rummaged through the rest of the clothes.

Seconds later she had unearthed four more packets of pills. Kaylee didn't know which emotion took precedence—boiling rage or acute despair. But since she needed a clear head so that she could think, she pushed both emotions aside.

She had known drugs and anorexia were common problems among models, but her agency had always stressed the importance of the whole person, of making the inside as beautiful as the outside.

She was adamant that all girls maintain their health in body and spirit and not sacrifice either for a page in a magazine or a walk down an aisle. Her philosophy had served her well.

Until now.

The big question was how to deal with this latest kick

in the teeth. She told herself that after she'd had a bath and a good night's sleep she'd come up with a strategy.

Ha.

Fifteen minutes later, Kaylee turned into her drive, only to receive her second shock of the evening.

She braked suddenly, her heart slamming into the back of her throat.

Twenty-Two

Cutler knew he shouldn't have come to her place. Yet here he was camped out at her house, waiting for her to come home.

What did that say about him?

He wasn't sure he could answer that question even if he dug deep into his soul, prepared to be brutally honest with himself. At this point he simply wasn't up to that task. Despite the disruption to his life that had all to do with her, there was something about Kaylee that not only turned him on sexually but affected him emotionally.

A haven in the time of a storm.

Was that crazy or what? Especially when she was at the eye of the storm.

He should be at the hospital with his mother. After all, it was his fault she was there.

After she had passed out in his arms, he'd called 911, then Trevor. By the time the ambulance arrived at the hospital, Mary had regained consciousness and was insisting on going back home.

Both he and Trevor, however, had remained united in their effort to see that at least the E.R. doctor examined her. Her cardiologist had been called, and he had said flatly that she wouldn't be going home before the next morning.

Later, after Mary was settled in a room and resting, he had told Trevor what had happened. His dad hadn't been happy and wasted no time in taking Cutler to task.

"I told you to leave it be, boy." His features were hard with worry. "Now see what you've done."

"Even though I'm sorry as hell about what happened, I had to ask."

"Well, don't ask again," Trevor had said coldly, then added, "When she wakes up, I think it'd be best if you weren't here. I'll call you tomorrow."

Realizing if he hung around he'd definitely be adding insult to injury, he'd hauled it. Straight to Kaylee.

Along with simply seeing her, he wanted to know the truth about her involvement in her father's scheme. While Edgar had vehemently denied her culpability, he wasn't so sure. The more he'd thought about it, the more convinced he'd become that Kaylee had to be in the know.

Too bad his heart didn't agree with his head.

He knew Kaylee was fiercely independent and proud, two characteristics he admired most about her. He felt that and her fighting spirit would have stopped Edgar from continuing down such a crazy path.

Yet he couldn't discuss the horrifying situation with her. The risk to his mother was too great. His heart had skipped several beats when he saw her car arrive home. What was he going to say to her?

Their last time together had left him with a physical

longing that had shocked him, especially after the visit from her father. One would have thought he'd want to be as far away from her as possible, that the sight of her would repulse him.

Was that why he was here? To test his response to her? No. As crazy as it was, he knew he wanted her.

The second she got out of the car and leaned against it, he felt that stirring in his loins.

Staring at him wide-eyed, Kaylee said, "I should ask what you're doing here."

"Are you? Asking, that is?"

"No."

"Thanks," he muttered brusquely, shoving his hands into his pockets.

"Something's wrong, isn't it?"

"Am I that easy to read, even in the moonlight?"

"Yes."

He tried to smile. "I'm not sure that's good."

"Do you want to talk about it?"

"Does that mean you're going to let me in?"

"Should I?"

"Probably not," he said with tormented but blatant honesty.

He hadn't touched her, but it was all he could do not to grab her, yank her against him, then kiss her until she begged for mercy.

As if she could read his mind, he heard her sharp intake of breath. But then she turned and made her way toward the front door. Once inside, she flipped a switch and a lamp bathed the room in soft light.

"I'll get us something to drink."

He grabbed her hand. "Forget it." His voice was deep and thick.

"Then have a seat." She swallowed hard. "I need a minute."

"Hurry," he said huskily, then eased onto the sofa, leaned his head back and closed his eyes.

She wasn't gone but fifteen minutes. Even so, she made good use of the time, stripping off her clothes and stepping into the shower. She had felt dirty after finding the pills, as if she needed a good cleansing. More than that, she needed time alone to regroup, to gather her wits about her.

Even if her insides were quivering like jelly, she wasn't sorry she'd invited him in. Since he'd kissed her, she had wanted to see him, *had wanted to touch him.* No matter how many times she had told herself he was forbidden to her, she couldn't get him out of her head.

Ridiculous?

Of course.

Did she care?

Not tonight.

What was happening to her?

With no answers readily available, Kaylee stopped thinking. She put on a silk robe that more than covered her, then made her way back to him. It took her only a second to realize he was asleep, which gave her an opportunity to study him.

Even his dark stubble failed to hide the lines of exhaustion that were etched in his face. His clothes and hair were mussed as though he'd also had a bitch of a day. She had known the instant she saw him that something was wrong. He'd looked almost ill. And still did.

Now, as she perched beside him, though not too close, she fought the urge to reach out and smooth those lines with her fingertips. Just the thought sent erotic chills through her. Each time she saw him alone, the danger to her heart increased.

As she watched, he opened his eyes and stretched. "Sorry, I fell asleep," he said huskily. "Been waiting long?"

"No. Actually, I just sat down."

His eyes traveled over her. "I'm glad you got comfortable."

She averted her gaze. "It's been a long, hard day."

"I know about that."

She picked up on the bitterness in his tone and frowned. "What's going on, Cutler?"

She heard the tremor in her voice, but couldn't help it. She was struggling with his being there and couldn't seem to hide it.

"It's my mother."

"What about her?"

"She had another spell with her heart."

"Is she all right?"

"Yes, according to her doctor, although he's keeping her overnight in the hospital for observation."

"I'm sorry."

"Me, too," he said in a terse tone. "Especially since it was my fault."

"I doubt that," she said, more to herself than to him.

"Oh, it was my fault, all right, but—" He broke off abruptly.

"But what?" she pressed.

His features twisted. "I don't want to burden you with my problems."

"What if I want to be burdened?"

His eyes burned into her and her heart turned over.

"You look like you haven't had such a swell day yourself," he said, shattering the hot moment of intimacy.

She sighed. "It's okay if you don't want to talk to me."

"It's much too complicated, Kaylee."

"I understand."

"No, you don't. Hell, I don't even understand."

A short silence fell between them.

"Back to your day," he finally said, his eyes trapping hers again. "I've never seen dark circles under your eyes."

"The day's been a bitch. I—" This time her voice failed. Though she knew she was going to have to deal with the drug problem, she wasn't ready to involve the law yet. And Cutler was the law.

"Go on."

"Never mind." She forced a smile.

He gave her a semblance of a grin. "You don't want to share either."

"Right."

Another silence fell between them, during which Cutler reached out a finger and trailed it down one side of her cheek. Her insides fluttered.

"I want you, Kaylee," he whispered.

"I want you, too, only—"

"Only what?"

She moved her head from side to side, tears perilously close. "You...you don't understand."

"Try me."

The same finger that trailed her cheek now made its way down her neck into the V of her robe. She stiffened when that calloused fingertip grazed the tops of her breasts. Her breath rushed in and out of her lungs.

"I would never hurt you," he said, his eyes darkening. "I want to make slow, passionate love to you." He reached for one of her hands and placed it over the hard mound behind his zipper. "That says it all."

"Cutler—"

"You just said you wanted that, too."

"I do, but…" Her voice played out again while her blood beat like a drum in her ears.

A hand gently parted her robe, exposing her. "Your breasts are beautiful," he said in a strained whisper. "They're firm, like newly ripened peaches."

"Oh, Cutler, I couldn't stand it if you felt sorry for me."

His hand stilled and he frowned. "Is that what this is all about? You think I feel sorry for you because you have a limp?"

"No, because I'm…I'm scarred."

"Scarred?"

She nodded, dislodging a tear.

"God, it's okay," he said, reaching for her and pulling her close against him.

"No, it's not okay," she said in a muffled cry, her throat pulsating painfully.

"Kaylee, look at me." He pulled slightly back and lifted her chin.

Their eyes met and held, tighter than magnets.

"I'm going to take your robe off."

The fear of him seeing the rest of her body sliced through her like a jagged shard of glass.

"Cutler, please—"

"Shh," he whispered. "It's going to be all right. Perfect, in fact."

She didn't know which was hotter, his hands or his eyes. But both were powerful and persuasive, rendering her useless.

He lifted her to her feet, then pushed the robe off her shoulders, sending it pooling around her feet.

"Oh, no," she whimpered, grasping at it to cover herself.

"Don't." He trapped her hands to her sides as his eyes slowly perused her body, seemingly not missing one ounce of flesh.

"I told you I was scarred," she whispered through the tears now clogging her throat.

He didn't say anything. Instead, he dropped to his knees in front of her and began kissing the welts that crisscrossed her stomach. A moan started low inside her as she ran her fingers through his hair.

Wordlessly he rose and kissed her passionately on the mouth. Then he eased her down beside him on the sofa.

It was moments later that *her* fingers began playing havoc with him. She found, then fumbled with his zipper. His response was to deepen the kiss before helping her release his penis from the confines of his pants.

With their eyes locked, he lifted her onto the throbbing head.

She gasped.

He froze.

"Am I hurting you?" He ground out the words.

"Only if you stop."

In the dim light she watched his eyes glaze over as she continued to slowly slide onto him, all the way. They both let out a long moan before he leaned forward and kissed her on the lips.

She clung to him while he clamped his hands on her hips and frantically moved her in long, deliberate strokes. She felt her thighs spread farther apart, giving him full access. And he was taking full advantage, too, in a way that made her gasp each time he penetrated higher and deeper.

Then tightening his muscles, he unloaded in her with one powerful thrust. Was this really happening to her? Was this good-looking, charismatic man making love to her?

Yes.

And she was sweating, dissolving under the heat, melting as if she were a wax figure.

Finally they both cried out and grew still, breathing heavily.

Holding him tightly with tears rolling down the sides of her face, Kaylee caught a glimpse of the stars through the window and thought they seemed brighter than she could ever remember.

Twenty-Three

"Are you sure you should be working?"

"Now, Trevor, don't hover."

He sighed as he took a seat in front of Mary's desk in the church office.

"I'm sorry, my dear, but you just got out of the hospital."

"And you're worried," Mary said with a limp smile.

"Of course I'm worried, and you should be, too."

Mary picked up on the censure in her husband's tone even though he spoke with his usual gentleness. Never once during their long marriage had he ever raised his voice to her. Maybe that wasn't a good thing.

"You look deep in thought," he said.

"I was thinking about how kind you've always been to me."

"Maybe too kind."

She smiled for real. "You read my mind. Because you never cross me, you gave me the confidence to be stubborn."

"As a mule, just like now."

Mary's smile faded. "I don't mean to cause you worry."

He reached across the desk and sought her hand. "You've caused me nothing but the greatest of joy."

Mary felt tears prick the back of her eyes. She blinked furiously, fearing she would cry, which was not like her. She rarely resorted to tears; in fact, she couldn't remember the last time she'd even been tempted.

But since Cutler's bombshell, she had wanted to sob her heart out. She'd held herself together, fearing if she opened that valve to her heart, she wouldn't be able to close it.

"Mary—" Trevor cleared his throat as if he had trouble finding the right words.

"It's okay. I'm okay, really." She squeezed his hand. "You can't get bent out of shape every time I have a flare-up with my old ticker."

"I don't find any humor in this, Mary."

She gave him a look. "I'm not trying to be humorous. I'm just trying to get you to accept things as they really are."

"How about you, my dear?"

Mary tensed. "I don't know what you're talking about."

"When were you going to tell me?"

She didn't pretend to misunderstand him. "When the time was right."

"I'm sorry about all this."

She looked away. "My son has upset me terribly."

"And your heart took the brunt of that strain," he said in that same gentle tone. "Which has upset me."

Tears pricked again, but still she refused to let her emotions have free rein.

"He has a right to know, Mary."

"That's not your decision." Her tone was much harder than she intended.

His face flushed with color. "Sorry if I offended you."

"Oh, Trevor, you didn't offend me."

A silence followed her words. Finally Mary got up and walked to the window, where she stared out at the flower garden. The sight that greeted her calmed her instantly, and for that she was grateful.

"I couldn't tell him," she said, still facing the window.

"I know it has to be hard."

She swung around, then said flatly, "It's impossible, actually."

Trevor's face lost its color. "Don't you think you owe him the truth?"

"No."

Trevor spread his hands, opened his mouth, then shut it.

"I know you don't approve of my decision."

"You're right, I don't. But I'm going to back you, nonetheless."

Mary swallowed hard. "At this point, nothing good can come of baring my soul."

"Do you think Cutler will leave it alone?"

"I pray that he will."

Trevor sighed deeply. "You know Cutler better than that. He's so much like you, which means he won't walk away."

"And I shouldn't expect him to. Isn't that what you're saying?"

"That's not my call."

"I can't…talk about it. I wish I could, but I just can't."

Trevor got up, walked to her and took her in his arms. She clung to his warmth. "If you can't, you can't," he said. "I can't bear the thought of losing you. It's for that reason I'm so fearful. If this thing explodes…"

Even though he let his voice trail off, Mary knew the rest of that sentence, too.

"Why did this have to happen now?" she asked, disentangling herself from Trevor's arms.

"I'm surprised it's taken this long."

Mary was taken aback and didn't try to hide it. "But why?"

"Rarely are secrets taken to the grave."

"He...he—" Mary broke off with a shudder. She couldn't bring herself to even say Drew's name out loud. The thought of doing so made her fight for her next breath. She turned away so that Trevor wouldn't pick up on her acute agitation.

"Are you all right?"

There was no fooling him. She wasn't surprised, though. They had been married for so long and he knew her so well.

"I'm not going to pass out, if that's what you mean," she said, facing him once again.

"That's reassuring," he said with rough but obvious relief.

"If you don't mind, I'd like to be alone for a while."

Trevor leaned over and kissed her on the cheek. "We'll get through this, my dear."

"With God's help."

"I'll see you this evening." He gave her an anxious look. "Meanwhile, if you need me or you feel the least bit off center, you call 911."

"I promise. But I'll be fine."

Trevor caressed one cheek. "You'd better be. I need you, my dear."

"I need you, too. And Cutler." Mary's voice cracked.

Frowning, Trevor peered more closely at her. "I'm not at all sure I should leave you."

"Please. I need to be alone."

"I—"

She shook her head and smiled. "I'm okay. I'd tell you otherwise."

"Since when?"

She forced a smile, then gave him a shove. "Go dig in the dirt."

After giving her another close look, Trevor nodded, then walked out.

Mary immediately stepped out into the garden, where she took a deep breath, pulling the scent of the roses deep into her lungs. When she released her breath, she felt less shaky. Still, she eased down into the glider, fearing her legs weren't as steady as the rest of her, and lifted her eyes toward heaven.

Oh, God, she whispered silently. She wanted so much to break down and sob her heart out. But again she wouldn't allow herself to lose control.

She had vowed long ago she would never shed another tear over the traumatic, life-changing incident that had robbed her of so much of herself. It had taken her years to mend her broken heart, her broken spirit and her broken pride. She'd thought she had the battle won. And she had.

Until now.

Dear God, why? Mary cried from that dark part of her soul where many scars dwelled.

That was when she heard that still small voice whisper, "You can run, but you can't hide." Suddenly her heart almost stopped beating, but for an entirely different reason. Had she run? No, of course she hadn't.

She had taken the needed time to heal, to face the pain and deal with it. The only thing she hadn't done was tell another living soul the truth except Trevor, and he would never betray her.

But someone had.

Others had been involved, of course. You couldn't birth a child alone. Yet she hadn't worried about the outsiders, because most people didn't care. They had their own problems, their own crosses to bear. She might have been the gossip flavor of the day, but that was all.

And again, it had been so long ago. Who would benefit by resurrecting old gossip now? She was certain Trevor knew the answer, but she hadn't asked him. She didn't want to know. She didn't want to know anything. She just wanted the past to stay buried.

Unfortunately, life didn't always work that way. As a minister who dealt with sin and pain on a daily basis, she was more aware of that than most.

Then why was she so shocked that her secret was no longer a secret?

Cutler.

She had protected him like a mother cub nursing a newborn, never suspecting that he would ever learn the truth. In retrospect, how naive was that? How unrealistic?

Even so, she made no apologies. At the juncture, she had done what she'd thought best for his welfare and her sanity. She had no regrets.

Or did she?

Feeling her heart rate quicken and a stab of pain in her chest, Mary reached in her pocket for her medication. If she was going to have to retravel that hard and wounding path, she needed earthly help.

Once she'd swallowed a tiny pill, she closed her eyes

and delved deep in her conscience. Were Cutler and Trevor right? Was it soul-cleansing time?

Should she confess the truth to her son and let the chips fall where they may? If so, would she be able to glue her own soul back together? Once more?

Mary couldn't answer that question, and that was what frightened her the most.

Cutler finished another beer, his fifth, before tossing the empty bottle into the trash can, flinching when it struck the other ones. He waited for glass to fly, but none did.

He was at the fridge ready to grab another one when his hand stalled. What the hell was he doing? Getting stinking drunk wasn't the answer. Even if he hit the sack in a stupor, he'd still have to face his demons when he awakened.

Hell, maybe he'd get lucky and not wake up.

Swallowing an expletive, Cutler made his way out onto his balcony, but the stifling heat and humidity that greeted him did little to enhance his mood. But in all fairness to summer, it wasn't the weather that had him going.

His nuts were in a vise and he hated that. Until this point in his life, he had been in control of his destiny, but now he no longer felt certain about anything. Except that he couldn't be responsible for his mother's death. A cold chill shot through him. He knew what he had to do.

Marry Kaylee.

Sweat replaced the chill as he left the deck, walked back inside and made a beeline for the fridge. Only one more beer, he told himself, then he'd make a pot of coffee. Once he'd downed it, he'd shower and go from there.

He tossed his head back and guzzled half the beer before setting it down on the table beside the sofa. Then burying his head in a soft cushion, he closed his eyes, only to see Kaylee printed on the back of his eyelids.

Even though the thought of a forced marriage still grated on his last nerve, he could do a lot worse than Kaylee. At least she turned him on. He thought about the other night when they had made love on the sofa, then later in the bedroom. There hadn't been one inch of her flesh that hadn't felt his lips and tongue.

He squirmed deeper into the cushion after peering down and seeing the bulge in his jeans. For someone who wasn't experienced sexually, she'd either been a fast learner or she simply had innate talent.

Her lips and tongue had done a number on his flesh that he wouldn't ever forget. Besides the hot chemistry between them, he liked her. She was smart, savvy and independent.

It was that independent streak that bothered him.

When he did ask her to marry him, what if she told him to get lost? Feeling his gut burn, Cutler polished off the remainder of the beer, then wished for another. He refrained, however, as the next thing on his agenda required complete sobriety.

Instead, he walked into the kitchen and made coffee. He gagged down two strong cups, then headed upstairs to the shower.

Fifteen minutes later he was dressed and out the door.

"Mr. Rush will see you shortly."

Cutler merely nodded to the housekeeper, who turned and left him alone. He released a pent-up breath, realizing that he was sweating profusely. Nerves. That was the culprit. Even so, he wouldn't dare let on that he could easily bite a tenpenny nail in two.

This was his party and he aimed to run the show. While he waited, his eyes scanned the room. Everything in the study was so perfect, it gave him the creeps. For that matter, the entire house gave him the creeps. It was like a mausoleum. Too elaborate. Too cold. Too showy.

"Ah, sorry to have kept you waiting."

Cutler whipped around and faced his nemesis.

Twenty-Four

He had to force himself to look at Drew Rush, the man who could or could not be his father.

"Ah, McFarland, what can I do for you?"

"We need to talk," Cutler said without preamble.

Drew smiled, though it never reached his eyes. "I have no problem with that. Would you care to sit down?"

"I'll stand."

Drew shrugged. "Fine. How 'bout something to drink?"

"No, thanks."

"If this visit's about your campaign—"

"It's not," Cutler interrupted.

Drew's lips quirked. "If you'll excuse me, I'm going to have a drink."

While Drew's back was to him, Cutler said, "I know who you are."

Drew's body visibly tensed. That was the only reaction to Cutler's terse comment. But that was enough for Cutler to know he'd struck a nerve.

"I repeat. I know who you are."

Drew seemingly took his time turning back around. "What does that mean?"

"I think you know."

"What I know is that your manners need an overhaul, especially when you walk into someone else's home and behave like a fool."

"This isn't a social visit, Rush."

"Go get a life."

Cutler smirked. "Just so you'll know up front, I'm immune to your insults."

"You ought to start this conversation over, sonny boy, take a different approach. I don't think you want me for an enemy."

"I don't give a shit what you think."

"It's only because I'm a gentleman that I'm letting you take your frustrations out on me. So what's your beef? All I did was contribute to your campaign. Perhaps my donation wasn't enough, huh?"

Drew's attempt at dark humor fell on deaf ears. "I don't want your money," Cutler spat out. "In fact, I plan to return it."

This time Drew's lips stretched into a thin line. "You're trying my patience, boy. If something's stuck in your gullet, you'd best spit it out before you get thrown out."

"I came after the truth."

"Ah, imagine a D.A. wanting that." Drew's sarcasm deepened.

"This is not a game, Rush."

"You bet it's not a game, and I'm fast losing patience. I have other things to do besides stand here and listen to your incoherent babbling."

"I know the truth about you and my mother."

Dead silence.

"Ah, so that's what you meant by your opening statement," Drew said in a blasé tone, as though Cutler had said something as mundane as it's dark outside.

Cutler ignored his second attempt at dark humor and said, "Do you have the guts to tell me?"

"You're pushing your luck."

"My question stands."

"So you think you know the truth."

"Yes," Cutler lied. It was inconceivable to him that Drew would admit that he had fathered him, especially since the truth had been hidden for such a long time.

Drew's features suddenly changed, becoming cynical and twisted. "I doubt that. Not if you heard it from that sanctimonious, holier-than-thou bitch, that is."

Those denigrating words loaded Cutler's cannon instantly. His blood pressure shot to stroke level, and his heart pumped overtime. It was all he could do not to rearrange Drew's smug features. Because he knew how critical this meeting was, he held on to his temper. "I assume you're referring to my mother."

"That I am, and I make no apologies for it."

Rage almost choked Cutler. "Okay, let's hear your version of the truth."

Drew shrugged his gym-sculptured shoulders. "We had a one-night stand and she got pregnant. It's as simple as that."

Gritting his teeth, Cutler said, "Doesn't sound simple to me. Sounds damn complicated."

"I'll admit her getting pregnant definitely muddied the waters."

Cutler was getting sicker and sicker by the second. "So you're not denying you're my father?"

"Only by blood," Drew said with rough fierceness.

Cutler struggled for his next breath. He had hoped that Edgar Benton had been full of himself. Instead this encounter was proving to be his worst nightmare come true.

"I begged her to have an abortion, but she wouldn't even consider it. In fact, she looked at me like I had just crawled out of a sewer." Drew's voice and eyes were bitter as quinine. "I won't ever forget that either." He paused.

"I insisted on the termination of rights papers to ensure Mary wouldn't try to blackmail me later either emotionally or financially."

Cutler recoiled. "Obviously you never cared about her."

"That was a two-way street, sonny boy."

"I don't believe that."

"Not caring what you believe ranks right up there with not caring what you think."

"My mother isn't that kind of woman."

"Oh, really?"

"Have you always been such a bastard?"

"According to your mother. After all this time, I suppose she's still claiming I took advantage of her."

"And you didn't?" Cutler's tone was low and harsh.

"Hell, no. I didn't rape her."

The mention of rape sent shock waves through Cutler's entire body. Yet he continued to stand stonelike— except for his eyes. He could feel the venom shooting out of them.

"She might have said no, but I could tell she wanted it."

Cutler's throat shut down, rendering him speechless.

"And did I ever give it to her." Drew's chuckle was derisive. "Real good, too."

Cutler moved with the speed of lightning. "You sorry piece of garbage." His fists followed his words, flying out and smashing Drew in the face.

Drew crumpled to the carpet. He was out cold.

Cutler turned and walked out, taking with him the feel and sound of crunching bones.

Kaylee didn't know whether to laugh with giddiness or cry with bitterness.

What she did know was that she had done the unthinkable. She had broken a lifelong promise to herself.

She had let a man invade her heart.

How had that happened? Perhaps there was no clear-cut answer. Perhaps it was one of those unplanned things, a quirk of fate.

But the word *unplanned* had never been in her vocabulary. Until Cutler made his appearance.

With his attraction and charm, he had managed to creep into her heart. Even now she couldn't believe he'd made love to her. Equally mind-boggling, she'd loved him back, and she'd enjoyed every moment of it.

Just thinking about the way he had dropped to his knees and kissed the scars on her stomach before working his lips and tongue back up to her mouth made her knees knock. Not only had he set her flesh on fire, but he had melted her frozen heart. That was dangerous stuff. Heady stuff.

She hadn't known a man's touch could be so exhilarating. She hadn't known what making love was all about, certainly not from bumbling, fumbling Kenny. While she had endured, it was an experience she hadn't enjoyed.

Not so with Cutler.

She couldn't seem to get enough of him. Nor he of her. After their burning passion for one another had been quenched, he had held her in his arms, making her feel so special, so beautiful, *so normal.*

"God, I loved every second I was inside you," he'd whispered against her neck while spooning her.

She could barely hold back her tears. "Me, too."

"You're so tight," he added in a strained voice. "I was so afraid I was going to hurt you."

"You…didn't." She felt him turn hard again.

He nipped her neck with his lips. "And you smell so good and taste so good."

She turned in his arms just in time to meet his hot, seeking lips. They kissed until both were gasping for breath.

"God, I can't get enough of you," he whispered, his hands kneading one breast and then the other.

"Oh, Cutler," she'd moaned, especially when he'd eased her onto her back and had begun using his tongue to take her to new heights.

A knock on the door jarred Kaylee back to earth.

Licking her dry lips, she said, "It's open."

Sandy walked in, only to pull up short, narrowing her eyes. "You okay?"

"Of course," Kaylee almost snapped. "Why?"

"Sorry, you just looked flushed, like you might have a little fever."

She had better watch herself, Kaylee thought, feeling

the flush on her face grow hotter. She couldn't be wearing her heart on the outside for everyone to see. This thing with Cutler was just a passing fancy headed down a one-way street. So for her own self-protection, no one must ever know she'd been with him.

The only excuse for her actions was to plead temporary insanity.

"I thought maybe your leg might be bothering you."

Kaylee shook her head. "Uh, no more than usual. But thanks for caring."

"That goes without saying." Sandy paused. "I know something's up, so let's hear it."

"Trouble."

Sandy's face fell. "I'm not sure I want to hear it."

"Trust me, you don't."

"Only, misery loves company." Sandy smiled a weak smile.

"You got it, friend," Kaylee said. "So have a seat. It's share time."

She told Sandy about the prescription drugs, leaving nothing out. When she finished, a heavy silence filled the room.

"God, I can't believe it."

"Me either," Kaylee said, rubbing her temple.

"We have to call the cops." Sandy's voice was a whisper.

Kaylee raised her brows. "Why are you talking so low?"

Sandy cleared her throat. "Didn't realize I was."

"We're alone, remember."

"Chalk it up to paranoia," Sandy responded with a shrug. "So what do you propose?"

"I know you're right, and we probably should involve the cops, but— "

"You'd rather handle it in-house."

"I'd like to try, anyway."

Sandy wrinkled her forehead. "That might be the best route, but it's dicey."

"I know."

"What about asking your friend?"

"What friend?"

Sandy look slightly affronted. "Did I say something wrong?"

"No, why?"

"You snapped at me."

"Sorry, didn't mean to."

"The D.A. What's his name?"

Kaylee schooled her features to show none of her churning emotions. "Cutler McFarland."

"Could you talk to him?"

"Maybe later." Kaylee reached for a pen and pad. "Meanwhile, let's put our heads together and see what we can come up with."

Twenty-Five

"Want to play some more, baby?"

"No," Drew said, slapping her on the butt. Hard.

"Ouch! That hurt."

"I meant for it to. Now, do like you're told and get the hell out of here."

"One of these days you're going to get what's coming to you."

"Good thing you're out of range, or you'd get what's coming to *you*."

The young girl's face lost its color before she bounded up and out, slamming the door behind her.

Drew let out a sigh of relief. Alone at last. He didn't know why he fooled with one airheaded bimbette after another. There were plenty of classy women who would love to give him a piece of their ass. And more.

It was the "and more" that scared the hell out of him. He'd had it with marriage. Two times down the old aisle was enough for him. As it was he already paid too much alimony—not that he couldn't afford it. It was the fact that he was forced to do something against his will that he hated.

He didn't like tight corners.

And Cutler McFarland had just backed him into one. He rubbed his jaw and flinched. No bastard hit him and got away with it. But Cutler had, and that was what galled him. That was why he'd banged that dizzy broad tonight. He'd been so full of rage, he'd wanted to take it out on someone.

Only his ploy hadn't worked. He was still mad enough to kill. After Cutler had knocked him flat on his back, he'd been addled for hours afterward. During that time, his rage had almost gotten the best of his better judgment.

Charging after that bastard would have served no purpose. When it came to Cutler, he'd decided to bide his time. One way or the other he'd get his pound of flesh. After all, he was in no hurry and didn't have anything to lose.

Cutler, on the other hand, was on a timetable and had lots to lose.

Mary McFarland, however, had been a different matter. After he got his head back on straight and put ice on his jaw, he'd jumped in his vehicle and driven to her house, where he'd waited for hours, hoping to catch her alone.

It never happened.

Her husband hadn't left her side all evening. Finally he'd driven home and immediately called the bimbette. Now, however, Drew felt his anger rise again along with numerous questions.

Why now? Why did she tell Cutler the truth after all this time? What had happened to make her open herself up to his wrath? To add insult to injury, she had broken a promise she had sworn to keep.

He'd get her for that, too.

After walking to the mirror in his bathroom and peering into it, he muttered a curse. He was a mess. No wonder he'd caught strange looks and dodged endless questions from his friends. He was more than a mess, actually. He looked like a freak.

One side of his face was a purplish-black, soon to be a greenish-yellow. He clutched both sides of the sink, giving in to another bout of rage that threatened to choke him.

He couldn't decide who was at the top of his ruin list—his son or his son's mother.

The second Cutler let himself in to his condo, he knew something was not right. Someone was there. When his nostrils got a whiff of perfume, he knew who that someone was. His stomach clenched with anger. But by the time he'd made his way into the living room and tossed his briefcase on the nearest chair, he had gotten his anger under control.

"Surprise, surprise," Julia Freeman said in her lilting voice, a huge smile on her face.

In spite of her upbeat demeanor, however, Cutler noticed the wary look in her expressive brown eyes. It was obvious she wondered what kind of reception she'd receive. Well, she was right to question. He was more than a little pissed off to have an uninvited guest, especially this evening when he'd had the day from bloody hell.

Who was he kidding? He'd had the *week* from bloody hell. Since he'd gone to see Drew, his world had soured. Nothing had gone right.

Hence the last thing he wanted was the company of another person, even if she was an attractive lady with red hair and dainty features. Any man in his right mind would be proud to have her as a companion. And he had fit into that category until he'd met Kaylee.

Ah, Kaylee. His heart gave a start, but as much as he'd love to think about her now, he couldn't. He had to take care of the business at hand, and that was getting himself out of his present jam.

"Say something," Julia said in a pleading voice. "Please."

"Julia—"

"I know it was presumptuous on my part to invade your space like this," she interrupted in a hurried voice, "but I haven't seen you in so long." Julia paused and took an obvious breath as if she realized she was talking too fast and too much. "I didn't know what else to do."

"You could've called." Cutler tried hard to keep his voice as gentle as possible and still get his point across. Dammit, that was what he got for letting her have a key. In retrospect, it had been a dumb-ass thing to do.

"Would you have seen me? Tonight, that is?"

He hesitated, hating to hurt her, but that was exactly what he was going to have to do.

"Your hesitation says it all." Julia's voice was as glum as it was unsteady.

"It's been a hell of a day," he said tersely, hating being put in this position—having to defend himself when he shouldn't.

"Aren't they all."

The undercurrent of anger in *her* voice refueled his anger. "What do you want me to say?"

"That you're glad I'm here, that you're glad I have dinner prepared and the table set with candles and wine."

He saw tears brimming in her eyes, making him feel more like a heel than ever.

"Only, you're not glad I'm here, are you?"

"You want me to be honest?"

Her chin jutted. "Absolutely."

"Then no, I'm not."

Her chin started to wobble. "I don't know why I keep giving you the power to hurt me."

He crossed to her then and took both her hands in his. "Look at me."

She met his direct gaze.

"I care a lot about you. You've been and still are a good friend."

Julia jerked her hands out of his and turned her back. He watched her clench and unclench her fingers.

He gave her a few minutes, then said, "Please, Julia."

"It's okay, Cutler. I'm not going to disintegrate on the spot because you don't love me."

He was taken aback. "Love. Surely you—"

"Don't love you? Of course I do. I always have. The sad part about it is that you never cared enough to notice."

"That's a low blow, and you know it."

"Do I?"

"Look, Julia," Cutler said, raking his hand through his hair, "it was never my intention to hurt you."

"I've heard that before." Her tone was bitter.

"Not from me, dammit." He'd wanted to get through this brouhaha with as few recriminations as possible, but from the way things were going, that wasn't in the cards.

"I should go."

"Not this way, Julia. I value our friendship and I want it to continue."

She was quiet for a long time. "Is that all I'll ever be to you, Cutler, a friend?"

"That's all."

She gave him a watery smile. "Then I guess I'll have to accept that, won't I?"

"I'm sorry if I've hurt you. It was never my intention."

"I really do know that, though it's hard for me to admit."

"I don't want to lose your friendship."

"You won't." She smiled. "But you may have to give me some time to regroup."

"Take all the time you like."

She was quiet for another long moment, then asked, "Is there someone else?"

His heart lurched. "What makes you ask that?"

"I don't know, actually. It's just a woman thing, something we feel here." She placed her hand on her chest, indicating her heart.

Cutler blew out his breath, not knowing how to answer that. He'd always prided himself on never lying about his feelings for any woman.

"There is someone, only—" He deliberately killed the remainder of the sentence, knowing he was close to stepping into shark-infested waters.

"It's okay, Cutler. It really is. I only want your happiness."

"God, Julia, you're making me feel more like a heel than ever."

She stood on her tiptoes and kissed him on the cheek. "You're a good man, Cutler McFarland, because you're honest. Most men would have opted not to be so brutally honest."

He blanched at her blunt assessment of him, then said, "I'm not most men."

"Oh, don't I know that." Julia tempered her words with another genuine smile.

"Something smells really good," Cutler said with a lopsided smile.

"Ah, so you noticed."

"Shall we make good use of your culinary skills?"

"Are you sure that's what you want to do?"

It wasn't. But he wasn't about to admit that. It wouldn't kill him to sit down and have a decent meal. Once she was gone, he'd have time to resume his tormented thoughts. A respite might put things in perspective. Yeah, right, he told himself, smirking inwardly.

"Some man's going to get a jewel when he gets you."

Julia smiled as she poured the wine. "Thanks for saying that."

"The truth comes easy." Once they were seated, he reached for his glass and held it up and out.

Julia clicked his glass. "To friendship."

"To friendship," he responded with heartfelt relief.

Cutler awakened bathed in cold sweat.

Sitting straight up on the sofa, he cut his eyes to the clock. Ten o'clock. Julia hadn't been gone that long. Still, he must've just dozed off. Too bad the nightmare had awakened him. He could have used the sleep. Letting go of several expletives, he got up and trudged into his bathroom, where he splashed his face with water.

He remembered now. He'd been dreaming about his altercation with Drew Rush. *Again.*

It was in that moment that his stomach revolted. He barely managed to raise the lid on the toilet before he lost his entire dinner. After brushing his teeth, he made his way into his room and fell on the bed, feeling as though his body had been drained of all its vital ingredients.

Yet he found it impossible to close his eyes again.

Rape.

His mother raped?

No way.

That couldn't be.

Not his mother, who was a pastor.

Rush was full of shit.

Had to be.

Only, Cutler knew better. Gut deep he knew that his mother had indeed been raped by that vile man and that he was the product of that rape.

His stomach heaved again and he thought for sure he'd have to make another run to the toilet. But following several deep breaths, his stomach settled and his head cleared.

No wonder his mother had guarded the circumstances of his birth. Who could blame her? Certainly not him. How could a mother tell her son he's the outcome of such a heinous act?

She couldn't.

Unless she was forced. Yet how could he not force the issue? Rush needed to get his just deserts. For his mother's sake.

He made a vow to himself. No matter what it cost him,

Drew Rush *would* be held accountable for his sins. Cutler would delight in being judge, juror and executioner.

First, though, he had to protect Mary and her reputation. He couldn't take a chance on Benton following through with his vow to expose his real father, dragging his mother's name through the mud, if his demand wasn't met.

Desperate men did desperate things.

And to his way of thinking, Edgar Benton was desperate.

Because of that, Cutler could no longer put off the inevitable. He reached for the phone beside his bed and dialed the number.

Answer, dammit, he fumed. Then he heard a sleep-filled voice say, "Hello."

"Kaylee, I'm coming over."

"Cutler, what—"

"I'll be there shortly."

He hung up the receiver and lunged out of bed.

Twenty-Six

Kaylee was aghast.

Yet she was curious, too. What on earth could have prompted Cutler to call her after ten o'clock?

Realizing she would only be wasting her time speculating, she got out of bed and went into the bathroom. She wasn't about to put on makeup, though she looked a fright. Too bad. He'd have to take her as she was or not at all.

After brushing her teeth and taming her hair a bit, Kaylee made her way into the kitchen, where she started a pot of coffee. Then she checked the fridge to make sure she had some almond tea made. She did. Remembering that she had some orange muffins left from the bakery, she reached for them, only to freeze.

What was she doing? Playing the hostess at this time of night was crazy. Besides that, he wouldn't expect it. She certainly didn't want anything to eat. Just the thought made her queasy.

But then, Cutler did a good job of that. He only had

to come anywhere near her and her entire body reacted. The last time she had seen him they had made love all night.

Even if he never touched her again, she would never forget him. In the space of several hours he had changed her life. He had made her feel like a desirable woman, something she'd never before felt.

For that, she would be forever indebted to him. While he had known that, he hadn't used it to his advantage, or at least not yet. Waves of panic washed through Kaylee. She feared she wouldn't be able to resurrect the wall he'd so easily torn down.

Right now she could walk away from Cutler with her heart intact. If she let him touch her again, an easy flight wouldn't be possible.

Be careful, she warned herself, just as the phone rang. Had Cutler changed his mind? If so, was she relieved? Or perturbed? Because she didn't want to pursue the answer to either question, Kaylee simply reached for the receiver.

"Hello."

"Hi, sweetheart, did I wake you up?"

"Hey, Uncle Drew."

"You don't sound like you were asleep."

"It's not that late," she countered with a smile in her voice.

"I know, but it's late to some folks."

"Not me, so don't worry." She paused, growing more puzzled by the second. Something was up with him, too. He rarely called, and never in the evening. But there were exceptions, she reminded herself. Cutler's abrupt, out- of-the-blue call had apparently tapped into her paranoia.

"What can I do for you, Uncle Drew?"

"What? You mean I just can't call and say hello?"

"Of course you can." She paused. "Is that what you're doing?"

Seconds of silence ticked off the clock.

"No, actually it's not."

"Daddy's okay, isn't he?" She couldn't imagine what had prompted her to asked that. Yes, she did. That same paranoia working on her.

"He's fine, sweetheart. At least, he was earlier today."

"Good."

"Are you busy?"

"Now?"

"I know it's late, but I'd like to talk to you."

She felt a frown mar her forehead. "Actually—"

"Sorry. No one wants company this time of night."

It was on the tip of her tongue to tell him that was exactly what was about to happen, but since he didn't give her a chance, she held her silence.

"We'll talk another time."

"You can't tell me on the phone?"

He hesitated again.

"Look, if it's something—"

"It's not," he cut in. "Trust me, there'll be another time."

"You promise?"

"Now, sweetheart, remember who you're talking to. Have I ever let you down?"

"No, and I don't want to let you down, and I feel like I'm doing just that."

"Baloney. You're doing no such thing."

"If you're sure."

"I'll call you the next day or so and we'll get together."

"That had better be another promise."

"Count on it."

When she replaced the receiver, Kaylee remained un-moving. Two strange happenings in one evening. Though they weren't related, it unnerved her. She'd hated having to turn Drew down. Of all people. At the same time, she was certain Cutler was on his way.

Ten minutes later she was still thinking about Drew's call when the door chime sounded. Taking a deep breath, Kaylee made her way to the door and opened it. She didn't know what she'd expected, but not someone who looked as if he'd been soundly whipped.

"I know you'd like to have my head on a platter," he muttered, crossing the threshold, not stopping until he reached the middle of the great room.

Kaylee attempted a smile. "Looks like someone beat me to it."

His lips quirked. "That bad, huh?"

"That bad." She swallowed hard as he was staring at her with a look that she couldn't read. But for whatever rea-son, her heart kicked into overdrive. She'd best find out what he wanted, then send him on his way.

His disheveled and anguished appearance could easily bring about her downfall. Keeping her distance was of the utmost importance so there would be no repeat perfor-mance of the other evening.

"I've made some coffee."

"I don't—"

"I'll pour us a cup," she interrupted, her tone indicating it was nonnegotiable.

"Fine."

Once in the kitchen, she didn't tarry, and soon set a tray on the table in front of the sofa where he sat.

Still, neither reached for the cups.

"Come here," Cutler said brusquely, patting the seat beside him.

She hesitated, drawing her lower lip between her teeth in order to keep it steady.

"Please." His voice was ragged. "I'm not going to pounce on you."

She gave a start.

"Though I'd like to," he added in a strained whisper, a vein beating in his neck.

God, she didn't want to care about him. She didn't want to *love* him. Suddenly she froze, not daring to breathe. Love? Where had that word come from?

"Kaylee, it's okay."

"No, it's not," she said in a husky whisper.

His eyes darkened on her. "I would never hurt you. You have to know that."

Her bones turned to water at the tenderness in his voice. All the more reason to keep her distance. "I know, because I'm not going to give you a chance."

Admiration flared in those dark eyes. "Did I ever tell you that I like your style?"

"If you're trying to seduce me with kind words, it won't work."

His lips quirked again as he snapped his fingers. "Damn. Must be losing my charm."

She couldn't stop her smile any more than she could refrain from sitting beside him. "So what's on your mind?"

"Us."

She blinked with a racing heart. "Excuse me?"

"You heard what I said."

Why couldn't she stop thinking about touching him? It would be so easy to reach out. Kaylee wound her fingers tightly together, and sat straight as a block of wood.

"Relax," he said, his voice a decibel lower than usual.

"I am. Relaxed, that is."

"Sure you are."

She cut him a look. He was smiling at her, which was almost her undoing.

"You asked me up front if I'd like your head on a platter? Well, I just might take you up on that."

Cutler's smile widened, which went a long way toward easing the torturous tension between them. "You'd certainly be within your rights, especially since visiting hours are technically over."

She lifted her shoulders in a shrug. "I'm a night owl." She intended that comment to sound glib, but she wasn't sure she'd pulled it off.

Instead of commenting, he reached out and placed a hand over hers. She stared at his, noticing his long, tapered fingers sprinkled with just the right amount of black hair. His thumb rubbed across the back of her hand, scalding her insides.

She looked down and tried to pull away. He tightened his hold.

"Kaylee," he said in a hoarse, urgent voice, "marry me."

Twenty-Seven

Kaylee's mouth fell open and her eyes widened. "What did you say?"

"I said marry me."

She slammed her mouth shut; at the same time her head spun and her stomach lurched, as if she'd just been shoved out of a plane.

"I mean it, Kaylee. I want to marry you."

"You don't…can't mean that."

"You know me better than that."

"No, I don't. Actually, I don't know you at all."

"Yes, you do. You know that I don't make statements like that lightly, that I'm a man who says what he means and means what he says."

"That's the craziest thing I've ever heard."

"Why?"

Again she opened her mouth, only to slam it back shut. Frankly she didn't know how to respond. She was too shell-shocked.

Cutler's next words bore testimony to the fact that he

knew she'd had a major blow. "Hey, you're not going to pass out on me, are you?"

Suddenly she giggled, realizing that she was close to hysterics.

"I had no idea a proposal of marriage could be funny."

The shadow that fell across his face stopped her giggling instantly. Pain? Was that what she saw mirrored there? Oh, God, she couldn't believe this was happening.

"Kaylee, say something."

"I don't know what to say, Cutler. For the second time in my life I'm at a loss for words."

"When was the first time?"

She stared at him closely. "Do you really care?"

"Of course I care."

His tone had a slight snap to it, and deservedly so. She flushed with shame and that was also deserved. But dear Lord, she was still so confused, so blown away by his proposal that she wasn't thinking or talking straight. "So when was the first time?" he asked again.

"After the wreck, when my life changed so drastically."

"I figured as much. I don't know if I've ever told you how sorry I am about that." Cutler paused. "I'd like to know a few of the details, if it's not too painful to talk about. Even now."

Kaylee explained how the wreck had happened, how she'd been thrown through the windshield and the painful aftermath. She broke off with a shuddering breath, then said in a small voice, "I may never be able to have children."

"There are worse things, you know," Cutler said in a gentle tone.

Kaylee didn't feel the need to respond. Anyway, what else was there to say?

"You're a real trouper, Kaylee Benton. And I admire the heck out of you."

"Thanks, but that was a long time ago, and I've adjusted."

"That you have, and in a wonderful way, too."

"What's going on, Cutler?" she demanded, her gaze nailing his.

"A proposal of marriage."

"I'm serious."

"Me, too. I've never asked a woman to marry me before."

"Dammit, you know what I'm getting at."

"Is marrying me that abhorrent to you?"

"You know better than that," she snapped, then stiffened. "But that's not the point."

"I beg to differ. That's exactly the point."

Kaylee stood, looped her arms across her chest for protection, then looked at him out of defiant eyes.

He stood, clenched his hands at his sides and returned her look. "I want to marry you, Kaylee. It's as simple as that." A note of urgency underlined his words.

She gave him an incredulous look. "I can't believe you said that. You asking me to marry you is anything but simple."

"I don't see it that way."

"I might as well butt my head up against a brick wall as to try and reason with you."

This time humor did rearrange his mouth, softening it. "I don't mean to be difficult."

"Yes, you do."

He laughed outright, which helped to dispel the growing and suffocating tension.

"Say yes, Kaylee."

So much for the lessening tension. His soft plea shot the

tension back up, sending her hand to her heart as pains shot through her chest like tiny darts.

"Aren't you forgetting something, Cutler?"

His eyes narrowed. "What would that be?"

"Love." She watched his face drain of color before she plowed on. "You don't love me. We both know that."

"Nor do you love me."

"So again, I don't get it. Why would either of us want to marry the other?"

"What if I do love you?"

"Stop it, Cutler," Kaylee lashed back. "I didn't just fall off a turnip truck."

Color darkened his face. "I never implied that."

"Yes, you did."

"I don't want to turn this into a verbal slinging match."

"So satisfy my curiosity. Love aside, why would you want to be saddled with a woman who's a cripple when you could have any woman you want?"

He reached out for her.

She backed away, thrusting out an arm. "No. Don't touch me."

That vein in his neck began beating overtime. She watched it for a moment, thinking that if something didn't give soon, she'd lose what little control she had left.

"I don't think of you as a cripple, for God's sake," he muttered at last.

"I'm just calling a spade a spade."

"That's crap."

"Perhaps it's because you want to appear more sympathetic to your voters."

He strangled on an expletive.

"That's the only possible reason I can think of for your sudden and off-the-wall proposal."

"I care about you, Kaylee, more than I ever thought possible." He paused and shoved a hand through his already disheveled hair. "And let's just say it's time I settled down."

"Since when?" she asked bluntly.

"Since I met you."

"You expect me to believe that?"

"It's the truth," he said in a hoarse voice. "I know I can make you happy."

"What about the woman you're seeing?" Kaylee swallowed hard. "Can't avoid the gossip, you know."

"She's a friend."

"I've heard that before." Her voice dripped with sarcasm.

"Not from me you haven't."

"No matter." Kaylee laughed with derision. "I'm *not* marrying you."

He swore, then pulled her against his chest. Before she could get her bearings, his lips adhered to hers with such force that it literally took her breath.

It was only after he heard her moan that his lips relaxed and his tongue snaked into the hot cavity of her mouth. That was her undoing. Heat boiled up inside her. Sure that her insides were about to explode, she clung to him, returning the kiss with equal fervor.

She didn't know how long he held her captive. She didn't care. As much as she despised herself, she was exactly where she longed to be—locked in his arms with his lips against hers. A lifetime of that would be heaven on earth.

But that was the fluff fairy tales were made of. And she was no Cinderella.

Clearly struggling for breath himself, Cutler stared deeply into her eyes. "Fair warning—you're mine, Kaylee Benton, and I don't intend to give up."

With that, he thrust her away, turned and walked out the door.

Kaylee crumpled in a heap on the floor.

Keeping her arms tight around her, she rocked back and forth, whimpering. Only when she could no longer stand the sharp pains shooting up and down her leg did she try to get up.

Miraculously, she did that and more. She made it into her bedroom and into the tub, where she lay back and closed her eyes, letting the hot, sweet-smelling water penetrate her muscles and bones.

If only that soothing balm could reach her head. While the water worked magic on her body, her mind remained immune. What had she done to deserve to have her life turned upside down once again?

Tears trickled down Kaylee's face into her mouth. She licked her lips and tasted Cutler. She moaned and sank farther down into the tub. What if she just kept on going until her whole body was immersed?

Frightened by that irrational and crazy thought, Kaylee jerked herself upright and opened her eyes. Still, his image swam in front of her and she struggled for a decent breath.

Had he really asked her to marry him?

Yes. She might be well on her way to losing her mind, but she hadn't as yet. As much as she might want to pretend that conversation never happened, she couldn't.

But why?

More to the point, why her?

She didn't for a minute buy his lame explanation. So if the most important ingredient, love, didn't enter into the equation—and it didn't—then what did?

Who cares? a tiny voice inside her whispered. *As long as he asked you.*

Kaylee's body turned rigid. Somewhere in her subconscious was she entertaining the idea of taking him up on his offer, regardless of whether he loved her?

Absurd.

Ludicrous.

Impossible.

Yet *possible.*

If he carried through with his threat, which she felt he would, then he wouldn't give up. He was right; she did know the kind of man he was. He didn't waste words or time. He knew what he wanted and he went after it.

Apparently he wanted her.

A sense of excitement suddenly filled every corner of her mind. All she had to do was say, "Yes, I'll marry you."

But that same little voice whispered, *Not so fast.* With the excitement now thundering through her entire body, it was impossible to remain confined to the tub. After drying off, she slipped into a pair of lounging pj's.

Instead of crawling into bed, she made her way into the kitchen. She poured herself a glass of almond iced tea, then headed back to her room, where she made herself comfortable on the chaise lounge. But she could hardly raise the glass to her lips, her hand was shaking so much.

She had forever been envious of other women for having what she perceived she could never have—a husband who loved her. Tonight Cutler had offered her himself. So should she…

Kaylee's mind simply froze, unable to even contemplate such a thing. Yet the seed had been planted and she couldn't stop thinking about it.

So what if she threw caution to the wind and went with her heart instead of her head? Which carried the most weight?

Her heart won hands down. And she knew why. She had fallen in love with Cutler McFarland. She couldn't say the precise moment it had happened, but it had. So if she listened to that vital organ and said yes, what was the worst-case scenario? He would break her heart, and the marriage would end in divorce.

The best-case scenario, of course, was that their union would be a match made in heaven and they would live happily ever after.

Since there were no sure things in life, either way was a gamble.

And she was no gambler. Suddenly every cell in Kaylee's body came alive with new awareness and anticipation. She wanted to see him. Now. For the moment nothing else seemed to matter—food, drink, sleep, or even her next breath—so long as she was with him.

Her heart was throbbing so painfully now that unconsciously she splayed a hand across her chest. She'd made her decision. May God help her if she'd made the wrong one.

"How did you get in here?"

Drew shrugged. "Walked."

"Don't you dare be flippant with me," Mary snapped,

feeling her heart plunge to her toes. "I told you never to come near me again."

Mary watched Drew's eyes as he stood in the doorway of her church office looking her up and down. She recoiled visibly. As he read her aversion to him, his features contorted. For a moment she feared he might strike her. But then her reason returned and she knew better.

Drew wasn't an out-in-the-open kind of guy. He snuck in the back door, the coward's entrance, to do his grievous deeds. Even though he was no believer, he wouldn't do anything that might damage or sully his inflated reputation.

If there ever was a hypocrite, he was standing in front of her.

How in the name of God had she ever gotten involved with such a loathsome person? If she lived to be more than a hundred, Mary would never have the answer to that question. But then, the answer was no longer important. She had ripped that part of her life out of her soul and that was where it would stay.

"You should never have opened your mouth," Drew said in a cold tone.

"If you don't leave—"

"Shut up, bitch, and listen."

Mary gasped. Yet she didn't know why she was shocked at his behavior. He was a sociopath, and you never knew which way they would jump.

"If I signed over my rights to our son, you swore never to reveal the truth."

"And I've kept that promise," she said with as much dignity as she could muster, when she wanted to physically attack this man, rip his heart out and stomp on it as he had on hers so long ago.

He smirked. "And here I thought preachers weren't supposed to lie."

"I would rather be dead than have my son know he came from your loins."

Drew closed the distance between them with his hand raised.

Mary didn't so much as flinch, but said in a deadly tone, "If you ever touch me again, I'll kill you."

Drew stopped dead in his tracks, an incredulous expression on his face. Then he threw back his head and laughed. "I'll have to hand it to you, you've grown some balls since I was between your legs."

Mary forced herself not to react to those vile and inflammatory words, which was exactly what he wanted. He'd come there with the intention of starting World War Three, but she was having none of it.

"He knows," Drew said into the heavy and hostile silence. "The cat's out of the bag. He got in my face and demanded the truth."

"You...you told him?" Mary was horrified.

"That you accused me of rape? I sure as hell did. But I also told him it was your word against mine."

"You bastard," she spat out, feeling a tight squeeze inside her chest. Oh, God, she couldn't faint. Not now. Not in front of *him*.

"Me? You're the one who opened your big mouth."

"I did no such thing."

"If you didn't tell Cutler, then who did?"

"I have no idea," Mary said in a cracked voice. But at

least she was still upright and coherent. "Maybe you should look in your own backyard."

"What about that do-good husband of yours?"

"He would die before he'd betray me."

"For now, I'm going to give you the benefit of the doubt. But if I find out you did indeed lie to me, I'll be back."

"And do what?"

He loomed over her, his mouth drawn back in a snarl. "I don't think you want to know."

"You're as despicable as ever," she lashed back, then was sorry. She hadn't meant to lose her cool. In fact, she'd prided herself on how well she'd done. But there were limits to even her endurance.

The longer he stayed, the more repulsed she became, the more horrified at what this man had done to her.

"You had best restrain that son of yours." He crept closer. "Keep him away from me, you hear?"

"I have no control over Cutler and what he does."

Drew sneered. "Then you're both in big trouble."

Twenty-Eight

"You have a nice pad."

"Think so?" Cutler asked.

"Yeah. It looks like you."

He gave her a lopsided smile. "Should I take that as a compliment or an insult?"

"Depends."

"Lady, you drive a hard bargain."

"I'm just teasing," Kaylee said with a slight catch in her voice. "It's very tastefully decorated. I especially like the leather-and-fabric combo. And you have great taste in books and artwork."

"I enjoy both."

"Me, too. So that's something we have in common."

"Trust me," Cutler responded, his gaze smoldering, "we have a lot more in common than that." He cleared his throat, then went on, "Glad you like it. So that brings me to this question. Where would you rather live—your place or mine?" He grinned as he flicked her chin. "I vote for your place."

Kaylee's heart skipped a beat. "I haven't said I'd marry you, Cutler."

"You haven't said you wouldn't either."

Kaylee sighed inwardly and gave him a pointed look that told him how exasperated she was. "You're impossible."

"I'm determined."

"And cocky. And arrogant." She smiled. "Shall I go on?"

He shrugged with a grin. "Hey, I warned you that I wasn't giving up until you gave in."

And he hadn't. He'd wined and dined her for the past few days, and she'd loved every minute of it. Flowers, visits, heady kisses. But he hadn't made love to her again. It was as though he was waiting for the right time. Perhaps this evening was just that.

He'd invited her to his place for steaks. He'd baked potatoes, made a salad and grilled the steaks on his grill. The entire meal had been delicious and she'd eaten more than she had in a long time.

Now they were in his living room enjoying a glass of Baileys Irish Cream over ice.

"Thank you for dinner," she said in a husky voice, the heat from his body affecting her breathing.

"You're welcome." Cutler's tone was equally husky.

Over the rim of his cup their eyes met and held. For a second the world seemed to stand still. God, this man knew exactly what buttons to push without even knowing it.

"You're about the loveliest thing I've ever seen."

Her heart caught. "That's not true, but I like hearing it."

"I want you, Kaylee Benton, so much it hurts."

She heard the break in his voice as he set his cup down, then reached for hers, prying it from her hand.

"Cutler—"

"Shush," he said, pulling her against him and kissing her so hard and so deeply that all she could do was cling to him. When he raised his lips, he added, "Let me show you how much I need you, how much I want you."

His kiss had torn down whatever resistance she might have had. When he touched her, she turned to putty and made no apologies for it.

"Come on."

He helped her up and with his arms around her led her to the bedroom, where only a lamp burned in one corner, creating a soft, romantic glow. Without wasting time he wordlessly began undressing her, never taking his eyes off her.

Only when the last of her garments was tossed aside did she panic and place her hand across her chest and stomach, covering as much of her flesh as she could.

"It's okay, my darling," he said in a rusty-sounding voice. "You're beautiful the way you are."

"No…I'm not."

Suddenly the thought of him seeing her imperfect body again freaked her out. He had to be repulsed by it. God, she was.

"Look at me, Kaylee." His words were a plea.

She did.

"Do you see any pity in my eyes?"

"No," she whispered.

"Have you ever seen pity?"

"No," she repeated.

"That's because there is none."

"Do you feel sorry for me?"

"No, for chrissake."

"Is that why you want to marry me?" she whispered, her throat pulsating painfully, rivaling the loud beat of her heart.

"God, no. How can I convince you of that?"

"Make love to me," she said in an urgent voice.

"I thought you'd never ask."

Quickly discarding his clothes, he reached for her again. But she stopped him, her eyes roaming his body. "You're beautiful."

And he was—all muscle and brawn. With a long, swollen penis.

Her hand, as though it had a will of its own, shot out, then froze. She peered up at him through wide eyes.

"Touch me," he pleaded in a gravelly voice. "Please."

Her hand wrapped around the hard, throbbing flesh while heat boiled up inside her.

"Oh, God, Kaylee," he rasped. "I can't take much of that."

He gently laid her on the bed and, starting at the bottom of her feet, with his tongue, began working his way to that secret center of her. Once there, he spread her legs and thrust his tongue into that moistness.

"Ohh," Kaylee cried under the tender assault.

With his mouth and tongue on her, she wanted to believe this was really happening to her, yet she couldn't.

Why was she so afraid?

Love hurt. She didn't want to hurt ever again. But what she was experiencing at the moment was a different kind of pain. It was exquisite and all-consuming. It was love.

Once the orgasm slammed into her body, Cutler rose, slid himself inside her, then leaned over and sucked one nipple then the other, all the while moving in and out of her.

Feeling as if she was going to explode, Kaylee clutched

at him, digging her nails in his back as if trying to pull him inside her. As the kiss deepened her nails moved to his buttocks, where they dug in to his muscled flesh.

He was so real, so alive.

Just as she was. For the first time in her life.

"God, Kaylee," he muttered, emptying his seed in her at the same time she cried out, matching him stroke for stroke.

Later, wrapped tightly in each other's arms, they lay spent and unmoving for the longest time.

Finally he smoothed her hair back from her temple and kissed her. "I can't get enough of touching you."

"Good," she whispered.

"Do you want a big wedding?"

"I never said I'd marry you."

"Maybe not with words, but with your heart."

"Oh, Cutler," she cried, "you win. I'll marry you."

His hot, sweet lips meshed with hers. "You won't be sorry. I promise to honor and cherish you always."

He didn't say he would love her, but that was all right. For now she could settle for the others and be happy.

"And I you," she whispered against his lips.

Edgar's eyes filled with unshed tears.

"Oh, Daddy, I didn't mean to make you cry," Kaylee wailed, crossing to him and giving him a big hug.

When he pulled away, he didn't try to hide his emotions. Instead, he smiled through those tears and said, "I'm so happy for you, baby." Then his smile faded. "But I want you to be happy."

"How can I not be happy, Daddy? I'm in love."

"That was always my hope and dream for you."

"Well, it's come true."

"So what are the plans?"

"A simple ceremony, only family, performed by Cutler's mother."

"What about a honeymoon?"

Kaylee rolled her eyes. "You've got to be kidding. We're both up to our eyeballs in work."

"Ah, almighty work. Nothing must interfere with that."

"Now, Daddy, don't be sarcastic. Cutler has some big cases on the docket plus his reelection bid. And—"

Edgar snapped his fingers, interrupting her. "Guess that means I'm going to have to vote for the guy."

"You'd better," she said with a grin. "As I was saying, I have two big shows coming up. There's no way I can be away."

Edgar flicked her on the chin. "I'm okay with whatever, as long as you're happy."

"Well, I'm happy," she responded, feeling her own eyes well up with tears.

"Do we have a date for the joyous event?"

"Next weekend."

Edgar's eyes widened. "That soon? All right."

"After the ceremony, we're going to party at the country club. Cutler's taking care of all the arrangements."

"Oh, baby, things couldn't have worked out better."

Kaylee poked him in the chest. "Now maybe you can live your life instead of mine."

He frowned. "Should I take offense at that?"

She grinned, rose on her tiptoes and kissed him on the cheek. "Absolutely not. No one could ask for a more devoted father. Know that I adore you."

"Have you told Drew?"

Kaylee noticed the pensive shadow that replaced the animation on Edgar's face and commented on it. "Will that be a problem? Telling Drew, I mean?"

"No, not at all," he said quickly. "It's just that, like me, he's always been so protective of you."

"He'll be proud, I know." She smiled. "Cutler's quite a catch."

"That he is, my dear," Edgar said in a faraway tone. "That he is."

That conversation had taken place the day after she'd accepted Cutler's proposal. He had gone to see his mother at the same time and reported back that she'd been overjoyed, as well.

The next stop on her list had been her godfather. And while Kaylee hadn't been able to pinpoint what was going on behind Drew's eyes, the result was that she'd left feeling as though he was genuinely happy for her.

"You swore you'd never marry, my dear," he said over a piece of cheesecake and coffee at a bakery near her office.

"That's because I never thought anyone would want to marry me."

"I'm proud someone was able to prove otherwise."

"Me, too."

He opened his mouth as if he was going to say something, then shut it.

"What's on your mind, Uncle Drew? Surely you approve. You of all people should know what a catch Cutler is."

He averted his gaze. "I just want you to be happy."

"Oh, I plan on it. But I want your good wishes and your blessings. You know how I feel about you."

"Well, honey, you have both." Drew paused and cleared his throat. "Always know that whatever happens, I love you like you're my own."

"And I love you, too."

"I've failed at a lot of things in my life, Kaylee. Done a lot of things I'm not proud of."

"We all have, Uncle Drew."

"The one thing I'm most proud of is you and your contribution to my life. If sugar ever turns to shit, promise me you'll remember that."

Kaylee narrowed her eyes on him. "That's a strange thing to say, but then you've always been one to follow the beat of your own drum." She smiled. "Trite as that might sound."

Now, as Kaylee pulled her mind back to the moment at hand, she made a face, especially after looking at the stack of work on her desk. Getting ready for a style show and a wedding, simple though the latter might be, proved a daunting task. Yet she was up for the challenge; actually, she was up for anything, as her feet were barely touching the ground.

The phone rang beside her. Absently she picked up the receiver.

"Hey."

The sound of that husky voice never failed to send chills up her spine. "Hey, yourself."

"Want to grab a bite of lunch?"

"I'm sorry, no can do. I'm up to my eyeballs this morning."

Cutler chuckled. "So am I."

"You were hoping I'd play hooky and make it easier for you to do the same."

"That's right." He paused, lowering his voice. "See you this evening at my place."

"This evening," she murmured with a catch.

He chuckled again, then hung up.

Kaylee didn't know how long she sat there, her heart dancing with anticipation and excitement. Then she sobered. Was she living in a dream world? More so, was she making the biggest mistake of her life? Because she was head over heels in love, she was willing to take the gamble; yet in the secret part of her soul she wanted to believe Cutler felt the same about her.

If not, then...

"Yo," Sandy said, flouncing into her office. "Got a moment? No, make that lots of moments. I have tons to go over with you."

"Before we get down to business," Kaylee responded, "I have something to tell you. Have a seat."

Sandy's eyebrows shot up. "Mmm, sounds serious."

"It is."

"You found more drugs?"

Kaylee pinched the bridge of her nose. "No, thank heavens. I hate to admit this, but I've put that on the back burner of my mind."

"It's not an easy thing to deal with, I know. Don't let it go too long."

"I won't," Kaylee said with a sigh. "Thanks for keeping me on the straight and narrow."

Sandy nodded, then said, "So what's up?"

"Something good, actually."

"Ah, I could stand that."

Kaylee leaned her head sideways. "I'm getting married."

"Excuse me?"

"I'm getting married," Kaylee repeated.

Sandy jumped up and shouted, "Halle-damn-lujah!"

Twenty-Nine

His breath was warm and minty as he rained kisses over her cheek and neck.

"Mmm," she moaned before reaching behind her and circling his neck with her arm. "You're about to get something started you can't finish."

"Think so, huh?" Cutler kept on nibbling.

"I definitely think so," she said, breathing rapidly.

"Why don't we stay home, forget about going to the shindig?"

Kaylee peered up at him. "You know you can't do that, since this is a campaign dinner."

He straightened with a deep sigh. "I know, but damn, it's tempting, especially the way you look in that garb."

"Excuse me, Mr. McFarland, this is no garb. It's a designer gown." Kaylee smiled. "Do I sound like a snob, or what?"

"Whatever. While you look like packaged dynamite in it, you'd look a hell of a lot better *out* of it."

She flashed him a saucy grin. "You're bad."

"Oh, baby, but when I'm bad, I'm good."

Kaylee grinned, then slapped playfully at his hand that now rested on the creamy flesh spilling over the top of her sequined gown. "I think you're getting too big for your britches."

"We can remedy that, too." He stroked the overflow of the other breast. "I can take my britches off."

"You're impossible."

"You're perfect."

With a full heart she stood and went into his arms. He held her for the longest time. "What's perfect is our life together," she finally said. "You've made me so happy."

And he had. They had been married for a week, but that week had been heaven on earth.

"I feel the same way, my darling." Cutler stepped away. "I just wish we had more time together."

"We have our evenings."

"That's not enough."

She smiled. "For now, it'll have to be. We've both got so much going."

"I'll be damn glad when the election's over."

"What about those two cases?"

"Those, too, of course. The one where the woman killed her kids is about to end, thank God. But I still feel like I'm chasing my tail." He grinned. "Now, if it was your lovely tail I was chasing, I wouldn't be complaining at all."

Kaylee elbowed him in the ribs. "I think I've married a pervert."

He threw his head back and laughed.

Kaylee watched him, feeling a warm glow settle over her. Yes, marrying him even under less than ideal circumstances had definitely been the right thing to do. Not only was he a wonderful lover, both savage and sweet, but he was a gentle man, as well.

Until he was crossed, that is.

She'd seen that rough, dark side of him in the courtroom. There he turned into a pit bull, which worked both to his advantage and disadvantage.

"My, but you're looking serious all of a sudden, Mrs. McFarland." Cutler's eyes were questioning.

"I was thinking about your behavior in the courtroom."

He seemed taken aback. "What about it?"

"You take on a totally different personality, become a different person."

"Does that bother you?"

"No. Not as long as you don't try it on me." She tried to keep her voice light, but knew that she had failed.

He frowned, and his eyes darkened. "I promised you I'd never hurt you and I meant it."

"I know," she whispered, looking away.

"Hey." He gently turned her face back to him. "What's going on? Really? A few moments ago you were as bright as a patch of sunshine. Now, you appear upset. Did I say something?"

"No, silly. It's just that when I think of that dark side, it kind of unsettles me."

"Then don't think about it. Anyway, it's my courtroom persona."

"Actually, I saw traces of it at the reception."

His brows shot up and he looked suddenly wary. "Oh?"

"Your demeanor toward Drew."

A shadow fell over his face at the same time his jaw tensed. Ah, she had indeed struck a nerve.

"What about it?" he asked in a nonchalant tone.

He hadn't fooled her. She knew he was anything *but* nonchalant. She called his hand. "I sensed you don't care for him."

"I don't know him."

"Please don't insult me, Cutler," she said softly. "I'm much more intuitive than you're apparently giving me credit for."

"Don't you think you're overreacting?"

"Only because you're trying to hide something." She meant her bluntness to strike another nerve, and it did. He looked both guilty and irritated.

"Did Drew take a heavy hand concerning me?" She smiled. "He's a bit overly protective, I know, and often comes on strong. But he doesn't mean any harm."

"You don't know him at all."

Taken aback by the bitterness she heard in his voice, Kaylee gasped. "I beg to differ with you about that. I've known him all my life."

"I don't want to discuss Drew Rush." Cutler's tone was cold and clipped. "Not now. Not ever."

"Well, I do," she countered, not bothering to hide her own irritation.

For a few minutes they glared at each other. It dawned on her that they were having their first disagreement—argument, if you will—as a married couple. And while she hated that, she refused to back down.

Cutler spoke her thoughts. "I don't want to argue with you."

"Since you know how I feel about Drew and how important he is in my life, I think you owe me an explanation as to why you have your stinger out for him."

"Now's not the time to discuss this, Kaylee."

She dug her heels in. "Maybe not. But since the subject is opened, we might as well discuss it."

"Okay, you asked for it." If possible, his tone turned colder and more clipped.

Her eyes widened. "You're scaring me, Cutler."

"This is your party, Kaylee."

The atmosphere turned more tense.

"I'm listening."

His gaze slid away. "Did you know Drew had a son?"

"No." If she sounded shocked it was because she was.

Cutler turned to her once again, his features taut. "Well, he does."

"So he has a son. What does that have to do with anything?"

For what seemed like the longest time, Cutler looked at her with the strangest expression on his face. Her anxiety increased.

"Cutler, for heaven's sake, where are you going with this?"

"Drew is my biological father."

Kaylee felt her jaw drop, while a wave of emotion flooded through her. The room spun. She felt Cutler grasp her arm and lead her back to the vanity stool.

"I'm…fine," she said, struggling for her next breath.

"Yeah, right."

But once she was sitting, Cutler stepped back, rammed his hands into the pockets of his tux and stared at her through smoldering eyes.

"How…I mean…I—I don't understand," she stammered, peering up at him.

"I'm sure you don't."

"But how can that be? I mean it can't be."

Cutler blew out his breath, then said in a flat, harsh tone, "It can be because it is."

"How long have you known?"

"A while."

"Were you going to tell me?"

"Yes, only not tonight."

"I feel like I've been hit on the head with a baseball bat," Kaylee admitted with a tremor.

"I know the feeling."

"How did you find out?" Even though she was still reeling from stunned disbelief, she had managed to retain enough brainpower to press for the rest of the story, although it was apparent that Cutler was reluctant to share it.

"By accident."

"What about Trevor?"

"He adopted me right after I was born."

Kaylee pressed a hand to her chest hoping to halt her racing heart. "Your mother and Drew—" Her voice broke and she couldn't go on.

"Pretty disgusting thought, isn't it?"

"Yes and no." She took an unsteady breath. "I know Uncle Drew so well, but not your mother. Still, I would never have put those two together."

"They weren't together," he said with increased bitterness.

"God, I can't imagine how you must be feeling."

"Like my underpinnings have been jerked out from under me."

She went to him and put her arms around him. At first he stood unresponsive, like a block of wood, but then he loosened up and gave her a brief hug before pushing her to arm's length.

"There's more," he said, looking down at her through anguished eyes.

She felt so bad for him. What a blow to find out the man you thought was your father wasn't. It didn't matter how he found out, or even who told him.

"More?" Kaylee barely got the word through her frozen lips.

"It has to do with Drew."

"Uncle Drew?" she asked inanely, her mind still reeling.

Cutler swore under his breath, then lashed out, "Would you stop calling him that?"

Kaylee gave him an astonished look but didn't say anything. Frankly, she didn't know how to respond. She wanted to comfort him, not fight with him.

"Sorry," he muttered. "Didn't mean to bark at you."

"It's okay."

"No, it isn't."

She didn't want to argue about that either, so again she refrained from saying anything. Right now she just needed to be a good listener, let him release his pain in the way he saw fit. It was obvious he was hurting badly.

She knew how that felt, too. Although the circumstances were vastly different, she had traveled down one of life's painful and wounding paths. Taking a major blow, mental or physical, did something to the psyche.

And even though Cutler was strong and proud, he was human.

"What were you going to tell me about Un...about Drew?" Kaylee asked at last.

"My office is investigating him."

Kaylee gave him an incredulous look. "That's crazy."

"It's a fact." Cutler's voice was tight.

"Well, that's wrong," she snapped. *"You're wrong."*

"Hey, I'm not responsible for the investigation. Major Crimes was already on it when they brought me into the loop."

"You can tell them to halt the investigation."

"Even if I wanted to, I couldn't do that."

"You have to," she said, hearing her voice rise. "The charges have to be trumped-up. Drew would never do anything illegal."

"You can't know that, Kaylee, nor can I."

"I know him," she said fiercely, "and you don't."

He let out a weary sigh. "Let's drop the subject, okay?" His eyes pointedly dipped to his watch. "We have to go or we will be late."

Tightening her lips so as not to snap at him again, Kaylee reached for her bag and wrap. But the joy had gone out of the evening.

For both of them.

Thirty

"Hey, what a nice surprise."

Mary McFarland gave her son a weak smile as she walked through the door to his office. "I hope it's okay if I just barge in."

He made a face. "Of course it's all right. Since when do you have to have an appointment to see me?"

"Since you're up to your neck in work and almost never in your office."

"Okay, you've made your point." Cutler smiled, walked around his desk, gave her a hug, then pulled back and looked at her. "How are you doing? Really?"

"Fine." Mary stepped back and sat down.

Cutler, watching her carefully, took a seat in an adjacent chair, certain she wasn't fine. But then neither was he. Since he'd dropped his bombshell about Drew, nothing had been the same. Nor would it be. He just hoped the gaping hole in their relationship could one day be stitched back together.

Right now he wasn't sure about that.

"Are you happy, son?"

"Yes, I am."

"You sound surprised. That you're happy, I mean."

Cutler averted his gaze, reminding himself just how intuitive she was when it came to him. She might not be able to read him like a book, but she sure could read between the lines of his mind. He couldn't allow even that. It was too dangerous.

And unlike her, he hated secrets. Unfortunately, he'd go to the grave with his.

"Cutler?"

"I am a little, I'll admit." He gave her a sheepish grin. "You know how I've always felt about marriage."

"That's why I'm still shocked that you took the plunge. And so suddenly, too."

"Like I told you before the ceremony, Kaylee was such a catch, I couldn't take a chance on someone else getting her."

"What about love?"

He ignored the note of chastisement in her tone and said, "What about it?" Careful, McFarland, you're close to that slippery slope. You don't want to take a fall.

"You never said you loved her."

"What is this, Mother, an inquisition?" Now his tone was chastising.

She flushed. "No, and I'm sorry. When I came here, I had no intention of grilling you about your feelings for Kaylee. That's your business." She flashed him a deep and genuine smile. "But I can see how you're smitten. To know her is to adore her."

Cutler answered her smile. "I'm so glad you feel that way. She's one special lady."

Mary shook a finger at him. "You'd best remember that, too. Or you'll have to answer to me, young man."

"Gotcha."

Her smile disappeared as she reached across and took his hand in hers, then peered into his eyes. "I'm here about you."

Cutler knew what was coming, and he didn't want to discuss the past, not today, not after his verbal skirmish with Kaylee last evening. He still felt raw from that, especially since there was now a wedge between them. So far he hadn't come up with a way to repair the damage.

"Don't get that shuttered look on your face," Mary said in a soft but firm voice.

"Mom, please."

"And don't call me Mom in that patronizing tone either."

Cutler grimaced, holding up his hands in defeat. "The floor's yours. Go for it."

"By the way, am I interfering with your schedule?"

"I can give you another fifteen minutes or so, then I'm due in court."

"Fair enough."

"Want some coffee?"

"No, your dad and I drank a pot before I left."

Cutler nodded as he leaned back in the chair, crossed one leg over a knee and raised his brows.

"I'm guessing you told Kaylee who Drew is."

"I had no choice."

"How did she take it?"

"At first she was stunned, then she got upset, especially when I told her our office was investigating him for illegal business practices."

"That doesn't surprise me." Mary's features tightened. "Underneath that charming facade is an evil man."

"I know that, Mother, but she doesn't. She's never seen that side of him."

"Oh, God, Cutler, I'd give anything if you had never found out the truth." She paused and sucked in a breath. "That's terribly selfish of me, isn't it?"

"It's moot because I *know* the truth."

"I've always admired your ability to go forward and not look back."

Only not this time, Cutler told himself. He hadn't changed his mind. Drew *would* pay for the sins, which meant he, too, would have to wallow in the past. Like it or not.

"Drew can hurt you, son."

"Don't worry. I can take care of myself."

"He came to see me."

"That bastard," Cutler spat out, lunging up and pacing the floor.

"Calm down. Please," Mary said in a pleading tone. "You would've been proud of me. I held my own with him."

He gave her a gentle smile. "That doesn't surprise me. You were always made of the right stuff and I'm proud to be your son."

"Then let Drew be, Cutler. You'll only hurt yourself if you have anything to do with him. Don't make me beg. Please."

"He raped you, for God's sake."

Mary's face drained of color at the same time her hand flew to her chest.

"Dammit, Mother, don't you dare pass out on me."

"I'm not," she said, her voice holding a tremor. "It's just that you're so hardheaded, so stubborn."

"And you're not?"

His challenge was met with a new surge of color in her cheeks, which somewhat diluted his mounting fear. He hated to think that every time something unpleasant was discussed she would end up in the E.R.

"He never admitted he…did anything wrong." Mary shuddered, her eyes filling with tears. "And he never will."

Cutler knew she couldn't say the word *rape*. He had the same difficulty; just the thought filled him with such rage and disgust that he couldn't think straight. But under no circumstances could he lose control. That would surely send his mother toppling over that dark edge. More than ever, she needed his strength.

"If it'll ease your mind any, I don't want any details concerning your relationship with him."

"It wasn't a relationship," Mary said sharply. "It was a mistake, a gross error in judgment." Mary's sharp tone turned bitter.

"I know how hard this is for you."

"You have no idea."

"Mom, I'm sorry, but I can't make promises about Drew that I can't keep."

Tears spilled down her cheeks, and he wanted to comfort her, but he couldn't. Not when his own insides felt as if they were in a shredding machine.

Mary stood and took a succession of deep breaths. "Just promise me you'll be careful, that you'll watch your back."

"Now, that I can promise." Cutler leaned over and kissed her on the forehead. "You take care of you. I'll be all right."

"Don't forget I'm a survivor, Cutler."

"Like Kaylee." He smiled. "The two special women in my life are cut from the same bolt of cloth."

"But you're not." A flat statement.

Cutler was taken aback, and showed it. "What does that mean?"

"It means that you haven't had the hard knocks that a lot of us have, whether by choice or circumstances. Until now, that is."

"I can't argue with that."

"Finding out that you were a product of—" She broke off with another shudder.

"Puts me in that league. Is that what you were going to say?"

Mary nodded as though her throat was too full to speak.

"Trust me, I'll be fine. I've got enough of you in me. While I wish you had told me long ago the circumstances of my birth, I will get through this."

"Oh God, son, I pray so. But I'm frightened."

"Your fear is something I have no control over. Again, you'll just have to trust me, trust in the system."

"So you're going after Drew legally?"

"I'm making no promises there either." And he wasn't. If legal didn't work, then he'd take another route.

But what his mother didn't know wouldn't hurt her.

"It's time I was going."

Cutler nodded. "I'll talk to you later."

With a heavy heart he watched her leave. Because of Drew Rush his life had become a disaster. His mother was hurting and so was Kaylee.

And right now he couldn't do a damn thing about either.

* * *

The Neiman's show had gone off without a hitch.

For that Kaylee was profoundly grateful. Now all the agency's efforts could go into the Versace show. Yet she was scared, too, scared that she wouldn't be able to pull off a show of that magnitude.

Maybe her sudden lack of confidence stemmed from the conversation with her husband.

Her husband.

She still couldn't believe that she was married. Since she had spoken her vows, she'd had to pinch herself mentally over and over in order to convince herself that she was now Kaylee Benton McFarland.

While she remained ecstatically happy, she couldn't deny that Cutler's shocking and disturbing news had knocked the props out from under her.

Drew and Cutler—father and son?

How could that be?

It was too coincidental. Too unbelievable. *Not possible.*

Only, apparently it was. As was her husband's vendetta against his birth father—her godfather. And she was caught in the middle.

Kaylee's stomach pitched. How could circumstances have swung so quickly and so drastically? It had been so long since her life had changed on a dime, she'd become complacent and forgotten that nothing was sacred or forever.

But why now? her heart cried.

She had everything she'd always wanted—a great career, a great father, a caring godfather, loving friends and last but not least, a doting husband.

However, Cutler's declaration of war against Drew had put her happiness and security in grave jeopardy.

Only if you let it, her subconscious whispered.

While she dearly loved Drew and knew in her heart that he was innocent of the alleged charges against him, she could not let her allegiance to him rank above her love for and loyalty to Cutler.

Yet right was right and wrong was wrong. And Cutler was wrong. He just had to be. That left only one alternative, and that was prove it to him.

"You look deep in it."

Kaylee thought about venting to her assistant, who'd just bopped into her office. But if the truth ever got out, she was determined it wouldn't come from her. If Cutler wanted it known that Drew was his father, then he'd have to be the one to tell it. She sensed he wouldn't. It was something he was apparently ashamed of.

"I am. Too deep for my own good."

Sandy sat down with an inquiring look on her face. "Tell me you're still happily married."

Kaylee smiled. "I'm still happily married."

Sandy ran a hand over her brow as if to wipe off imaginary sweat. "Whew! You had me worried there for a minute."

"So far, I have no complaints." That she was willing to air, that is.

"Well, let me tell you, you did good. He's a hunk of eye candy, if I ever saw it."

"I always thought you had great taste, and now I know it." Kaylee grinned. "No pun intended, of course."

"Of course."

They both laughed; then Sandy said, "I've got a ton of stuff to go over with you. But first I have to tell you something."

Kaylee groaned. "Are you going to rain on my morning or my entire day?"

"Your entire day."

"Thanks."

"Sorry."

Kaylee set her chin. "Let's have it."

"Nicole's been beaten up again. She's all black and blue."

Thirty-One

"McFarland, wait up."

Cutler froze in disgust. He didn't have to turn around to know who had hailed him, and it irked him no end that he couldn't ignore the summons.

"Ah, Judge," he said, turning slowly as James Jenkins strode up to him, stopping so close that Cutler smelled his breath. Instinctively he backed up.

If possible, Jenkins's features contorted even more, which made him that much more unattractive. He was a small, scrawny man with a thatch of curly gray hair and tobacco-stained teeth. No wonder he had to bribe women to sleep with him, Cutler thought, then felt a twinge of guilt. Since his office hadn't been able to prove that allegation, he should withhold judgment. However, that wasn't easy; his gut told him Jenkins was as guilty as sin.

"What can I do for you?" Cutler asked.

"Stay out of my affairs. That's what you can do for me."

"And if I don't?"

"Listen, you dirtbag, you don't know what trouble is until you've crossed me."

"Are you forgetting who you're talking to?" Cutler asked. "I'm well acquainted with your tactics in the courtroom."

"You haven't seen anything yet, boy."

"I'm just doing my job, Judge."

"You're more than doing your job. You've got a vendetta against me because I don't kiss your ass in court."

"You're entitled to your opinion," Cutler pointed out in an unruffled tone, though inside he was seething. It was a struggle not to deck the cocky little bastard. For a moment he thought seriously about doing just that and to hell with the consequences. Then his sound judgment kicked in. Jenkins wasn't worth losing his career over and that was exactly what would happen.

Granted, the judge might be unlikable and unethical, but he was still a judge. When it came to the legal system, judges walked on water. Besides, if he played his cards right and did his job, he'd nail Jenkins. It boiled down to timing and patience.

"McFarland, you'd better hope you don't appear before me anytime soon."

"Is that a threat, Judge?"

Jenkins was close enough for Cutler to see the spittle on the sides of his mouth. It was all he could do not to visibly flinch. But he held himself steady. Spittle or not, he wasn't about to let Jenkins know that he'd rattled him in any way.

"You're damn straight it is."

"I guess we'll let the chips fall where they may, then."

"I do my job and I do it well."

"If that's the case, then you don't have anything to worry about."

Jenkins punched Cutler in the chest with a finger. "Now, you—"

"If you don't remove your finger, I'm going to break it," Cutler said with a smile.

The judge's finger froze and his face paled. Though he removed his finger, he didn't back down. "Call off your dogs, McFarland."

"Can't do that."

"Okay, don't say I didn't warn you." Jenkins raised a hand again as if to poke Cutler in the chest, then obviously thought better of it, because he lowered his hand just as quickly as he'd raised it. "I'll find your Achilles' heel. Make no mistake about it, and then I'll use it to sink your ass."

Cutler's thoughts jumped to his mother, sending a shudder through him. Yet he continued to smile. "If you'll excuse me, Judge, I have work to do."

"I'm going to take pleasure in knocking your dick in the dirt, boy. And it's coming. Count on it."

Cutler's smile held steady. "Have a nice day, Judge."

With that, Cutler pivoted and walked down the hall, his piss factor so high, he figured anyone who passed him could see his burning rage. No doubt about it, his personal hit list was growing.

Not only was he bound and determined to nail Drew, he would nail Jenkins right along with him, though for totally different reasons, of course. Yet in his mind, the two were alike. Both disrespected and mistreated women, and that amounted to two faults he couldn't, *wouldn't* tolerate or dismiss.

"Hey, McFarland."

Cutler groaned as he pulled up short. Again. He whipped around with no more excitement than he had moments ago. Actually, he'd rather have had a root canal than face his opponent, Winston Gilmore.

Cutler clenched and unclenched his hands, then jammed them into his pockets. This was another bastard he'd like to see get his comeuppance.

"Gilmore," he said by way of acknowledgment.

"How's it going?" A grin was plastered across the attorney's handsome face.

"Can't complain. How about you?"

"Couldn't be better," Gilmore said with a wide and confident smile that showed his pearly whites to perfection.

"Glad to hear it," Cutler responded.

As if Gilmore picked up on the hint of sarcasm in Cutler's voice, his face darkened and his eyes narrowed. "You're a cocky son of a bitch whose ass I'm going to enjoy stomping." He smiled. "In the polls, that is."

"That remains to be seen," Cutler countered with ease.

"You're really chalking up the enemies, my friend." Glee was in his voice again.

Cutler let the "my friend" pass, seeing no reason to carry the insults to a new level. All he wanted was to get out of the courthouse and back to his office before he completely blew his gasket and did something he'd regret, like putting a dent in pretty boy's smug face.

"I saw, even heard, a bit of your exchange with the judge," Gilmore said with more of that glee.

Cutler merely shrugged.

"You've always thought you were a law unto yourself, McFarland," he said for Cutler's ears alone, "but that's about to change. I find it's my honor-bound duty to show you otherwise."

"Like Jenkins, you do what you gotta do." Cutler didn't know why he bothered to respond. Nothing was getting accomplished. But then, this kind of verbal bashing was Gilmore's forte. He wanted to win and it didn't matter how low he played to reach that goal.

Cutler rued the day he'd ever gone out with Gilmore's wife. Even though they hadn't been married at the time, Gilmore had always held that against him, thinking he, Cutler, still had the hots for his wife, which couldn't be further from the truth. Convincing Gilmore of that was another story altogether.

"I'll see you around," Gilmore was saying, an idiotic grin still plastered on his face. "Or rather on the campaign trail."

Not if I can help it, Cutler thought. "Looking forward to it."

Cutler had taken two steps when Gilmore said, "Oh, by the way."

Though furious at being further held up, Cutler stopped and turned, not bothering to curb his irritation. "What?"

"How's your mother?"

A gut-knifng fear shot through him. "She's fine. Why do you ask?"

Gilmore's smile was too innocent to suit Cutler. Yet he made sure his fractured emotions didn't show.

"My sister attends her church."

Cutler lifted his brows, waiting for the hatchet to fall, if indeed it was going to.

"She was told your mother had been ill."

"Like I said, she's fine."

"Good, because Lucy's planning to get married and wants her to perform the ceremony."

"I'm sure she'll be delighted. Tell your sister to give her a call."

"Will do," Gilmore said before turning and striding off.

Cutler didn't know how long he stood there with his heart stuck in his throat.

"You look like you've been drawn and quartered."

"Thanks, Angel. I'll do you a favor sometime."

Angel grinned. "Don't mean to be insulting. I'm just calling it like I see it."

"You're right," Cutler responded in a reluctant tone. "It's been another one of those days."

"You kicked butt in court this afternoon. You should be feeling good about that."

"I won't feel good until the jury comes back with a guilty verdict."

"I don't see how they could do otherwise, after your closing. It's one of your best."

"We'll see. But thanks for the kind words. I could use them."

"I know you're pissed at the picketers."

"Actually, I wasn't even aware of them until I left court."

"I think several were arrested when they wouldn't stop shouting obscenities about you, calling you a woman hater—among other things."

Cutler's mouth turned down. "Whatever floats their boats. I feel confident I proved that Gail Sessions knew exactly what she was doing when she drowned those babies."

"I'm on your side. Unfortunately, those bleeding-heart liberals don't see it that way."

"And some of them just might be on that jury," Cutler pointed out.

"Like you said, we'll see, but not any time soon, I expect." Angel paused and cocked his head to one side. "Meanwhile, is there anything I should know about?"

Cutler told him about his encounters with Jenkins and Gilmore.

"No wonder you're out of sorts."

"That's an understatement," Cutler said flatly. "So has Snelling got anything on the judge yet, something we can sink our teeth into?"

"Not to my knowledge, but I'll check with him."

"Build a fire under his ass, if you have to. I'm sure he's still dragging his heels on purpose."

"He should just do his job and keep his opinions to himself," Angel said with censure in his voice.

"He's playing it cautious, since he'd like to move into this office one day."

"Seems as though a lot of people would like to occupy your chair." Angel grinned, then drawled, "That would be all right, if you wanted to vacate it, that is."

"Gilmore has a chance to whip me."

"Nah. That's not going to happen." The room fell quiet for a moment, then Angel said, "On a brighter note, how's married life treating you?"

Cutler perked up. "Great, actually."

Angel scratched his head. "Man, I still can't believe you took the plunge, and out of the blue, too."

"I can't either," Cutler responded much more seriously than he intended.

Angel gave him a puzzled look. "Do I hear a strain of regret in your tone?"

"Absolutely not. Kaylee's the best thing that ever happened to me."

And she was. Even though he wasn't in love with her and had married her under the worst of circumstances, he had no regrets. And while he was still in shock over that himself, he was making the most of it and having a hell of a good time.

The only hitch in their relationship was their disagreement over Drew. Even though that was a serious breach, he hoped that, too, would work itself out. Again, there were no sure things in life and he wasn't prepared to let Drew off the hook, marriage or no marriage.

"Give her my best."

"Will do. Anything new on Drew Rush?" Cutler asked.

"Still working on it, but so far I don't have enough to make an arrest."

"Keep your nose to the grindstone on that one, too."

"I'll let you know the second we get something concrete."

Following that conversation, they discussed several more ongoing and upcoming cases. When his assistant finally left, Cutler felt more spent than ever. What he needed was a beer, followed by a hot shower.

With his wife.

Thinking of Kaylee brought a smile to his face. He reached for the phone and punched out her cell number.

"Hello, baby," she said in that lilting voice of hers.

"Where are you?"

"On my way home. How about you?"

"Working on getting out of the office."

"Homeward bound?" Kaylee asked.

"As fast as I can get there."

"Want me to make something for dinner or do you want to go out?"

"Neither."

"You're not hungry?"

He paused and lowered his voice. "Only for you."

Hearing that tiny but obvious catch in her throat turned him on that much more.

"I can handle that," she whispered.

"I'll see you shortly."

Thirty minutes later he walked in and pulled up short. Kaylee was naked except for a pair of strappy sandals.

"I thought you'd never get here," she said in a sweet, husky tone.

Blood thundered to his loins as he reached for her.

Thirty-Two

"**O**hh, Cutler, yes."

"Don't hold back, baby. Let it go."

No way could she hold back even if she wanted to, not when his tongue had licked all ten of her toes, the insides of her legs and thighs, before moving up into her wet, hot center. Once there, he continued to make magic.

Kaylee tangled her hands in his hair and bucked as sensation after sensation rocked through her. He knew just where to touch, to nibble, *to suck.*

He'd been doing that since he had walked in the door and grabbed her. Clothes had been shed with haste, then after his hot mouth had devoured hers, he'd lowered her to the floor, where he'd licked and tugged on her nipples until she thought she'd go mad with desire.

"Take me here," she cried. "Now."

With his heated gaze centered on her, he pressed her against the carpet, spread himself over her and entered her with a deep thrust, not stopping until he'd ridden her hard and fast.

Their mutual cries were stymied by his lips clinging to hers once again. Afterward, when they could breathe, he swept her into his arms, took her straight to the bedroom and into the shower. There they soaped each other, all the while laughing and nibbling on each other's sudsy flesh.

Then he lifted her and backed her against the tile wall. Once she'd locked her legs around his waist, he thrust inside her again. This time their orgasms were hard, deep and quick.

Fifteen minutes later, after rinsing and toweling their bodies, they fell into bed.

"Want to take a nap?" she asked in a dreamy, sated tone.

He crooked his elbow and rested his head in a hand, then stared down at her. "Do you?"

She licked swollen red lips. "No," she whispered.

"Me, either," he said in a guttural tone, his eyes still heated.

"Want something to eat?"

"Yeah, you."

Her heart went into another meltdown. "Oh, Cutler, Cutler."

"Yes, Kaylee, Kaylee," he mimicked with suppressed humor.

Lifting her head a bit, she snaked out her tongue and traced his lips, not once but several times.

He groaned, the light in his eyes flaring with fire. "God, what you do to me."

"And you to me."

"No matter how many times I'm inside you, it's not enough."

"I feel the same."

"Right now I want you so much I'm about to explode." He took her hand and placed it on his hard, throbbing organ.

She shifted enough so that she could see and touch it. When her hand surrounded it and moved up and down, his head fell to the pillow and his moans grew louder.

"If you don't stop, I'm going to come."

"That's all right."

His eyes opened. "I want to be inside you."

"How about in my mouth?"

He drew in his breath. "Are you sure?"

Her answer was to scramble to her knees, then lower her head onto the engorged flesh, taking it as far into her mouth as she could without strangling.

"Oh, yes, yes," he whispered, sounding as though he was in agony.

She knew he was in agony, all right, but oh, such sweet agony as her lips and tongue continued to bring him untold pleasure.

"I'm going to—"

She felt his warm seeds spill into her mouth. Even then she didn't remove her mouth, not until she was sure he had completely emptied himself.

After she felt him go limp, she got up and went into the bathroom. A few minutes later she returned and crawled in beside him. For what seemed the longest time, they simply stared at each other.

"You're incredible," he said at last, his voice croaky as if he had a severe sore throat.

"You're pretty incredible yourself, mister."

"I've never kissed a softer mouth."

"I'm glad."

"Nor have I ever had anyone actually kiss me like you."

"Really?" she whispered, basking in the glow of his sweet and loving words of praise.

"Really. It's the nibbling, the gentle biting that makes my dick rise to the occasion instantly."

She giggled. "He likes me."

"Oh, baby, that's an understatement."

"Okay, so he's obsessed with me. How's that?"

"That's hitting the nail on the head."

"Speaking of head—" Kaylee deliberately broke off with a mischievous grin spreading over her face.

Laughing outright, Cutler grabbed her and rolled her onto her back. "I'm up for another round, my darling."

Her heart went crazy. "Do you hear me complaining?"

"Wouldn't do you any good."

"Hey, I'm easy," she said, laughter further enriching her words. "But then you already know that."

"You're so beautiful, so hot."

"Only for you," she whispered around the fullness in her throat. He made her feel so special, so wonderful she could hardly believe it. She'd never thought life could be this perfect, much less marriage. She couldn't imagine waking up without him beside her.

"Whatcha thinking?" Cutler drawled, tracing her lips with a finger.

She nabbed that finger between her teeth and sucked on it. He sucked in his breath, passion flaring anew in his eyes.

"You'd best be careful or you'll get something started I'll want to finish."

"Is that a threat or a promise?"

He smiled. "Both."

"Good. Either way I won't lose."

His eyes turned serious. "I'll never let you go, Kaylee."

"I'm not going anywhere, my darling. Ever."

He muttered something incoherently, then pulled her against him, burying her face against his chest, where he held her so tightly she feared she might smother. Yet she would never complain. She loved every moment of being against him. The most important thing was that she was *with* him.

"Round two's about to begin." His grin was leering.

"I'm ready," she whispered, feeling herself tingle all over with anticipation.

He maneuvered his way to the foot of the bed and began his love affair with her toes all over again.

Finally reaching the center of her, his tongue stabbed, sucked and nibbled repeatedly until she thought she might not live over the tender yet savage assault.

"Ohh," she cried again.

Somehow through the fog of her mind she heard him whisper, "Perfect" before he repositioned himself next to her, though not before he placed a hand between her legs, cupping her throbbing center.

She placed her hand on top of his and pressed.

"You're aching, aren't you?" he asked, his eyes probing.

"Yes, but it's a wonderful ache."

"I bet I know how to make it go away."

"I bet you do, too."

Cutler rolled over and took her with him. When he lifted her and the head of his spiked hardness met the folds of her softness, he stopped as though having met resistance.

"You're so tight." He ground out the words, his eyes questioning. "I'm not sure I can get in again. I don't want to hurt you."

"You won't." Kaylee's breath hung suspended.

He took a nipple into his mouth and she groaned, feeling suddenly as though nature had reawakened her insides, giving him access to the heart of her as a flower opens to the sun after a storm.

Once he was all the way inside her, he splayed his hands on her buttocks and began to move.

"No," she said. "Let me." She moved slowly but deliberately, making each thrust count to the max. Finally, when she couldn't take any more dallying, she upped the pace.

It was a toss-up to see who moaned the loudest and the longest. But it didn't matter, as wave after wave of pleasure rolled through them.

With one last cry she collapsed on top of him.

Cutler massaged his stomach. "Man, that was good."

"I thought so, too."

After their marathon session of lovemaking, they'd showered once again, then headed to the kitchen, where Kaylee had whipped up two omelets and opened a can of biscuits.

"Thanks," Cutler said, smiling at her out of still-glazed eyes after they had finished eating. "The old saying is the way to a man's heart is through his stomach."

She wrinkled her nose. "Only, we both know that's not true."

"You got that right, baby. It's through the old dick."

"That's where a man's brains are, too."

He chuckled. "You won't hear me deny that."

She answered his chuckle, then looked at the clock. "Can you believe it's nearly three and we're not asleep?"

"I bet we can take care of that."

"Only, I'm not sleepy."

He gave her a teasing grin. "Last one back in the sack has to make up the bed."

By the time they reached the bed and fell on it, they were both laughing so hard they couldn't get a decent breath. Soon, though, they were wrapped in each other's arms, naked, the covers on the floor.

After a lengthy silence Cutler asked, "Are you asleep?"

Kaylee sighed. "No."

"So what are you thinking?"

"How much fun it is to you-know-what."

"No, I don't know. Just say it."

"I can't," Kaylee wailed.

"Sure you can. It's just a word."

"Okay," she said, then got close to his ear and whispered.

He pushed her away from him and stared at her in astonishment. "Why, Kaylee Benton McFarland, I can't believe you said that."

Her eyes widened with a gasp. "You made me say it." She giggled. "Actually, I've always wanted to blurt that out, and now I have."

He laughed out loud. "You're something else."

"Do you think I'm terrible?"

"Because you said fuck? Or because you *like* to fuck?"

She felt a sting in her cheeks even though she knew he couldn't see that in the muted light of the bedroom. "Yes, to both."

He laughed again and hugged her. "Honey, trust me, if that's as bad as you ever get, then you'll be real good."

"Thanks. I guess."

He leaned over and kissed her on the nose. "Maybe we should try and get some sleep."

"I suppose so. We both have killer days tomorrow."

Cutler groaned. "How 'bout we shuck it all, run the hell away and spend all our time screwing our brains out?"

Kaylee stared at him wild-eyed.

He hooted.

"Did anyone ever tell you that you're a pervert?" she asked, jabbing him in the ribs.

"Don't you just love it?"

I love you, she almost said, but didn't. Instead she let out a deep sigh, and curled her body back into his and closed her eyes.

"Wake up."

"I am. Awake, that is," Cutler replied, shifting one leg over hers.

"I want to talk to you about something."

Instantly Cutler came alert. He didn't dare ask what. He didn't want to know. Actually, the last thing he wanted to do was talk. The evening and night had been too perfect to let anything mar it. Talking could definitely make that happen.

He suspected she wanted to discuss Drew, which was a subject that was taboo as far as he was concerned.

"Did you hear me?" Kaylee asked in a voice that was only a decibel above a whisper.

"I heard you."

He felt her pull back and look at him, though he was reluctant to meet her gaze. "It's not about Drew, Cutler."

He swallowed an expletive. "How did you know what I was thinking?"

She punched him in the belly. "Because I know you."

"I'm not sure I like that."

"Get over it."

He chuckled, glad the tense moment had passed. "So tell me what's on your mind before I ravish you again."

"You've got to be kidding."

"Kidding?" He reached for her hand and placed it on his erection. "Now tell me I'm kidding."

She gave it a hard squeeze, then moved her hand.

"How cruel is that?" he demanded in a strained but teasing voice.

"You'll live."

"I might not."

"Be serious, please."

"Okay, baby. I'm sorry."

"I was rummaging through the agency's wardrobe room the other day and found something I shouldn't have."

"Oh?"

"Several small packets of pills fell out of some of the pockets."

"What did you do with them?"

"I put them in the safe at the office."

He tensed. "Why did you do that?"

"I wanted to handle the situation in-house."

"And have you?"

"No, not yet," Kaylee muttered in a glum tone.

Cutler cursed.

"That wasn't a smart move, right?"

"Right, especially when you don't know what the pills are."

"My worst nightmare is that one of my girls is dealing."

He swung around and sat on the side of the bed with his back to her. "Bring the packets home tomorrow."

"I really don't want to involve the law."

He swung around. "You just did."

"Sometimes I forget who you are."

"That's a pretty lame excuse," he responded in a grave tone. Then seeing her lower lip tremble, he reached for her. "It's going to be all right."

"Oh, God, Cutler, I hope so, but I'm scared."

And well you should be, he wanted to add, but didn't.

Thirty-Three

"Shut the door behind you."

Though Edgar's heart flip-flopped, he did as he was told. His boss had "that" look on his face, which said he was not in a good mood.

Edgar suspected he knew why.

"Good morning," he said in a jovial tone, hoping to lighten things a bit.

"There's nothing good about it," Drew lashed back.

"Sorry," Edgar muttered under his breath.

Drew flapped his hand toward the plush chairs in front of his desk. "Sit."

Rarely was Drew openly rude to him. Edgar had seen this side of him more times than he cared to remember, but the barbs had always been directed at someone else.

"What's on your mind?" Edgar asked, having complied with the command.

"Do you know how Cutler found out I was his father?"

Edgar had promised himself he wouldn't react, that he'd take whatever was dished out to him with no expression and argument. Yet, sitting here in front of his old friend and boss, whose ire was clearly directed at him, he felt the urge to mess in his pants.

"Yes, I do."

"You told him, didn't you?"

"Why are you asking when you already know the answer?"

Drew lunged out of his desk chair. "Dammit, Benton, you don't have the right to question me."

When Drew called him by his surname, he knew he was in deep trouble. Today was no exception. The other times, however, had been work related.

"Then, yes, I told Cutler."

"You looked at the papers in the safe, right?"

Edgar nodded.

"Damn you to hell."

"I deserve your condemnation."

"You betrayed me," Drew said in a hard, unforgiving tone.

"I won't argue with that."

"I was so sure it was Mary who had spilled her guts, but when she so vehemently denied it, I believed her. If not her, then who? I thought back and remembered sending you to my house, to my safe."

Edgar didn't respond.

"It has to do with Kaylee, doesn't it?"

Edgar forced himself to sit as if he was frozen in a block of ice.

"The more I thought about Kaylee and Cutler getting married, it dawned on me that it was too much of a goddamn coincidence." Drew snapped his fingers. "And too quick."

"They fell in love."

"Bullshit."

"I can promise you Kaylee's in love."

"Did Cutler pay you for the information?"

Edgar blanched. "No, he did not."

"I should fire your ass, Benton."

"I wouldn't blame you if you did."

"If I had wanted Cutler to know the truth, I would've told him. Did you stop to think about that?"

Though Edgar still didn't react, he again fought the urge to mess in his pants. When he'd used the information he'd found in the safe that day to blackmail Cutler, he'd known it was only a matter of time before Drew figured it out, through the process of elimination, if nothing else.

What surprised Edgar was that it had taken Drew so long. He was one of the smartest and most astute men Edgar had ever known.

"The only reason you're still sitting in front of me is because of Kaylee. Not much is sacred in life to me. She happens to be the exception."

"Trust me, I'm grateful for everything you've done for her." Edgar cleared his throat. "She absolutely adores you and thinks you can walk on water. Do whatever you want to me, but please don't take this out on her."

"Underneath that good-ole-boy facade, Benton, you've got some big balls. Even though I could slit your throat for a little of nothing, I'll admit I admire you. Having said that, I've ruined a lot lesser men than you for a lot lesser infractions."

"Whatever you dish out, I have coming."

"And more. Get out of my sight before I change my mind."

* * *

"Hi, Daddy."

"Hi yourself, sweetheart."

"Come in and sit down."

Edgar strode toward Kaylee just as she walked from behind her desk. "First I want a hug. It seems like ages since I've seen you."

"It's only been a few days, but I want a hug, too." Kaylee smiled. "Hugs are always good."

"You betcha," Edgar exclaimed, grabbing her and giving her a hard squeeze. Afterward he sat down, where his eyes scanned the room. "You know, you really got a good thing going here."

Kaylee eased into the chair next to him.

Edgar frowned. "Your leg's bothering you." A flat statement of fact.

"Not really," Kaylee said in an evasive tone.

"Hey, kid, don't forget who you're talking to."

She gave him a limp smile. "I'm okay, really."

"Just okay's not good enough for my girl."

"But that's the way it is, and we can't change that. This bum leg is as good as it's ever going to get."

"I'd like to think that's not so. Medical science is coming out with new medicines and procedures every day."

Kaylee reached across and pressed his arm. "You've always been my cheerleader, and I suspect you always will be. Just in case I haven't told you how much I appreciate that, I'm telling you now."

"I know." Edgar cleared his throat, then added, "Let me take you to lunch."

"Sorry, Dad, no can do. You know the 'big' show is coming up real soon, and I'm nearly nuts trying to make sure everything goes off without a hitch."

"It won't be perfect, Kaylee."

"You're right, but I want it to be as close to perfect as possible."

"That's my girl." He grinned. "So what did you want to see me about?"

"How do you know I didn't just want to *see* you?"

He gave her a look. "Like you just said, you're too busy to waste time."

"Excuse me, but spending time with you isn't a waste of time."

"Whatever," Edgar countered with a smile in his voice.

"You're right, I do have a reason."

"I'm at your disposal."

Kaylee sank her teeth into her lower lip for a second. "It's about Uncle Drew."

"What about him?"

Was there a note of caution in his tone or had she imagined it? On closer observation, she thought she must've imagined it, because his demeanor was as calm as ever. "Did you know he's being investigated?"

Edgar was clearly taken aback. "No."

"Well, he is," Kaylee said flatly.

"I suppose Cutler told you."

"Yes, he did." She paused and took a breath. "I don't know much about Drew's work, how he makes his millions, but I can't believe he does anything illegal."

"Kaylee, you know I can't discuss Drew's business with you. As his employee and friend, that would be unethical."

"Sorry. I shouldn't have brought it up."

"It's okay. Hey, you don't worry yourself about that, you hear? If anyone can take care of himself, it's Drew Rush. Like you, he's a survivor. You should know that."

"Did you know that Drew is Cutler's birth father?"

Edgar didn't so much as blink. "Yes."

"How long have you known?"

"Just found it out."

"Me, too. I still haven't gotten over the shock."

"It's one of those things where truth is stranger than fiction."

"I'm still reeling."

"How does Cutler feel?"

"Vindictive as hell, to put it bluntly. However, he won't discuss any of the particulars or the details. I'm pretty much in the dark."

"Don't look to me to fill you in. I was stunned myself."

"I love Uncle Drew and I love Cutler. I feel caught in the middle."

Edgar leaned closer to her, his eyes piercing. "Don't you dare get caught in the middle. Those two will have to work it out."

"It's not that easy, Dad. Cutler's my husband and Uncle Drew's my mentor."

"Still, you stay out of it. Promise me."

"I won't promise, but I will try and take your advice."

"Don't just try—do it."

Kaylee angled her head. "You know more than you're telling me."

Edgar's expression remained bland. "Not about Drew and Cutler's relationship, I don't."

"You wouldn't lie to me, would you, Dad?" Instantly a

look of hurt crossed his face, changing his features. "Sorry. I know better than that. Forget I said it."

"I will." Edgar leaned back in his chair. "It'll all work out, honey girl. You just wait and see."

"I have to think that or else—" Kaylee broke off, pulling her lower lip between her teeth again.

"So are you happy?"

She flashed him a brilliant smile. "Ecstatically."

Sudden tears appeared in Edgar's eyes. "That's a praise."

"Oh, Daddy." She got up and hugged him again. "You're such an old softy."

"When it comes to you, I'll admit it. I've dreamed of this day since we lost your mother. You having a home and family, that is."

"I won't ever have a family, Daddy," Kaylee said in a soft but matter-of-fact tone.

He bowed his chin. "A husband's considered family. And he's good to you."

"So far, he's perfect."

Edgar rolled his eyes. "No man's perfect. You've just got newlywed-itis."

She grinned, then stood. "Thanks for stopping by."

He stood, as well. "Are you dismissing me?"

"Yes."

He grinned, then ambled out.

Later that morning Kaylee made her way into Sandy's office and closed the door behind her.

"So how did your visit with Nicole go?" she asked, coming straight to the point.

"I got nowhere," Sandy responded in an exasperated tone. "I might as well have been talking to a stump."

"I have no choice, then, but to go to her parents."

"Or let *her* go."

Kaylee sat down, her thoughts troubled. "I hate to do that. She's truly one of our brightest and upcoming stars."

"True, but if she can't walk the runway, what good is she to us?"

"None, as far as the agency goes. But we're about more than that, Sandy."

Sandy's face turned red. "You're right, we are. That was a selfish remark, and I apologize."

"No need to apologize. Right now all our nerves are frayed, especially the girls'."

"You said a mouthful there," Sandy said. "I don't think I've ever seen them so strung out."

"As we both know, there's a lot riding on this Versace show for them and for us."

"That's why they're nipping at each other's heels like crazy," Sandy said.

"How about Barbie and Jessica? Unless you haven't kept me informed, they apparently haven't tied into each other lately."

Sandy frowned. "Not physically, but the tension between those two is so thick you could slice it with a knife."

"Well, as long as they keep their mouths shut and do their jobs, we can live with the tension."

"I hope you're right." Sandy pushed a stack of photos aside and rested her chin in her hands. "So what about the packet of pills? Have you decided how we're going to handle that yet?"

"I told Cutler about them last night."

Sandy's brows shot up. "And?"

"He wouldn't say until he checks them out, has them analyzed."

"I've been keeping a close eye on all the girls. To date, I haven't seen any signs of anyone being high." Sandy shrugged. "But then, I'm no authority on the use of drugs."

"Hopefully when they realized the stuff was gone," Kaylee said, her features pinched, "they panicked and closed up shop. Either way, we're in for a world of hurt if this gets out of hand."

"Cutler will help us, won't he?"

Kaylee heaved a sigh. "Only if it's within legal boundaries."

Following that statement, they both sat in troubled silence.

Thirty-Four

"Y̲ou look lovely this morning, but then you always do."

Kaylee flashed Cutler a dazzling smile, which sent an electric current through him. He gave a start. If he didn't know better, he'd think he had fallen in love.

No way.

Love didn't enter into the deal. He'd made a bargain with her father that he would honor. But love? He couldn't allow himself to go down that path.

Love hurt. Love made demands.

Love possessed.

Look what had happened to his mother. Cutler shuddered visibly.

"What's wrong, darling?"

Cutler cleared his features. "Nothing. Why?"

"You just looked odd for a minute." A twinkle appeared in her eyes. "You're probably tired, since you didn't sleep much last night."

"And just whose fault is that?"

"Not mine," Kaylee responded with obvious innocence.

He snorted with a grin. They had spent the biggest part of the night making love. Neither could get enough of the other.

"We really should sleep more," Kaylee said in a musing tone. "With all we have on our plates."

"Not on your life, sweetheart." Cutler's tone was emphatic. "Hey, it's early yet. Let's get some more coffee and sit on the deck."

"Good idea. After the gully washer last night, it's a bit cooler this morning."

Soon they were sitting in the comfortable lounge chairs sipping on their beverages, the sweet smell of flowers wafting to their senses. Cutler broke the silence. "I'm acting like I don't have a thing to do today."

"Me, too."

Neither moved, however.

"Some days I feel like the boat I'm trying to keep afloat has holes in it and is sinking fast."

"You're not going to lose the election," Kaylee said with conviction, reaching out and taking his hand.

He squeezed it. "I wish I could be that sure."

"Just trust me."

"But it's more than the election. My workload's eating my breakfast, lunch and dinner."

"Which case is coming up next?"

"The abortion clinic."

"Ouch."

Cutler blew out a harsh breath.

"I know how you feel about being overwhelmed," Kaylee said. "I'm there right along with you."

"I know, and I'm sorry for you." Cutler's gaze was tender.

"It's not your fault my girls are using drugs. By the

way, thank you again for testing the pills and finding them to be illegal drugs."

"I'm here to help." He winked. "Among other things— like ravishing your lovely body."

"We both know that's not true," Kaylee said with a catch in her voice. "About my body, that is."

He drew his brows together. "Hey, I think you're lovely all over. Doesn't my opinion count for something?"

Her features brightened. "Indeed it does. In fact, it's only your opinion that counts."

"Good. Now, back to the drugs. I hardly think all of your girls are using."

"Probably not. I'm just afraid someone is actually selling out of the agency."

"Could be. And if that's the case, then the problem is much more serious. But then, I'm preaching to the choir."

"Sandy and I are meeting with the lot of them this morning." Kaylee sighed. "I can't imagine any of them confessing."

"Count on that *not* happening."

"So how do I handle it?"

"For starters, let them know you're on to their little sideline and you intend to find out who's involved, then deal with them accordingly."

"Should I tell them I've notified the police?"

"Not at this point. Wait and see what reaction you get."

"Even though they fight like cats and dogs, they stick together. Does that make sense to you?"

"Sure does," Cutler countered quickly. "They're pretty much all guilty of hiding secrets. In many instances, those secrets are the same."

"So to rat on thy cohort is to rat on thyself."

"Exactly."

"It looks like I'm facing an uphill battle," Kaylee acknowledged in a weary tone.

"I'm facing it with you."

She smiled. "Thank God for small favors."

"Do you have any idea who the culprits might be?"

"Not really. Three of the girls have been at odds, and there's a lot of tension. But like we just said, no one is willing to give the other up."

"Women," Cutler muttered.

"What can I say?" Kaylee's tone was lamenting. "Temperaments, good and bad, are a by-product of this profession."

"A hazard, if you ask me." Cutler smiled, then sobered. "You found the drugs in a pair of overalls?"

Kaylee nodded. "With lots of pockets."

"I'm guessing that more than one model wears the outfits."

"Right. Although we've narrowed it down to five girls. Those are the ones I'm going to zero in on."

"Still, you're doing the right thing by speaking to all of them. There's also the possibility that one of the others could have planted the drugs there for reasons we may never know."

"This latest debacle couldn't have come at a worse time. The Versace show is next week." Kaylee paused with a shudder. "More than that, it makes me sick to think those young girls are abusing their bodies in such a vile way. I thought anorexia was bad, but drugs…" She let her voice play out.

"Don't kid yourself. There are millions of bored, overweight housewives who are sucking down on amphetamines every morning with their glass of orange juice. They get two for one—a buzz and dead appetites."

Kaylee shook her head. "I can't imagine living like that."

They were quiet for a moment, listening to the birds chirp and watching a squirrel jump from one limb to another as if its legs were on springs.

"While we're on an unpleasant subject," Kaylee said into the silence, "there's something else I need your opinion on."

"Shoot."

She told him about Nicole's bruises and how the model refused to admit there was a problem.

"Man, you're getting hit with some heavy-duty stuff."

"Again, it couldn't have come at a worse time," Kaylee said ruefully.

"You said I'd win the election. I say this show will come off without a hitch."

"Nicole won't be in it for sure. And she's one of my stars."

"I thought makeup could perform miracles."

"She's too bruised." Kaylee's voice trembled.

"I'm sorry, sweetheart. You think it's her boyfriend who's using her for a punching bag?"

"No, I don't. I've met Scott. He's just not the type."

"Keep in mind you never know what goes on behind closed doors."

"True. Still—" She broke off and looked away.

"Why don't I do some checking into her background?"

"You can do that?"

His lips twitched. "I'm the D.A., honey. Remember?"

"Sorry." She gave him a sassy grin. "You can break the laws and get away with it."

He pulled his head back. "Whoa, girl. That's not funny."

"You're right, it isn't." Kaylee wrinkled her nose. "But I was only kidding." Cutler wished he could be sure about that—Drew jumping to mind. Since that remained a sore spot between them, they didn't discuss him. But the undercurrents were there with the potential to explode at any given moment.

As if Kaylee could read his mind, her face lost its color. Unwilling to delve into that taboo subject, he drained his cup, then stood. "I'll call you later." He leaned over and kissed her on the cheek. "Keep your chin up. Everything's going to be all right."

She rubbed a hand up and down his arm. "For you, too."

He grabbed her hand, squeezed it, then turned and strode off.

"Angel, bring me up to date."

Cutler had gone straight to the office and called in his investigator. He didn't have much time to play catch-up as he was due in court, so every minute counted.

"I wish I had better news, but I don't," Angel told him straightaway.

"That's not what I wanted to hear."

"I know, boss. Sorry."

"Before you give me what you do have, I want you to run a check on a young woman named Nicole Reed."

"Am I looking for anything in particular?"

"She's one of Kaylee's models who's a victim of abuse, or so it appears. Bruises and scrapes. You get the picture."

"I'll get right on it."

"Also, I want you to check on the drug dealers around this area."

Angel's big eyes became bigger. "What's that all about?"

"Another of Kaylee's problems. Someone's either using or dealing in or out of the agency."

"Man, I hate that for Kaylee."

"Ditto. That's why I'm trying to help. Now, back to matters at hand."

Angel opened his notebook. "Nothing new yet on Jenkins, though he did dismiss another suspicious case."

"How about Andrews or his sister?"

"It appears both have disappeared."

"Damn," Cutler muttered.

"But I haven't given up on them. We're still checking their residences every day."

Cutler nodded, his lips tight. "What about the priest? How are we doing there?"

"Somewhat better. I've found an ex-worker at the abortion clinic who thinks the priest doesn't walk on water. I'm supposed to speak to her this afternoon."

"If she knows anything, do whatever it takes to get her to testify. As you know, we have zilch. And now wouldn't be a good time to get crucified in court. No pun intended."

"Right. Speaking of campaigning, how's that going?"

Cutler snorted. "I wouldn't know. If I beat Gilmore, it sure as hell won't be from trying."

"You'll beat him," Angel said with assurance. "He's so full of hot air I'm surprised he stays on the ground."

In spite of his foul mood, Cutler laughed. Then he sobered. "I got a disturbing phone call this morning from a civil rights lawyer I've never heard of. Remember Cullen Bryant, the man I put on death row?"

"Yep."

"There's a chance he might be retried."

"Correct me if I'm wrong, but didn't you have an airtight case?"

"I thought so at the time, and I still do, but you never know."

"No, you don't," Angel said, "especially if you get a judge like Jenkins to hear the case."

"And that could very well happen."

"When it rains it pours, doesn't it?"

"Yep. The main thing about that particular case is his family. They raised so much stink the first time around, I can just imagine what's going to happen now."

"I'm here to tell you, it'll be a three-ring circus."

"And Gilmore will be the ringmaster."

Angel nodded. "I couldn't agree more. So put on hip boots and be prepared to wade in knee deep."

"Meanwhile, you pull the files so I can start reviewing them, making sure I didn't miss anything."

"Consider it done."

The phone rang into the sudden silence. Cutler jumped, then cursed.

Angel smiled and rolled his eyes.

"McFarland," Cutler snapped into the receiver.

After listening, he felt the color drain from his face.

"What?" Angel asked as he picked up on the changing mood.

Cutler dropped the receiver back into the cradle, knowing his face was devoid of color. "The verdict's in on the drowning case."

"Think we won?"

"I'm not betting on it, are you?"

Angel laughed with no humor. "Not in this lifetime. And certainly not with your luck."

"Don't you mean lack of?" Cutler's smile held no humor either.

"Yeah."

Cutler grabbed his briefcase. "Come on, let's go. Prolonging the misery won't change the verdict."

Thirty-Five

The interrogation had been a disaster.

As a result, Kaylee couldn't be more frustrated or confused. Or angry. Her insides churned so that she actually felt nauseated. That would never do, she told herself, striding out of her office to the break room, where she helped herself to a cold beverage. After downing several sips and walking back to her office, she felt better.

Not wanting any interruptions, she had told her secretary to hold all calls except from Cutler. She needed quiet time—thinking time, if you will. When she had broached the subject of the amphetamines with the girls, they had sat like stoic statues.

Still, she wasn't giving up. With Cutler's help and Sandy's and her vigilance, they would get to the bottom of this.

After taking another sip of her cold drink, Kaylee glanced at her watch. She had a meeting with Emily Austin, the Ford Agency rep, in a little over an hour. They planned to put the finishing touches on the schedule.

Despite the unexpected upheaval with the drugs, everything appeared to be on-target. She just prayed that the frayed seams would hold together until the show was over. Hopefully by letting the girls know she was privy to what was going on she had put the fear of God in them.

Since her accident, Kaylee had learned to live in the present. She saw no reason to change that philosophy now.

The phone buzzed. Ah, the verdict must be in. Only it wasn't Cutler on the other end, but rather her secretary. "Mr. Rush is here and insists on seeing you."

She didn't hesitate. "Send him in."

Seconds later a dapper-looking Drew opened the door and walked in. She met him halfway and gave him a hug.

He pulled back and smiled at her. "My, but you're looking good. There's a spark in your eyes I've never seen before." His smile widened. "Yep, married life definitely agrees with you."

"I have no complaints."

"And I'm thrilled."

Kaylee thought for a minute, then asked in a serious tone, "Are you really?"

Drew made a face. "Absolutely, my dear."

Kaylee wished she *really* believed that, but she didn't. "Do you have time to stay for a while?"

"If I'm not interfering."

"It wouldn't matter, Uncle Drew. I'd make time for you."

He sat down and she offered him something to drink. He turned her down. Afterward, a silence fell between them. She noted a slight strain in the atmosphere, which she hated.

"I can't wait for the big night," Drew said with enthusiasm.

With almost too much enthusiasm, Kaylee thought. Or was she just overreacting to him and the fact that she was wedged between him and Cutler?

"I can't either, though I'm so nervous."

"Ah, don't be. You and your agency will shine brighter than gold."

"If that's the case, I'll be able to pay you back in full."

A scowl removed the animation from his face. "I told you I don't want that money back. It's a love gift."

"I know what you told me, but I can't accept that."

"Yes, you can. You're a giver and that's good. But it's also good to learn to receive with the same grace."

"Wow, Uncle Drew, I've never heard you speak so eloquently. I'm impressed."

He gave her a sheepish grin. "Did get a tad carried away, didn't I?"

"A little, but it made me feel good."

"That was my intention all along."

They both chuckled, which helped remove the strain from the air. But only for a minute. Another silence ensued and the tension returned.

"You're here for a reason," she said, giving him a piercing look.

"I'm not sure I like your ability to read me so easily."

"Sorry," she said mildly.

His smile didn't quite reach his eyes. They remained dark and unreadable. "I just wanted to set the record straight."

"Please, Uncle Drew, I don't want to be between you and Cutler." Even to herself, her voice sounded anxious.

"I understand," he said with even gentleness. "And that's not my intention at all."

"Good."

"I want you to know that I'm not doing anything illegal."

"I believe you."

He looked taken aback. "You don't know how good that makes me feel."

"I'm glad."

"Cutler, I'm sorry to say, doesn't feel the same."

"I know."

"He's out to ruin me, Kaylee."

She grappled for a decent breath. "You said you wouldn't put me in the middle, but that's exactly what you're doing."

"How much did he tell you?"

Kaylee didn't pretend to misunderstand. "About the two of you?"

He nodded.

"Only that he found out that you were his birth father, a fact I find as unbelievable as I do bizarre."

"I can understand that."

Another silence.

"So he shared no details?" Drew pressed.

"None. But then, I didn't ask. I sensed the subject was much too painful for him to discuss."

"I never meant him to find out." His features twisted.

"I don't know what to say, Uncle Drew."

And she didn't. There was so much about Cutler she didn't know. Maybe time and longevity of marriage would take care of that. And maybe not. There might be areas of Cutler's heart where she would never be welcome. She feared that was because he didn't love her.

"I guess that's because there's nothing else to say." Drew

stood, reached for Kaylee's hand and helped her up. Then he looked deeply into her eyes. "I won't pretend I'm a saint. We both know better than that."

"None of us is."

"Please, then, keep Cutler in bounds. Don't let him throw everything away by his vendetta against me." Drew flicked her on the chin. "I'm counting on you, you hear?"

"I'll do my best, Uncle Drew," she said, wondering if her marker had just been called in.

"You have mixed feelings, don't you?" Kaylee asked Cutler.

"Of course, even though I think she was guilty as hell." Cutler's features were grim.

Kaylee shuddered. "I simply can't imagine what was going through her head when she held those babies under the water until they could no longer breathe."

"Nor can anyone else."

"Do you think she'll get the death penalty?"

"I'm not going to ask for it."

"I'm glad."

He smiled and pulled her into the crook of his arm. She nestled closer, basking in the warmth and security of those arms. While she was definitely rejoicing in his victory, it was a double-edged sword, especially for Cutler.

After the verdict had come in, Cutler had wanted to get out of town, knowing the media would be tracking him. He had opted to head to the ranch.

For two days they had done nothing but eat, drink, swim and make love. It had been a wonderful getaway weekend.

They had agreed that discussing work was taboo. Until now they had not broken that agreement.

Now, following a long bout of lovemaking, she asked, "Mind if I cheat?"

"Depends on how you want to cheat."

She made a face at him. "You know."

"You're excited about the show and want to talk about it."

"Right. But a pact is a pact."

"I'll give you a little leeway, okay?"

She ran her hands through the hair on his chest. "Thanks."

He moaned. "Ah, that feels so good."

She smiled, thinking again how much she enjoyed being married to this strong yet tender man.

"Two more days and your agency will be on the map for sure."

"Let us pray. While I'm about to burst with anticipation, I'm also scared to death."

"That's to be expected. But the evening will be perfect. The girls will be perfect. It'll be a night to remember. And when it's over, we'll celebrate with a few bottles of champagne."

"Is that a promise?"

"You betcha."

She gave him a come-hither grin. "Think you're up for a precelebration?"

He laughed, then grabbed her.

Recalling that conversation, Kaylee pinched herself backstage.

"Hey," Sandy whispered, sidling up to her as another model stepped out onto the runway. "You ought to be peeing up one leg and down the other."

"Sandy!" Kaylee exclaimed under her breath, though she couldn't stop the grin from spreading across her face.

"It's okay, kid, you can admit it."

"Mentally, maybe."

"I bet Cutler is, too."

"I know he's anxious, all right," Kaylee admitted. "Simply because he knows how much this night means to me."

Sandy craned her head. "I can see him in the first row. He's looking proud as punch."

Kaylee smiled. Cutler's presence and support wrapped her in a blanket of security. "He's my rock."

Sandy giggled. "And some rock he is, too."

"He is gorgeous."

"And he's yours." Sandy winked. "Which makes it all the better."

"Right on."

Sandy grinned, then switched the subject back to business. "So far, everything has gone off without a hitch. The girls are awesome, and the New Yorkers know it. You can see the admiration written on their faces."

"Who's had time to notice?" Kaylee asked in an astonished tone.

"Me," Sandy said in a lofty, unapologetic tone. "In between changes, that is," she added with a grin.

"Let's go to the back of the audience for a sec," Kaylee said. "Tonight of all nights, I'd like to see what the patrons see."

"Let's do it."

They had been standing in the back only five minutes watching the parade of lovely girls up and down the platform when it happened.

At first Kaylee had no idea what had caused all the commotion. Then she saw Barbie crumple on the runway, blood flowing down her back.

Then a cry rose from the audience. "Oh, my God, she's been stabbed."

Thirty-Six

Kaylee still couldn't believe what had happened, even though she was now at the emergency-room waiting room in the nearest hospital surrounded by scores of people.

Actually the room was a zoo.

Besides the models and staff, her dad was there, as were Cutler and his parents.

The only one significantly absent was Drew. She knew he'd been at the show, but he had obviously thought better of making an appearance here. His absence didn't matter. Nothing mattered except that Barbie cling to life. And next was that she, Kaylee, maintain her sanity amidst the insanity.

Cutler would see that she didn't crash under this tragedy.

Thank God for him, she had told herself countless times already. Following the pandemonium that had broken out after the hideous incident, he had taken charge.

At first she'd been so shell-shocked she couldn't respond, but then her adrenaline had kicked in and she had done her part in calming the models, who had been beside themselves with panic. Sandy had also jumped in and done her part, as though realizing that Kaylee needed to get to the hospital ASAP.

Once the ambulance, police and crime scene crew had arrived, Cutler had whisked her off the premises and they had headed to the hospital, where they now awaited word on Barbie's condition. She had been in surgery for several hours.

"What's taking them so long?" Kaylee wailed to Cutler, who hadn't left her side for one second.

"Hey, she's exactly where she should be. In the hands of competent surgeons."

"I know. It's just that I'm so frightened." Her voice broke.

He drew her to his side. "Sure you are, sweetheart. Maybe she'll pull through. Don't give up yet."

Kaylee shivered, seeking his warmth through his shirt. He felt so big, so secure, so perfect. In that moment she couldn't imagine her life without him.

She peered up at him, her eyes brimming with tears. "Have I told you lately how much you mean to me?"

They were off to themselves, which was a blessed relief, although everyone was subdued with the exception of the media. They were buzzing about, asking questions that no one could answer.

Kaylee certainly couldn't. She couldn't comprehend how or why this had happened. *Or who had carried out such an act of violence.* She knew that would be the second question Barbie's parents would ask when they arrived.

Somehow she had found the strength to call them herself. The next hurdle she had to jump was questioning by the police.

As for the fallout from the incident—well, she couldn't begin to cope with that yet, mentally or physically. Later the brutality of it would penetrate her dulled senses.

"Why don't I get you some coffee?" Cutler whispered against her temple, still holding her against his side.

"No," she whispered back. "I couldn't keep it down."

"Speaking of down. You need to sit."

"I can't do that either."

Cutler sighed. "That's probably a good thing, as here comes Ken Sowell, chief of detectives."

"I'm not surprised."

"Are you up to him questioning you?"

"Do I have any choice?" she asked, a slight tremor in her voice.

"Yep." He kissed her temple. "Remember, I'm the D.A."

She knew he was trying to interject a light note into the otherwise shattering moment, but she couldn't respond to that either, though she appreciated his efforts.

After somber introductions were exchanged, Sowell said, "There's an empty room adjacent to this one. Let's go there and talk."

They followed the big, burly detective into a sterile room, where they sat at a small dining-like table.

Sowell cleared his throat. "Let me say up front, ma'am, how sorry I am about what happened."

It was obvious he was uncomfortable with the job he had to perform. Kaylee figured that discomfort stemmed from the fact that the big boss was there. And though he didn't mean to be, Cutler could be, *was* intimidating.

"Thank you, Detective," Kaylee managed to say, but not before clearing her own throat.

Cutler squeezed her hand as if to pump her with courage. "Let's keep this brief, shall we?"

The officer's weathered features paled a bit more. "That was my intention, sir."

"Good," Cutler muttered, still not cutting him any slack.

"Mrs. McFarland, do you have any idea who'd want to hurt Ms. Bishop?"

Kaylee was appalled. "Of course not."

"You think it was one of the models?" Cutler asked.

"Don't you, sir?"

"Yes, since it's highly unlikely someone wandered in off the street."

"What we need is the motive."

"That is it, Detective."

"I refuse to believe one of my models did this to her," Kaylee said in an unsteady voice.

"You'd best readjust your thinking," Sowell said bluntly. "It's just a matter of proving which model."

Kaylee stared at Cutler, her insides roiling, then back at the detective. "I don't care how much animosity was between them, none of my girls is capable of such a heinous act."

"Tell him what you know, Kaylee," Cutler said in an even but firm tone. "Starting with the drugs and everything in between, including the catfight."

Sowell's dark eyes drilled her. "I'm listening, ma'am."

Kaylee complied with Cutler's softly spoken demand. Listening to herself relate the incidents, she realized all the models were now cast in a suspicious light, especially Jessica Riley, since she and Barbie had fought.

Yet she didn't believe for one second that Jessica could

mortally harm Barbie or anyone else. That was something she would have to convince Cutler and the detective of.

"The motive seems pretty clear to me," Sowell said.

"How's that?" Kaylee didn't bother to temper the censure in her voice.

"I'm betting the catfight has something to do with the drugs."

"I still don't believe it," Kaylee said, her tone bordering on hostility. "Which means you'll have to prove it."

"Trust me, I will," Sowell said, never changing the tone of his voice.

"Am I free to go now?" Kaylee asked. "I need to find out about Barbie."

The detective nodded, then stood. "Thank you, ma'am. I'll be in touch."

"Later, Sowell," Cutler said in a clipped tone before following Kaylee out of the room.

When they walked back into the waiting area, you could've heard a pin drop. Kaylee's heart faltered. One look at Sandy, who had come up to her, told the story.

"She…she didn't make it, did she?" Kaylee whispered.

"No, sweetie, she didn't." Sandy choked back the tears. "The doctor just came out and told us."

"God, no," Kaylee cried, shaking her head violently. "Please, no."

"Take it easy, sweetheart," Cutler said in an urgent voice.

In the background Kaylee could hear weeping, deep wrenching weeping. Yet it sounded as if it was coming from somewhere else, somewhere outside this room.

Somewhere outside herself.

"Dammit," Cutler cried roughly.

She felt his strong arms around her, then nothing more.

"Did I really sleep?"

"Yes, you did, and I'm glad. You more than needed the rest."

Cutler drew her naked body against the length of his. Once again she reveled in the secure warmth that invaded her limbs. She nestled closer. He held her tighter.

Neither spoke again for a long time.

Yet Kaylee's mind was no longer asleep. On awakening, she had been hit by the horror of the evening with the force of a sledgehammer. A precious young woman had been murdered in the prime of her life.

That just couldn't be. Only it was. Informing Barbie's parents of their senseless loss had literally sucked all the energy out of her, leaving her weak and listless. Afterward, she knew that was what had made her black out for several minutes. When she'd come to, Cutler had taken her home and put her in bed.

Quelling a cry of despair, Kaylee bit down on her lower lip.

"It's okay to cry, baby. Don't keep it bottled up."

Those gentle words of encouragement were all it took. The dam inside her broke and she sobbed until she couldn't sob anymore. All the while Cutler held her tightly.

Once she had regained control, she whispered, "Thank you for taking care of me."

"For better or for worse. Remember?"

"Well, this is the 'worse.'"

"I can handle it. It's you I'm worried about, though I know you're tough. You've already proved that."

Kaylee pulled back a bit and looked at him. His drawn features were shadowed in the lamplight. She realized the tragedy had taken its toll on him, too, if for no other reason than he was married to her.

"I refuse to believe Jessica is guilty."

"Why don't you let the police worry about that?"

"I can't. You know that. Not when the agency and the girls are my responsibility. I feel like I'm—"

"Stop it," Cutler ordered in a harsh tone. "Don't you dare go down that road. No way can you be held accountable for what those girls do. It's impossible for you, Sandy, or anyone else employed there to ride herd on them every minute."

"You're right, but maybe if I'd done something about the drugs."

"You did. You started trying to find out who was responsible."

"Do you think Jessica will be arrested?"

"I don't know. As soon as I get to the office, I'll see what the crime scene boys came up with."

"Please do, and let me know immediately."

"Meanwhile, you have to prepare yourself to deal with the media. When you arrive at the agency, they'll be all over you like mosquitoes on stale water. Count on it."

Kaylee shuddered. He drew her closer, then said, "Things are going to be crazy for a few more days, then it'll settle down. Someone else's misery will usurp yours. Trust me on that."

She realized the cynicism she heard in his voice was his

job talking. He dealt with human garbage on a day-to-day basis and was used to it.

"I hate for you to have to worry about this…me…when you have so much going on yourself."

"Hey, my shoulders are wide and strong. I can handle the load. I just want you to stand down and let the legal system work."

"I'll try, but I'm making no promises."

Cutler gave her a lopsided smile. "Now, why does that not surprise me?"

She stared at him for the longest time, feeling as though her heart might explode with love for him. Leaning in, she kissed his lips, then whispered, "Make love to me. Please. Now."

"My pleasure." He ground out the words, his lips adhering to hers in a deep hot kiss that turned her bones to mush.

When he pulled back, she surrounded his erection with her hand and began kneading it.

He groaned, then nudged her legs apart. She placed his penis at the entrance to her vagina.

He entered her with a hard, swift thrust that literally took her breath. As if he sensed that, he stopped.

"No," she whispered, digging her nails into his back. "I want to know that I'm alive. Ride me hard."

He did.

Thirty-Seven

"That son of a bitch is just asking for it."

"You okay, boss?"

Drew glared at his adviser, who was staring at him from under his overabundant eyebrows. "Do I look okay?"

"No."

"I'm about to have his head on a platter."

"Are you sure you want to mess with Cutler McFarland?"

"Shouldn't you be asking why he wants to mess with me?"

"He's the D.A., Drew."

"I don't care if he's Sir-fucking-Lancelot." Drew's tone spilled over with venom.

Glen scratched his head in perplexity. "I know you have power and friends in high places, but so does he. What's the deal with the two of you, anyway?"

"He's out to get me."

"And if we have to turn over our records, he's liable to do just that."

Drew's features contorted. "Not if you want to remain upright."

"Are you threatening me?"

"Yes," Drew said without hesitation.

"Ah, hell, Drew, get off your high horse. You know I'm on your side. Always have been and always will be. You've been good to me and my family. I'd never mess in my own playhouse."

"I'd hope you wouldn't be that stupid."

Glen's response was a sigh.

"How long do we have to get the records together?"

"Two days."

Drew cursed.

Glen lowered his overweight frame into a chair, then stretched his legs out in front of him. For some reason his casual stance raised Drew's ire even higher.

"Sit up, for chrissake," he barked.

Glen straightened as if he'd been shot. "Sorry."

"I didn't call you in here to relax."

"Whatever you tell me to do, I'll do," Glen said in a no-nonsense tone. "If you say keep 'em, I'll keep 'em."

"And get my ass hauled to jail? I don't think so."

"Your attorney wouldn't allow that."

"I'm not going to take that chance. Besides, there's really nothing in the books that will incriminate me."

"I didn't think so."

"It's just the idea that the son of a bitch is trying to nail my hide to the wall."

"You never told me why that is, either."

"It doesn't matter. The only thing that matters is that he gets nailed instead of me."

"Got any ideas how to bring that about?"

"Find me something that stinks, that I can rub his nose in."

Glen rose. "That ought to be real easy. You know how the press is. You just gotta hint that something smells foul and they take it and run with it."

"I got an idea. Talk to Winston Gilmore, his opponent. Rumor has it that they don't get along, that Gilmore has the red-ass for McFarland."

"I've heard that, as well." Glen paused, looking thoughtful. "Think it has to do with Gilmore's wife and McFarland. If I recollect, they had a thing going, which is probably what gave Gilmore that red-ass." Glen grinned. "No man likes to think about his wife humping another man, especially one whose job he's after."

"Exactly." Drew eased back in his chair, feeling a surge of renewed confidence. "All the more reason we need to put our heads together with Gilmore. I know he's not above hitting below the belt."

"I'll get on it."

Once Glen was gone, Drew swiveled his chair so that he was looking out onto the roof deck that was littered with expensive furniture and plants. If it weren't so blasted hot, he'd like to meander out there and sit, but his blood pressure was already elevated.

Thanks to his son.

Son.

He fought the urge to puke. He'd never had paternal instincts and didn't now. Most other men he knew would kill to claim a son like Cutler McFarland, who was good-looking, successful, charming. The list of assets could go on indefinitely.

Truth was, he didn't give a rat's ass. He wanted no part of Cutler or his life. The only thing Cutler had that he was remotely interested in was Kaylee. Outside of himself, she was the only person he cared about.

He didn't know why she'd gotten under his skin or even how. But he actually loved her as much as he was capable of loving anyone. Maybe it was because she had always loved him without any strings attached.

He'd been the one who had attached the strings, because he'd wanted her to need him, to want him in her life. So far, she had been the daughter he'd never had, and he didn't want to lose that human side of himself.

Now, however, his relationship with her was threatened—thanks to her relationship with McFarland.

Who would have thought they would meet, much less end up married? Of all the men in Houston, Texas, how the hell had she picked Cutler?

It was certainly one of life's freaking unexpected turns.

No matter, he had to deal with it. That was why he was having to walk a chalk line behind the scenes. He didn't want Kaylee to know he was going for her husband's jugular. Not at this point, anyway. If Cutler didn't heel soon, though, he might have to rethink the situation.

He couldn't allow Cutler to take him down and his empire with him. If it meant losing or crushing Kaylee and her father in order to preserve what he deemed sacred, he'd do it.

Maybe it wouldn't come to that, he told himself. Maybe teaming up with Gilmore would take some of the piss and vinegar out of Cutler. If not, then he'd resort to plan B. Drew chuckled with suppressed glee.

There was no doubt in his mind that his last resort would definitely bring McFarland to his knees.

"Shh, Nicole, stop crying now. It's going to be okay."

"No, it's not," the model wailed, pushing Kaylee to arm's length. "My life's never going to be okay, thanks to him."

Kaylee didn't try to put her arms around her again, even though Nicole was trembling as if she was having a hard chill. "Sit down, child, before you fall down."

For once, Nicole complied without an argument.

"Who's him, Nicole?"

Nicole looked up at Kaylee through the tears brimming in her eyes. "What?"

"You said him, that your life wouldn't be okay because of him."

"I didn't say that."

"Yes, you did. And you're not leaving this room until you tell me who `him' is."

"I can't."

"Or won't?"

"Both."

Kaylee sat beside the model on the sofa, took her hand, then spoke in a soft tone. "You can trust me. You have to know that. I only want what's best for you."

"I know," Nicole wailed again.

"Then who's abusing you, honey? Who's using you as a punching bag at will?"

Nicole lowered her head. Kaylee watched Nicole's shoulders shake with sobs. Kaylee raised her head, fighting back her own tears. But she couldn't afford to lose control. Something evil was happening to this young woman, and she would uncover it.

Today.

This minute.

"Nicole."

The model raised her head, but continued to stare straight ahead. Kaylee noted the thrust of her chin, and her heart faltered. How was she going to get Nicole to confide in her? Surely there was something she could say that would turn the tide. She just hadn't found the right combination yet.

"He's…he's a powerful man."

Kaylee sat still, her heart hammering like crazy.

"He's…he's rich, as well." Nicole paused and took a wrenching breath.

"Go on, honey." Kaylee squeezed her hand. "It'll be okay, I promise."

Nicole turned her big, fright-filled eyes on Kaylee. "Can you keep that promise?"

"I don't make promises I can't keep." God, Kaylee prayed she could put her money where her mouth was, so to speak. But then Cutler's words jumped to mind—*I'm the D.A., remember?*—and she felt her confidence return.

"Nicole, tell me his name."

Still she hesitated.

"Don't back down now," Kaylee said, trying to temper the urgency she heard in her own voice. The last thing she wanted was to spook the girl, confident she wouldn't get a second chance.

It was now or never.

Nicole licked the tears off her trembling lips, then stammered, "He's…he's a judge."

Kaylee's jaw dropped. "A judge?"

"Yes," Nicole cried, jumping up and pacing the floor.

"It's okay," Kaylee said again, rising with the use of her cane.

"How can you say that?" Nicole cried again. "If he finds out I told you, he'll hurt me real bad. He told me he'd make sure I never walked down another runway."

"His name," Kaylee demanded through tight lips, her anger reaching new proportions. "What's his name?"

"He'll pour acid in my face."

Kaylee managed to stifle a horrified cry. "He'll have to go through me first."

"Don't for one minute think he couldn't."

"His name, Nicole. You have to tell me."

"Can I whisper it?"

"If that will make you feel better."

With a terrorized look on her face, Nicole's eyes scanned the room. "It will. I'm afraid the walls have ears."

Masking her own brand of terror, Kaylee went to Nicole and placed her ear close to the model's lips. "Tell me."

"Mmm, darling, that was delicious."

"Thank you, kind sir," Kaylee said, taking a bow from her position by the cabinet.

Cutler grinned and rubbed his stomach. "I don't think I've ever tasted any better lasagna."

Kaylee gestured with a hand. "To hear you talk, you just polished off an extraordinary gourmet dinner."

Cutler rubbed his stomach again. "It's not just talk, woman, it's the truth."

"You're prejudiced, but thanks anyway."

Cutler's eyes darkened. "Come here."

"You follow me instead." Kaylee crooked a finger.

"Ah, 'into the boudoir' said the spider to the fly."

"No, into the sunroom."

Cutler's face fell. "Oh."

Kaylee laughed, but then her features turned serious. "We need to talk."

"I know," he said with equal seriousness.

After she served the coffee, they sat in silence for a long while, with Kaylee basking in the fact that despite all the troubled spots in her life, she was a happily married woman. When the walls came tumbling down around her, she knew there was haven to be found in Cutler's strong and secure arms.

This evening for sure.

"You've had a bad day, right?" Cutler asked, breaking the silence.

"No different from yours, I'm sure."

Cutler let go of a harsh breath at the same time he massaged the dark stubble on his cheek.

"If the press doesn't leave me alone," Kaylee said, "I'm going to take out a hit on them. Or at least one reporter."

Since Barbie's death, she'd been called on a daily basis, not to mention the inciting article that had run in the paper. She couldn't forget the television coverage either. Her life, her career, had been turned topsy-turvy, especially since no arrest had yet been made.

Detective Sowell had interviewed all the models and employees. So far, she'd been kept in the dark, a fact she hoped to correct.

"I know about reporters," Cutler was saying, "and what a pain in the ass they can be."

"Will you bring me up to date on the investigation?"

"The crime boys haven't found much except the weapon, and it was wiped clean."

"They're looking hard at Jessica," Kaylee responded with a frown. "But I still say she didn't do it."

"We'll see. I have someone tracking the drugs, along with the perp who sold to one or more of your girls."

"I know you're doing what you can. It's just taking so long."

"That's the name of this game, sweetheart. Gathering evidence is grunt work—tedious and boring as hell. Nothing like TV portrays it."

"In other words, I need to cool my heels and wait."

"That's about the size of it."

Kaylee sipped on her coffee, then changed the subject. "Tell me about your day in court. Do you have the evidence to convict the priest?"

"You never know. What I do know is that two controversial cases in a row are not helping my bid for reelection. The media's still crucifying me because I sent a woman suffering from postpartum to prison."

"And you're setting yourself up for that same kind of bad coverage with the priest."

"Exactly. Can't win for losing, but that's part of the job."

"Before I tell you about a conversation I had today, I'd like to ask about you and Drew."

Cutler visibly stiffened. "What about us?"

"I wish you could patch up your differences."

"That's not going to happen."

"But he's your—"

Cutler raised his hand and stopped her. "No, he's not my father. Never say that again. And I'd rather not talk about him at all, if you don't mind. Remember, we agreed to disagree. Let's leave it at that."

"I don't want to argue with you."

"Nor I with you."

She leaned over and gave him a long, hot kiss.

His eyes darkened and he reached for her. She pulled away. "Not yet."

"You've become a little tease."

She sat down across the room. "I found out who's been abusing Nicole."

"That's good news. I've had Angel working on her background."

"You can call him off."

"It's the boyfriend after all, huh?"

"Nope."

"Okay, you've got my attention. Who is it?"

"A judge."

Cutler went visibly still. "Did you get a name?"

"Sure did. The Honorable Judge James Jenkins."

Thirty-Eight

Nah, Cutler thought, the building's not high enough. If he jumped it wouldn't kill him, it would just maim him and that wasn't an alternative. Then he muttered several expletives. He ought to be ashamed of himself for thinking such a morbid thought.

Granted, he was *stressed* and *stretched* to the max, but he was also happier and more content than he'd ever been in his life. Thanks to Kaylee. Who would ever have thought he'd adjust to married life when that had never been on his dance card?

Although it still stuck in his craw that he'd been bribed into doing something that went against the very fiber of his being, he had no complaints, which absolutely boggled his mind when he thought about it. Such as now.

Maybe an inner mellowness that had heretofore been totally foreign to him was the glue now holding him together, compliments of Kaylee.

She was truly one special woman. Despite her handicaps, she never whined or held pity parties. Perhaps she had in the past, but he seriously doubted that. She was strong, kind, genteel and lovely. The list of assets could go on and on.

Yet she had spunk, too. And she could be as stubborn as hell. When it came to Drew, he considered her stubbornness a minus. But in all fairness to her, Kaylee wasn't privy to the rest of the story and he could never tell her.

Still, it concerned him that Drew would eventually cause problems between them, problems that might not be resolvable. He wouldn't think about that right now. Not until he had the evidence to arrest Drew's ass, that is.

When, not *if,* that happened, he suspected their relationship would really be tested. For now, though, he intended to make the most of their time together and let the chips fall where they may.

He had lived that way his entire adult life and he saw no reason to change now.

His phone buzzed. It was his mother. "Hey, it's good to hear from you."

"I'm calling to see if your finger's broken."

Cutler didn't pretend to misunderstand. Chuckling, he said, "Not the last time I checked."

"That's good news."

"So how are you, Mother?"

"Worried about you."

"That's a waste of time and energy," he said in a semi-scolding tone.

"Probably, but that's what mothers do."

He sighed. "I worry about you, too."

Silence.

"Have you had a change of heart about Drew?"

He heard the hesitancy in her voice and knew how hard

it was for her to even speak his name. More than likely she felt violated all over again. And he felt his blood boil all over again. He wished he could lie to her, but he couldn't. Besides, she'd see right through him. That was another "mother thing."

"No, I haven't."

Another silence.

"We need to talk, son."

"We've already talked."

"So we need to talk again."

She wasn't about to cut him any slack. That was her way of doing things, so it was no use arguing. But he had to try, for both their sakes. Continuing to talk about Drew kept the wound festering.

He dreaded the moment he'd have to tell her he'd arrested Drew. And that moment *would* come. He just couldn't pinpoint when.

"There's nothing left to say, Mom."

"I don't want what happened to me to poison your life, Cutler. I couldn't live with that."

He curbed his impatience. "Let's don't go down that road again, Mother, please. That bastard's—"

"Cutler—"

"Sorry. Look, this is not something we should discuss over the phone."

"Then come see me."

"I will. As soon as I can. I promise."

"I guess I'll have to be content with that."

He didn't say anything.

"How is Kaylee? I've been so distraught over that girl getting murdered."

"It's been tough on her."

"Both of your lives have certainly been turned bottom side up. I'm just grateful you have each other."

"Me, too, Mom."

"I'll see you soon," Mary said, following another short silence. "And I love you."

"I love you, too."

Once the receiver was back in place, Cutler dropped his head in his hands, feeling as if the walls were caving in on him. Then he straightened and mentally pulled himself up by the bootstraps.

"You rang?"

Cutler looked up with a start. Angel was standing in the doorway.

"We got the bastard," the investigator said with blunt enthusiasm.

Cutler motioned him in.

Angel gave Cutler the thumbs-up sign. "Oh, the sweet, sweet taste of victory."

"Are you sure you're not celebrating prematurely? Until Nicole Reed actually testifies, we don't have the bastard."

"Now that we've found Andrews and his sister, it'd be nice if she would reinforce the Reed girl." Angel paused with a grim sigh. "So far, though, Peggy Trent flat refuses."

"Think I might change her mind?"

Angel rubbed the beginnings of a beard. "You want a shot at her?"

"Not if it won't do any good."

"I don't know. Andrews says he's been working on her, but he hasn't been able to budge her either."

Cutler muttered an expletive, then said, "Jenkins is the lowest of scum in my book, and I have a full book. He uses his power to prey on the innocent and the weak."

"The vulnerable, as well."

Cutler's mouth stretched into a thin line. "I'm going to take delight in de-nutting that piece of garbage."

"Want me to tell Snelling to pick him up?"

"ASAP."

Angel grinned, shooting another thumbs-up. "Consider it done, and with great joy."

Cutler answered his grin, but it was short-lived as Detective Sowell stuck his head around the door. "Just thought you'd like to know we're about to arrest Jessica Riley."

Cutler stiffened. "You find something?"

"Nope. But we've had less and gotten a conviction."

"Need I point out, Sowell, that you're not the prosecutor?"

"Trust me, I'm aware of that." Sowell nodded toward Angel. "He's seen what we have. Maybe you'll take his word for it."

"I think we're good to go, Cutler," Angel said with an almost guilty look on his face.

Cutler let an expletive fly, then reached for the phone, his thoughts on Kaylee. He felt it only fair that he give her the heads up.

"Are you feeling okay?"

"No, San, I'm not," Kaylee said with unusual candor, surprising even herself.

"You sick to your tummy?"

"How did you know?"

"You've been looking kind of green around the gills lately."

Kaylee gave her a look. "In English that means I look like hell."

"No, it simply means you look green."

"Whatever."

"You could go to the doctor," Sandy said in a matter-of-fact tone. "Has that occurred to you?"

"I despise doctors."

"Considering your history, I can understand that, but—"

"I should go anyway."

"Right."

"Rest easy. I have an appointment this afternoon. It's my nerves. I can tell you that."

"Wouldn't surprise me," Sandy replied, indicating Kaylee should come in and sit down.

"Let's go back to my office. That way I don't have to balance all those folders."

Sandy got up immediately and followed Kaylee. Soon they were poring over a stack of new portfolios.

Finally they looked up and shook their heads simultaneously.

"Not a promising one in the bunch," Kaylee said, her mouth turned down.

"And that's a shame, too." Sandy pushed the last of the folders aside.

"At the moment we don't have to worry about adding more girls." Kaylee pinched the bridge of her nose. "Since the jobs aren't happening."

"Hey, lighten up. Things will take a turn for the better soon."

"Not until they find out who...who killed Barbie." Kaylee shuddered, drawing her arms around her. A week after the fact she still couldn't believe what had happened. The incident had surely impacted her life as much as her accident, only in a different way.

"I can't believe it, either," Sandy said.

"Am I that easy to read?"

"Not usually, but Barbie's center front in my mind, too."

"It's put a dark cloud over this agency and everyone who works here. And I'm not sure the atmosphere will ever be the same."

"It probably won't, but that doesn't mean things won't be good again."

"I hope you're right." Kaylee paused. "Jessica wants to come back to work. I have to decide if I'm going to let her."

"I wish I could make that call for you, but I can't."

"I wouldn't let you even if you could," Kaylee said. "That's something only I can do."

"I know you don't want to talk about it, but it still blows my mind to think that one of our girls could kill in cold blood for packets of pills, for crying out loud." Sandy blew out a breath of frustration.

"I'm having difficulty with that scenario, too, but then we've never been addicted to drugs."

"And I wouldn't have thought any of our girls were either."

"I know, San. This whole thing blows my mind, too. I still wake up at night in a cold sweat, much like I did after my accident."

Sandy reached over and covered Kaylee's hand with one of hers. "I hate this for you. Thank God you've got Cutler."

Kaylee smiled. "He's still my rock."

"You told me he was overseeing the investigation, so has he said anything about where the girls got the drugs?"

"I don't think they, meaning the detectives, have tracked down the source yet. I'll ask for an update this evening."

About that time, her cell rang. She smiled and said, "It's Cutler now." After answering, she listened, feeling the color slowly recede from her face. When she'd flipped her cell closed, she stared at her assistant.

"What?" Sandy asked, clearly panicked.

"Detective Sowell is about to arrest Jessica for Barbie's murder."

The heat was oppressive, so oppressive that Kaylee dreaded stepping outside. She had no choice, however, as she was due at the doctor's office shortly.

Good thing, too, she told herself, as her stomach was not in good shape. She hadn't let on just how bad she felt, because she had just finished having lunch with her daddy and Drew. She'd had the luncheon date for two days and hated to cancel, knowing she would have disappointed them both.

"Honey, are you all right?" Edgar had asked after they'd walked to the door of the deli.

"I'm fine, Dad. I'm just tired."

"I can understand that," he said, "considering what you've been through."

She turned to Drew. "Thanks so much for lunch."

"You're welcome, honey. I just wanted you to know that I'm behind you one hundred percent and that good things will come your way again." He kissed her on the cheek. "Your uncle Drew will see to that."

She hugged him closely, feeling tears prick her eyes. "You're too good to me."

"Not near as good as I'd like to be."

Kaylee turned to her daddy and hugged him. "I'll talk to you soon."

Now, thirty minutes later, she sat in the doctor's office. He was running behind, which didn't exactly sit well with her. But now that she was here, she decided to stay, though patience was not her strong suit. Idleness gave her too much time to think. The thought of Jessica in police custody added to her nausea.

The fact that she'd had lunch with Drew and hadn't told Cutler didn't help the situation either. She shouldn't feel guilty, but for some reason she did. What a mess. She loved both men and couldn't bear the thought of losing either.

Suddenly Kaylee lowered her head into her hands, feeling totally overwhelmed. This time in her life would pass, too, she kept telling herself. She had gone through tougher times than this and survived. But she was tired of survival mode. She wanted life to get back on an even keel and stay there.

People in hell wanted ice water, too, and didn't get it.

"Mrs. McFarland, the doctor will see you now."

Following a detailed examination and having given what seemed like a quart of her blood, not to mention answering countless questions, Kaylee was finally free to dress and was waiting in the doctor's office.

As soon as he walked in a short time later, she smiled and asked, "What's the verdict, Dr. Hayden? Am I going to live?"

"With good reason, too."

Kaylee didn't know quite how to take those words and said as much. "That's a strange thing to say, Richard."

"Not if you're pregnant."

Kaylee's mouth dropped open and the room spun for a second. "Pregnant? That's impossible."

He gave her a wide grin. "Oh, it's more than possible, my dear. It's a fact. You're going to have a baby."

Thirty-Nine

D.A. Bungles Case

The article underneath the headline bluntly accused Cutler of gross negligence in the trial of Cullen Bryant, who was now scheduled to be retried. The writer went on to say that McFarland had refused to consider a witness's statement when he first presented the case, a witness that the opposing counsel was now confident would exonerate their client. Adding insult to injury was the condemnation of the family, who blamed Cutler for their loved one spending ten years on death row for a crime he didn't commit.

"Oh, Cutler, how awful."

After Kaylee spoke, she stared at her husband from across the breakfast table, her heart hurting for him. When she picked up the paper each day, she always gave the front page a cursory glance. Rarely did she pay attention to detail. This morning, however, the headlines had reached out and slapped her in the face.

She had considered withholding the paper, but that wouldn't have been right or fair. Besides, he'd find out about it as soon as he reached the courthouse. Deciding it was better that he air out his frustrations at home with her, she had brought the paper to the table, only to place it on the floor beside her chair.

She hadn't handed it to him until they had finished breakfast, followed by several cups of coffee. She had learned that her husband was a bear until he got his caffeine fix for the day.

Before she'd looked at the headlines, she had considered sharing her news. Last evening he had been so tired, so distracted, she hadn't wanted to tell him.

She was determined to make the occasion special, with candlelight, flowers, the whole nine yards. To be honest, she had wanted to hold her news close to her heart for a while longer, until *she* could come to grips with the phenomenon.

Kaylee remained in a state of shock, albeit a wonderful state. She was going to have a baby. All the way home yesterday, despite all the present upheaval in her life, she had giggled and pinched herself.

As to Cutler's reaction, she had no clue. At times she felt he'd be ecstatic, while at other times she wasn't so sure.

Now this—this horrible and upsetting turn of events.

"Son of a bitch," Cutler spat out, tossing the paper onto the floor.

Kaylee knew he was about to choke on his rage. "I'm so sorry, darling. I know this couldn't have come at a worse time."

"There's never a good time for this kind of adverse publicity, especially when it's a setup."

"Who would deliberately—" She broke off, realizing how incredibly naive she sounded. He was in a political dog fight—the dirtier the better.

"Gilmore and Rush."

She blinked. "Drew?"

"Yes, Drew." Cutler's tone was low and harsh.

"You mean they would team up against you?" She heard the incredulity in her voice.

Cutler laughed a heartless laugh. "In a freakin' minute."

"Do you have proof of Drew's involvement?"

"Yeah." Cutler placed his hand on his belly. "Right here in my gut."

Kaylee grappled to accept such an outlandish explanation. She didn't think for a minute that Drew would stoop that low. Gilmore, yes. After all, he wanted to win the election and backing such an inflammatory article would definitely benefit him.

But Drew? No way.

"I think you're way off base," she said.

Cutler's eyes narrowed on her. "You just don't get it, do you?"

"I get it, all right," she responded in a tight voice, taking umbrage at his question and his tone.

He made an impatient gesture with his hand, then looked away.

Both infuriated her. How dare he treat her like an irritating child with whom he had no patience? "I get that where Drew's concerned, you've got your stinger out for him."

"For good reasons."

"Which brings me back to my original question—do you have proof?"

Cutler's gaze leveled on hers. "If I did, would you believe me?"

"I guess I wouldn't have any choice."

"You guess." His features twisted. "That's not exactly what I wanted to hear."

"Look, like I've said before, I don't want to fight with you about Drew. I know what a blow it was when you found out he's your father, but—"

"That has nothing to do with the fact he and his company are dirty or that he's trying to bury me politically."

"It has everything to do with it," she countered hotly. "Even though I don't know the details or the circumstances surrounding your birth, and don't want to," she added hurriedly, "your animosity toward Drew goes too deep for it to be just job related."

"I need to get to the office," Cutler said, standing abruptly.

"It's going to be okay," she said with feeling.

"I know. Somehow we'll get through this. Both of us."

"Ah, both of us." She forced a smile, desperately trying to put things back on track. "That has such a nice ring to it."

"This has nothing to do with you, Kaylee."

"Yet it has everything to do with me," she reminded him with a slight catch in her voice, knowing they were perilously close to a danger point in their marriage.

As if Cutler sensed that as well, he suddenly looked weary, gaunt and almost defeated. She'd never seen him quite like that.

Her heart turned over and she longed to reach out to him and tell him that everything was going to be just fine. But she couldn't do that; nothing might ever be the same again. While that thought terrorized her, she knew it to be true.

Sudden frustration darkened his eyes. "I have to go, especially now that I have to deal with the fallout from that trash in the paper."

"I don't want you to leave mad."

His gaze softened on her for a moment. "I'm not mad, certainly not at you."

Kaylee got up, went to him, looped her arms around his neck and kissed him deeply. His tongue played tag with hers for the longest time, then he pushed her back, his breathing labored.

"If you aren't careful," he said in an unnatural-sounding voice, "you'll get something started you can't finish."

She pulled back and gave him a saucy grin. "Who says I can't finish it?"

He chuckled as he swatted her playfully on the rear. "Tonight. I'll collect on that promise tonight."

Her eyebrows moved up and down. "Maybe I'll be out of the mood by then."

"Not to worry," he said with conviction. "I'll fix that."

"Go on, get out of here." Then Kaylee sobered as she walked him to the door. "I've hired a lawyer to get Jessica out on bail."

"Don't get your hopes up too high. The judge may not grant it."

"Are you going to fight it?"

"No."

Kaylee released a sigh of relief. "Thank you."

He flicked her on the chin. "Don't thank me yet. I'm hoping to review the evidence today. I'll let you know how strong our case is."

"Fair enough." She kissed him as he walked out the door.

* * *

"We picked up the judge."

"Kicking and screaming, I would imagine."

Mike and Angel had been waiting for him in his office when he arrived. He'd barely set his briefcase down on his desk before the chief of detectives had given him the news.

"And use of some words I haven't heard in a long time," Snelling added.

Cutler smiled, as did Angel.

"I just hope the Reed girl doesn't get cold feet."

"She won't," Cutler said, sitting. "I was a bit concerned myself at first, but I think she's made the commitment."

"Even as we speak, she's being interviewed," Snelling said.

"It won't be long until the good judge is behind bars." Cutler gave a thumbs-up. "Equal justice couldn't happen to a more deserving fellow."

"I couldn't agree more," Snelling said. "And by the way, McFarland, I owe you an apology."

Cutler's eyebrows shot up. Snelling apologize? Not something he thought he'd ever hear. But hey, miracles happen. His marriage to Kaylee bore testimony to that. Forcing his mind back on matters at hand, he asked, "How's that?"

"Jenkins. I didn't think you'd get the bastard, but you did."

"Coming from you, Snelling, I'll take that as a compliment."

Snelling's face reddened, but he didn't respond.

Cutler, however, knew what he was thinking and said as much. "Don't worry, I'm not about to get the idea that you like me."

Snelling's color deepened, but again he refrained from saying anything.

"Look, I'm in a pissy mood this morning," Cutler said by way of easing the tension in the room. "But then I think I've earned the right."

Mike and Angel looked at each other, then back to him.

"The paper. Apparently you haven't seen the headlines." Cutler reached into his case, took out the newspaper, then pitched it to them.

Following moments of silence, Angel muttered an expletive. Mike whistled under his breath. Both looked back at him.

"Gilmore," Angel said without a question mark.

"I'm thinking he had help." Cutler's features were grim. "Drew Rush."

"Wouldn't doubt it," Mike injected. "Talk about pissed off. When Rush handed over his records, I thought he was going to have a coronary."

"If that pissed him off," Angel chimed in, "just wait until he finds out we have someone who's willing to testify against him."

Cutler's mouth went slack.

"Who?" Mike asked, narrowing his eyes on the investigator. "Why haven't I been told?"

"One question at a time," Angel said, obviously reveling in the attention he was getting.

Cutler glared at him. "Out with it."

"He's an ex-employee of Drew's. And to make a long story short for now, they got crossways somehow and the man saved some recorded messages. He figured they might come in handy in case he wanted to blackmail Rush."

"Do you have the tapes?" Cutler asked, feeling a new rush of adrenaline.

"Not yet. Tommy Evans is his name. Said he needed more time. I have no choice but to wait him out."

Mike Snelling looked at his watch, then rose. "If there's nothing else, I have a meeting. Keep me informed."

"You keep me informed on the judge," Cutler said.

Snelling nodded, then left.

The door had barely clicked behind the chief before Angel turned to Cutler and said, "I think I'm being followed."

Cutler's forehead furrowed. "You? By who?"

"I don't know."

"That smacks of something Rush would do," Cutler said. "Not that he'd actually follow you. He's the type who hires someone to do his dirty work."

"You think he's got the balls for that?"

"Sure do."

Angel scratched his head and at the same time peered closely at Cutler. "What's with you and Rush? My gut tells me it's something personal with you."

Cutler hesitated, but only for a moment. He should've told Angel a portion of the truth shortly after the fact. Sooner or later he'd hear it from another source. Cutler didn't want that. "Your gut's right. The bastard's my birth father."

Angel looked as if he'd just been sucker punched.

"Don't ask me any of the details, because I'm not going to tell you. Out of respect for my mother." Cutler paused with a grimace. "But there's nothing good about it. I will say that."

Angel shook his head as though to clear it. "Man, I don't know what I expected you to say, but it sure wasn't that."

"Keep it to yourself," Cutler muttered.

"That goes without saying."

A short silence ensued, then Cutler asked, "Did you get a look at the person you think is following you?"

"Sort of. Remember the key word here is *think*."

"Hell, Angel, your gut remains alive and well. If you think you're being tailed, you are."

"If Rush is behind it, then he got wind I talked to Tommy Evans."

"That would be my guess."

"What do you think he'll do?" Angel asked.

Cutler thought for a moment. "Hire the smartest team of lawyers to get his ass out of the crack."

"We need to pick him up."

"Not until we have enough to make the charges stick."

Angel gave Cutler a pointed look. "This could get a whole lot nastier than it is now."

"Maybe not. If Rush and Gilmore are indeed in cahoots, then perhaps they've accomplished their goal. That article may very well sink my ship."

The room fell silent.

Drew Rush didn't bother to suppress his fury.

How dare that bastard try to best him? The fact that the newspaper article had the power to sink Cutler's political career was of little consequence to Drew now.

If the D.A. was bound and determined to bring down his empire, despite the countless warnings, then let the games begin, Drew told himself. He paused in his heated thoughts and peered at his watch. Glen was due back at any moment with his report.

Meanwhile Drew couldn't settle down, and that in itself irked him. He had two deals that were just about to jell and they needed his undivided attention. But no, that bastard son of his was wreaking havoc with his life's blood.

Dammit, he'd worked his ass off to get where he was and no one was going to do an end run on him and get away with it. Least of all someone who was of his own blood.

A knock on the door interrupted his thoughts.

"It's open."

Glen Yates came in and without mincing words said, "You're right. McFarland's office has talked to Tommy Evans."

Drew's insides coiled.

"Tell me what you want me to do, boss, and I'll do it."

"For now, leave me alone."

Drew wasn't far behind his exiting assistant. He should've gone to plan B from the get-go. The idea that he might be getting soft in his old age made him cringe. Then he brightened. Actually, the timing might be even better, he thought with a sense of relief as he made his way to his vehicle.

Thirty minutes later he turned into the driveway of the home of the head elder in Mary McFarland's church.

He grinned a huge grin. Then he let the fireworks begin.

Forty

Her body was tingly and hot. So hot, she thrashed on the bed. Trying to pinpoint the cause, Kaylee opened her eyes and realized the origin of that wonderful sensation pelting her.

Cutler had her legs spread and his tongue was working its magic. What a way to wake up and start a day, having the man you love *make love* to you as if you were a precious piece of china.

Kaylee moaned again, sinking her fingers into his hair.

As though he sensed she was on the cusp of an orgasm, his efforts intensified. Instantly her cries of pleasure filled the air.

"It's your turn," Kaylee murmured when she could find her voice. Reaching for his erection, she guided it to the wet, pulsating entrance of her vagina.

Without taking his glazed eyes off her, Cutler drove into her, then rode her long and deep until they both were hurtled into hard orgasms.

A while later she lay nestled against his warm chest, his

arm tightly around her. He was the first to rouse enough to speak. "So we're going to have a baby?"

Kaylee had told him the news earlier that evening following a candlelight dinner. Instead of answering him right away, she let her mind wander back to that heady time.

"What's with all the trappings?" he'd asked, staring at her from across the beautifully decorated dining-room table. "Are you trying to make us forget what a shitty week we've had?"

"Partially."

He'd smiled and gotten up and come around her chair, where he'd kissed her softly on the lips. "Let's continue this conversation in the living room." Moments later they were settled in the comfortable room.

"Well, for whatever reason you fed me so royally, I enjoyed the hell out of it. For the first time in a long while my gut is unkinked."

"Mine, too."

He kissed her again, this time on the end of her nose. "You're more beautiful tonight than I think I've ever seen you. In fact, you're glowing."

"That's because I have something to tell you."

"Oh?"

She smiled. "Something special."

"Ah, that sounds intriguing."

"Want to guess?"

"New York's tapped you for another show."

She gave him an incredulous look. "After that last fiasco, you've got to be kidding."

"Not in the least. In spite of the tragedy, they were pleased with your efforts. Remember, they told you that you'd done an outstanding job."

"That's what Emily Austin said, but I didn't…don't believe a word of it."

"They'll be knocking again. You just wait and see if I'm not right."

"I'm not about to hold my breath. You can count on that."

"So what's your news?"

Now that she was about to divulge her heretofore closely guarded secret, she felt a rush of panic. What if he…

"Kaylee?"

She pulled away so that she could look him directly in the eye. Not only did she want to hear his reaction, she wanted to see it in his eyes. More often than not, the eyes spoke louder than the mouth.

"I'm pregnant, Cutler."

He sucked in his breath and stared at her wide-eyed. "Pregnant," he repeated as though he hadn't heard her correctly. "Did you say pregnant?"

"That's exactly what I said."

"But how? I mean—" He broke off abruptly.

Her lips twitched. "The how should be a no-brainer."

As if he realized what he'd said, Cutler grinned, but that grin was short-lived. His face turned gravely serious. "I didn't think you…you could have a baby."

"Me, either."

Words failed him.

"How do you feel about a baby, Cutler?" she asked in a soft, uncertain voice.

"I don't know." He looked dazed, as if she'd just punched him in the solar plexus. "I mean, I'm so shocked because I never thought it was possible."

Kaylee got off the sofa and turned her back to him, feeling a squeeze on her heart. You can get through this, she told herself. Consider it just another bump in the hard and wounding path that's been your life.

Suddenly she felt his hands on her shoulders. She stiffened.

"Hey," he said, his hot breath caressing her ears, "don't think for one moment that I'm not delighted about the baby."

She looked back at him, knowing her heart was in her eyes and not caring. "You're not sorry?"

"Oh, sweetheart, how could you think that?" His lips touched her forehead, her cheeks, then her mouth. "Surprised, yes. Sorry, no. God, no."

She wilted against him, and to her dismay began sobbing.

"Shh," he said over and over. "Don't cry. This is truly a blessed day."

He was holding her so close that she had trouble breathing. She didn't care. The fact that he wanted the baby was all that mattered. The other loose ends in their life would fall into place, or they wouldn't.

"It's time to celebrate," he whispered into the silence.

He'd lifted her into his arms and carted her off to bed and made love to her off and on all night and again this morning.

"Darling, I asked you a question."

Kaylee jerked her mind back to the moment at hand. "Yes, we're going to have a baby."

"I didn't dream it, then?"

"No, you didn't dream it," she responded with a smile.

"So how long have you known?"

"A couple of days."

His brows furrowed. "And you're just now telling me?"

"I had to get used to the idea myself. In fact, I couldn't believe it either. Still can't."

"You're okay, right? You and the baby both are okay?"

"Dr. Hayden said I'm in great health and he saw no problem with me carrying the baby. He advised me not to gain too much weight because of the pressure on my leg. Otherwise, he sees no problem."

"Thank God," Cutler muttered, continuing to stare at her with that look of awe.

"I'm so relieved you're okay with this."

"You really doubted that?"

"Yes, I did," she said honestly. "Babies are a real commitment and responsibility and I simply didn't know how you'd react, especially to more responsibility."

"Well, now you know," he said with a tender grin, followed by a kiss that led to much better things.

"You take it easy today, you hear?"

Kaylee pecked Cutler on the cheek. "Hey, don't start treating me like I'm breakable, because I'm not."

"But you are under a lot of stress at the agency right now."

"No more than you," Kaylee countered.

"But I'm not pregnant."

She grinned, then pinched him on the cheek. "Think again. This is your party, too."

He laughed out loud. "Touché."

Suddenly Cutler's cell rang. "McFarland."

The second after he flipped his cell closed, Kaylee asked, "What's wrong?"

"I'm not sure. That was Mother. She wants to talk to me."

"She didn't say what about?"

He shook his head. "I know her and whatever it is, I don't think it's good."

"Maybe you're just imagining things."

"Maybe so."

"Let me know."

He kissed her briefly. "I'll talk to you later and see you this evening."

Kaylee arrived home much earlier than planned. But she'd had no choice. It was as though her body simply refused to cooperate any longer. She had told Sandy that it had shut down.

"Go home and go to sleep," Sandy had ordered.

Kaylee had told her assistant that morning that she was pregnant.

Following a bout of laughing and hugging, they had finally settled down and gotten some quality work done, though a shadow continued to hover over the agency as a result of Barbie's murder, Jessica's arrest and Nicole's dilemma.

Perhaps that was why she had used up what little energy she had so early. Now that she was home and had changed into something comfortable, she already felt better.

She hadn't heard from Cutler all day. She had tried to call him on his cell, but he hadn't returned her calls, which was not like him. Most likely he'd just gotten tied up in court.

If something serious had been wrong with Mary, he would've called. She just wished he'd get in touch with her or come home. As if her fairy godmother was looking out for her, the utility-room door opened and in walked Cutler.

She was halfway to him when she pulled up short, her hand going to her chest. "Cutler, my God, what happened?"

His face didn't have an ounce of color in it. His lips were twisted into a thin, bitter line. Even though she wasn't within touching distance of him, she knew he'd been drinking. The strong smell of alcohol assaulted her senses.

She tried to squash the burgeoning panic inside her by breathing deeply.

"When I find him I'm going to kill the bastard."

"Cutler, what are you talking about? *Who* are you talking about?"

"Rush, that's who."

"Drew?"

"Yes, Drew," he lashed back.

She reeled against the venom in his tone and in his eyes. "What's happened now?"

"He crucified my mother."

"How could he do that? He has nothing to do with Mary anymore."

"He's using her to get to me. Because our office has the goods on him and he knows an arrest is imminent, he went to one of the elders in Mother's church."

"Maybe there was another reason for the visit. You can't know what was said. Why not talk to Drew?"

Cutler's features contorted. "I don't want to be anywhere near that bastard."

"If only you'd get to know him."

"Get to know him?" Cutler laughed an acid laugh. "That's the joke of the century. How you can continue to defend that lowlife scumbag is beyond me."

Kaylee flinched under his choice of words and the harshness of his tone. Yet she refused to back down. This time Cutler was way out of line. "The Drew I know is a good man."

"He raped my mother, for chrissake." He strode up to her. "Now do you still think he's a good man?"

Kaylee stumbled back. "I...I don't believe that."

"Are you calling my mother a liar?"

"Of course not," she cried. "You're putting words in my mouth."

"Your father got screwed." Cutler shook his head. "*We* got screwed."

Kaylee blanched. "My father? What does he have to do with any of this?"

Cutler didn't answer. Instead he continued to stare off into space as if she hadn't spoken.

"Cutler," she demanded, grabbing his arm and turning him around, "answer me."

"It was all for nothing," he muttered, staring at her out of unseeing eyes. "All for nothing."

"Cutler, please, you're scaring me. You're not making any sense."

He stared at her for the longest time with the saddest look on his face. Her heart climbed into the back of her throat, rendering her speechless.

"Look, I gotta go. I gotta be by myself and think."

With that, he turned and walked back out the way he'd come in, slamming the door behind him. Kaylee didn't, *couldn't* move long after she heard his car leave.

Finally she crumpled to the floor and sobbed.

Forty-One

"Come on in, honey. What a nice surprise."

Kaylee practically pushed her way inside the door, then pulled up short. "Are you alone?"

A flush stained Edgar's face. "Of course. Why would you think otherwise?"

"Never mind."

"Rebecca and I don't live together," her father added in a rather huffy tone.

Kaylee didn't bother to acknowledge that declaration, knowing it would take the conversation in an altogether different direction. She didn't want that. She had come on a mission, and she had no intention of letting anything or anyone distract her.

"Sit down, and I'll get us some coffee."

Kaylee shook her head. The thought of coffee made her want to throw up. But then the thought of anything in her stomach made her feel the same way. "I have to talk to you."

"Honey, what's so urgent that you're out at seven o'clock in the morning?"

"Sit down, Dad."

His frown intensified. "Where's Cutler?"

"He didn't come home last night."

Edgar gasped. "What the hell—"

"I don't know. That's why I'm here."

A veil seemed to descend over Edgar's face with her looking right at him. The fear that had been growing inside her climbed to a fever pitch. The room suddenly spun.

"Dammit, Kaylee, don't you dare pass out on me."

She took several gulping breaths and the room righted. "I'm not going to. I'm all right."

"Like hell you are," Edgar responded. "Whether you like it or not, I'm going to get you something to drink."

"A Coke, then."

Once he'd walked out of the room, Kaylee fought back tears. If she didn't get control of her splattered emotions, she wouldn't make it through this encounter.

Moments later Edgar returned with a glass of iced Coke and a cup of coffee. He handed her the glass. She took a sip and sat down.

"Are you and Cutler at odds, honey?"

"I guess you might say that."

"What's going on?"

"I was hoping *you* could tell *me*."

While Edgar looked taken aback, Kaylee noticed that he shifted his gaze and that his hand shook slightly as he sipped on his coffee.

"Me?" He set his cup down. "Why ask me?"

Kaylee leaned her head sideways, her eyes delving into his. "Because of something Cutler said."

Edgar stood and turned his back. Her fear continued to

mount. When she had come here, she'd told herself she was nuts, that Cutler had simply spouted empty words. Now she wasn't so sure. Something was definitely not right.

Instead of confronting her father, this visit should be a joyous occasion. She should be telling him that he was finally going to have the grandchild he'd always wanted.

"Dad, look at me."

Edgar turned around, though she sensed he did so reluctantly. His face appeared carved out of concrete. "What did Cutler say?"

His voice told the rest of the story. She could taste her fear. "To quote, 'Your father got screwed. *We* got screwed.'"

"Is that all he said?"

"No. He said it was all for nothing."

"He didn't explain that?"

"No. He just left."

Edgar rubbed his forehead, then blew out a harsh breath. "I hate that you two are quarreling."

"Daddy, stop playing games."

"What do you want from me?"

"The truth," she said in a hard but quivering voice.

Edgar opened his mouth and then slammed it shut, looking suddenly panicked, as if someone had a gun to his head and was about to pull the trigger.

"Kaylee—"

"The truth, Daddy. Now. Did you have anything to do with Cutler marrying me?"

He flinched visibly, as if she had just pulled that trigger and shot him through the head.

"You've never lied to me. Please don't start now."

"It's not that simple, honey."

"Don't honey me, damn you. Did you have anything to do with Cutler marrying me?"

He flinched again as hurt filled his eyes. "You're happy, aren't you?"

"Daddy!" she cried, then, bending over, grabbed her stomach.

With the speed of lightning he crossed to her and knelt beside her. "Are you ill?"

"If you don't want me to lose my baby, you'd better answer my question."

"You're...you're pregnant," he said in an awed voice.

"But maybe not for long." She bit the words out tersely.

His eyes widened while a myriad of emotions stampeded across his face, some she could read and some she couldn't.

"I never intended for you to know this, Kaylee. But yes, I asked Cutler to marry you."

"*Asked?* Or bribed?"

"Okay, bribed, dammit."

"With...with what?" she managed to stammer, hanging on to her control by a mere thread.

Edgar blurted out about finding Cutler's birth certificate and parental termination papers in Drew's safe.

"Why?" That word was a plaintive cry. "That doesn't explain why Cutler would—" Sobs clogged her throat and she couldn't go on.

"Oh, God, honey, don't do this."

"Answer me," she cried again.

"I told Cutler I'd use this information against his mother."

Hot searing pain robbed Kaylee of her next breath; she felt the room spin again.

"I know you perceive what I did as the ultimate betrayal." Edgar's words seemed to tumble over each other in his effort to get them out fast enough. "On the contrary, I did what I did out of love for you." His eyes were pleading. "You have to believe that."

Kaylee couldn't say anything. With tragic clarity her worst fear had come to fruition. She had always known a man could never love her as she was or for whom she was, especially a man like Cutler. And she'd been right.

Their marriage had been a sham from the beginning and still was.

Edgar reached out to her. "Kaylee, please."

By sheer force of will she rose, then stumbled back. "How could you? How could you?"

Then she turned and walked out.

Somehow she reached her vehicle, and with tears drenching her face she cranked the engine and drove off, feeling as if her heart had been ripped from her chest and stomped.

This time Kaylee wasn't sure she would ever recover.

"Son, you look awful."

Ignoring her words, Cutler asked, "How are you?"

"Come here," Mary said in a tender voice, patting the cushion beside her.

Cutler sat down, and she took his hands. For the longest time they sat in silence. Then Mary looked him straight in the eye and said, "Let it go, son. It's not worth it."

"I can't, Mother," he said harshly. "There's too much water under the bridge. I'm drowning."

She tightened her hold. "No matter. You can still let it go."

"Because of me, you're going to lose your pastorate."

"I don't think I am. But even if I do, I can and will survive."

"If I had left Drew alone—"

"He broke the law. You had no choice but to arrest him."

"But look at the price."

"I have a loving and forgiving congregation. I'm going to be fine." She raised his hand and kissed the back of it. "I'm sorry I told you that Drew went to an elder."

"You couldn't have kept that a secret."

"That's why I told you. But what I didn't tell you, because you didn't give me a chance, is that I lost my appetite for vengeance long ago. I'm begging you to do the same. I've chosen to be blessed rather than bitter."

"Oh, Mom, I've done something awful, something I probably can't ever fix."

"Does it have to do with Kaylee?"

"How did you know?"

"A mother thing."

"I let my mouth overload my ass."

If she was shocked by his words, she didn't show it. Instead she asked, "What happened?"

He told her everything, from the time Edgar had walked into his office until now. "And in a fit of anger and need to get even, I all but told her our marriage was a sham."

"And is it?"

"God, no."

"Do you love her?"

He didn't even have to think. "Yes, more than life itself."

"Have you told her that?"

"No," he said in a strained, harsh voice.

"Don't you think it's time you did?"

He didn't say anything for a moment.

"Cutler?"

"It's way past time," he said.

"Then what are you waiting for?"

He leaned over, hugged her, then whispered, "Thank you, Grandma."

She ignored Cutler's string of expletives. She stilled herself against even the sound of his voice.

"Kaylee, let me in. Please."

Silence.

"Please, open the door. I'm begging you."

She remained unmoving in a fetal position on the sofa, trying to pretend he wasn't there. Thank goodness she'd had the locks changed so he couldn't get in. She would've preferred to have been in the bedroom, but when she'd returned from her dad's place, the sofa was as far as she could get.

"Don't make me have to kick it in."

"Go away," she cried.

"I'm not leaving until you hear what I have to say. If you still want me to go then, I will." He paused. "And that's a promise."

She knew she couldn't avoid him forever. Sooner or later she would have to see him. Realistically she would never be free of him because of the child growing inside her. Thinking of that miracle, tears poured down her face.

She hated him. She hated her father.

The truth was that she didn't hate either of them. She loved them both. That was what was tearing her to pieces.

The two men she loved most in the world had betrayed her. What about Drew? She couldn't forget him. He had betrayed her, too.

"Kaylee, please. I'm begging you to talk to me."

Forcing herself upright, she made her way to the door and opened it. She waited until he had crossed the threshold before she said, "It's over, Cutler. Get your things and get out."

"Kaylee, I can explain."

She laughed without mirth or emotion. "There's nothing to explain. My daddy offered you a bribe and you took it. And the fact that it was for a noble cause makes no difference. You still betrayed me."

"I won't deny that."

"Enough said."

"No, it's not enough said. We've just gotten started."

"You don't love me, Cutler," Kaylee responded in an emotionless voice. "You never did and you never will."

"That's where you're wrong. In the beginning I didn't love you. I'll admit that. I was attracted to you, wanted you in my bed. But love, no. I didn't want any part of that." Cutler laughed bitterly. "But you see, somewhere in between, I fell in love and now I can't bear the thought of living my life without you." He laughed again. "So you see, the joke's on me because I'm not prepared to lose you."

Kaylee placed her hands over her ears, then cried, "Stop it. It's time the lies ended."

"As God is my witness, I'm not lying. I know I was wrong to let my vendetta against Drew consume me. I'm going to work hard on letting that bitterness go. I don't care about anything but you and our child. If I win reelection, fine. If I don't, that's fine, too. You're all I need to make my life complete."

"I wish I could believe that," Kaylee whispered in a tear-clogged voice.

"You can. I swear you can." He dropped to his knees in front of her, then peered up at her, tears streaming down his face. "Please give me a chance to prove my love for you."

Kaylee's mind reeled. Could she ever trust him again? Could she let go of the demon inside and accept herself for the imperfect person she was? More than that, could she ever forgive her husband and her father?

She didn't know the answers to those questions. But the one thing she did know was that she didn't want to live her life without Cutler. But again, she was so afraid.

"What…what if I step out on that limb of trust and it breaks?" she whispered.

He rose to his feet and with his mouth working, he reached for her. "I'll be there to catch you, my darling."

Epilogue

His kisses were sweet and deep, and he was holding her so tenderly.

"Hey," she whispered against his lips, "you've got to stop treating me like I'll break. I promise I won't."

Cutler pulled back and smiled down at her. "Are you sure?"

"Yes, I'm sure. Women have babies every day." She grinned. "It's no big deal."

"It was a big deal for me, thank you." Cutler's face turned somber. "I was afraid something was going to happen to you, that you might—" He broke off.

Kaylee saw his mouth work and knew that his emotions were still running high. But then, so were hers. The birth of their son two months ago had been an awesome and blessed event. Surprisingly, the pregnancy and delivery had gone extremely well; as had their wonderful life together.

When she had first married Cutler, she'd been ecstatic even though she had known he didn't love her as she loved him. During this past year, through the months of carrying the baby, circumstances had changed.

He had changed.

Once Cutler had declared his love for her, he had become a different person. Along with being her lover, he had become her best friend. They had the awesome threesome, she kept telling him—friendship, laughter and love.

"An unbeatable combo," he'd said, and he had been right.

Even though Cutler had won reelection and remained as dedicated to his job as ever, their life hadn't been all flowers and honey. During that year, before their son, Nate, was born, they'd had their share of bumps in the road. The abortion/priest trial, long and tedious, had been a disaster for Cutler, as had the Cullen Bryant retrial. Both losses had been blows to his professional pride.

During that time her business had floundered as well, having taken a licking with the conviction of Jessica for the murder of Barbie.

Kaylee still had trouble coming to grips with that unnecessary tragedy. As it had turned out, both drugs and jealousy had been the motives for the stabbing. The pills had belonged to Jessica. Her boyfriend had been her supplier. The evening she'd stabbed Barbie she'd been high, and with that combined with her seething jealousy, she'd gone over the edge.

The idea that one beautiful young woman was dead and another was serving a life sentence was unthinkable and unbearable to Kaylee. Nonetheless, it was a fact.

Cutler had been learning to live with the undisputable fact that Drew Rush was his biological father and that he was the product of rape, rather than of love. To this day, Cutler struggled to deal with his torturous past, and his only comfort was that Drew was serving time—not for rape, but for his criminal business misdeeds. Cutler took comfort that when Drew entered his prison cell, he no longer wielded any power over anyone.

"What are you thinking about, darling?" Cutler asked, breaking in to her thoughts.

It was early on a Sunday morning. Since Nate was sleeping later than usual, they were taking advantage of the time by relaxing in bed themselves.

"Us. The good times and the bad."

"Such as?"

His finger began circling her breast, fuller now following the birth of their son. "How do you expect me to answer when you're doing that to me?"

He tweaked a nipple. "You like it, huh?"

"I love it," Kaylee said with a catch.

"Your breasts are so incredible."

"I was afraid they would sag since I'm nursing Nate." She smiled. "Not that I would care."

"Nor I. Watching that little mouth latch on to and suckle your breasts is an experience I'll treasure always." His eyes darkened. "Not to mention what it does to my libido."

She grinned. "I'll have to say you're a good sport about sharing your territory with your son."

"I have to keep in mind that he's a growing boy and needs you much more than me."

They both chuckled, then held each other in a long, sweet silence.

"Thank you for your patience," Cutler said at last.

"What do you mean?"

"My ongoing battle with Drew and who I am."

She sighed. "You've come a long way toward releasing your bitterness and hostility."

"But I still have a long way to go."

"He'll be out of prison soon, won't he?"

"I guess that's what has me turned inside out again."

"You know, darling, it's okay if you can't ever forgive him. As long as you don't let it fester inside you, that is."

"That's what I keeping telling myself. But I never want him in my life or in our son's."

"I feel the same. I just can't believe it took me so long to see the real man under that facade."

"In your defense, he was good to you, which I see as his only redeeming grace."

"Daddy's glad to be out from under him, too. He's a different man since Drew's empire toppled and he went to prison."

"I just keep reminding myself of what Mother told me."

"Consider yourself blessed instead of bitter." Kaylee smiled at him. "That's the best advice a mother could give a son, especially a mother who's been so wronged."

"She's a remarkable person."

"Yes, she is," Kaylee responded. "I've come to love her like a second mother."

"And she loves you, too." He kissed her. "But what's not to love about you, Kaylee Benton McFarland?"

She jabbed him in the ribs. "I'd say you're a bit prejudiced."

"Ah, really."

They both laughed again. "I guess I'd better go check on our son. He's too quiet to suit me."

"What time is everyone due?" he asked.

She and Cutler were having their families for brunch. She had prepared everything the night before, so there wasn't much to do. Anyway, they didn't really care about the food. They wanted to play with the baby. He was the apple of everyone's eye.

"I told them to come whenever."

"Oh, brother, we'd better get cracking." Cutler tossed back the covers, exposing his nude body.

Kaylee whistled.

He grinned, raising his eyebrows up and down. "Think we have time for a quickie?"

"We've already had several quickies," she pointed out in a teasing voice.

"But he's not satisfied."

They both looked at his erection.

"Think you can wait until after we check on our son?"

"Barely."

She rolled her eyes before she got out of bed. "You know what, I may decide not to go back to work."

He looked at her. "Are you serious?"

"I had a call about selling the agency. I'm thinking seriously about taking the offer."

Cutler looked taken aback. "And stay home with Nate?"

"Yes, and have another baby." She grabbed his hand and brought it to her lips. "I love being a mother."

His gaze heated. "I just love you."

"And I love you."

Cutler swatted her on the butt. "Come on, let's go see about our son."

Soon they were bending over his crib, watching their son's tiny chest move up and down. Kaylee thought she might suffocate with love. She turned to Cutler, who was looking at her with that same emotion.

"From my heart to yours," she whispered, physically moving her hand from her heart to his.

"And mine to yours." He kissed her deeply. "Forever."

Her eyes glowed. "Forever."

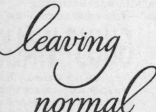

MARY LYNN
BAXTER

32142 IN HOT WATER	___ $6.99 U.S.	___$8.50 CAN.
66731 PULSE POINTS	___ $6.50 U.S.	___$7.99 CAN.
66686 HIS TOUCH	___ $6.50 U.S.	___$7.99 CAN.

(limited quantities available)

TOTAL AMOUNT	$ _____
POSTAGE & HANDLING	$ _____
($1.00 FOR 1 BOOK, 50¢ for each additional)	
APPLICABLE TAXES*	$ _____
TOTAL PAYABLE	$ _____

(check or money order—please do not send cash)

To order, complete this form and send it, along with a check or money order for the total above, payable to MIRA Books, to: **In the U.S.:** 3010 Walden Avenue, P.O. Box 9077, Buffalo, NY 14269-9077; **In Canada:** P.O. Box 636, Fort Erie, Ontario, L2A 5X3.

Name: _____
Address: _____ City: _____
State/Prov.: _____ Zip/Postal Code: _____
Account Number (if applicable): _____
075 CSAS

*New York residents remit applicable sales taxes.
*Canadian residents remit applicable GST and provincial taxes.

MIRA®
www.MIRABooks.com

MMLB1005BL